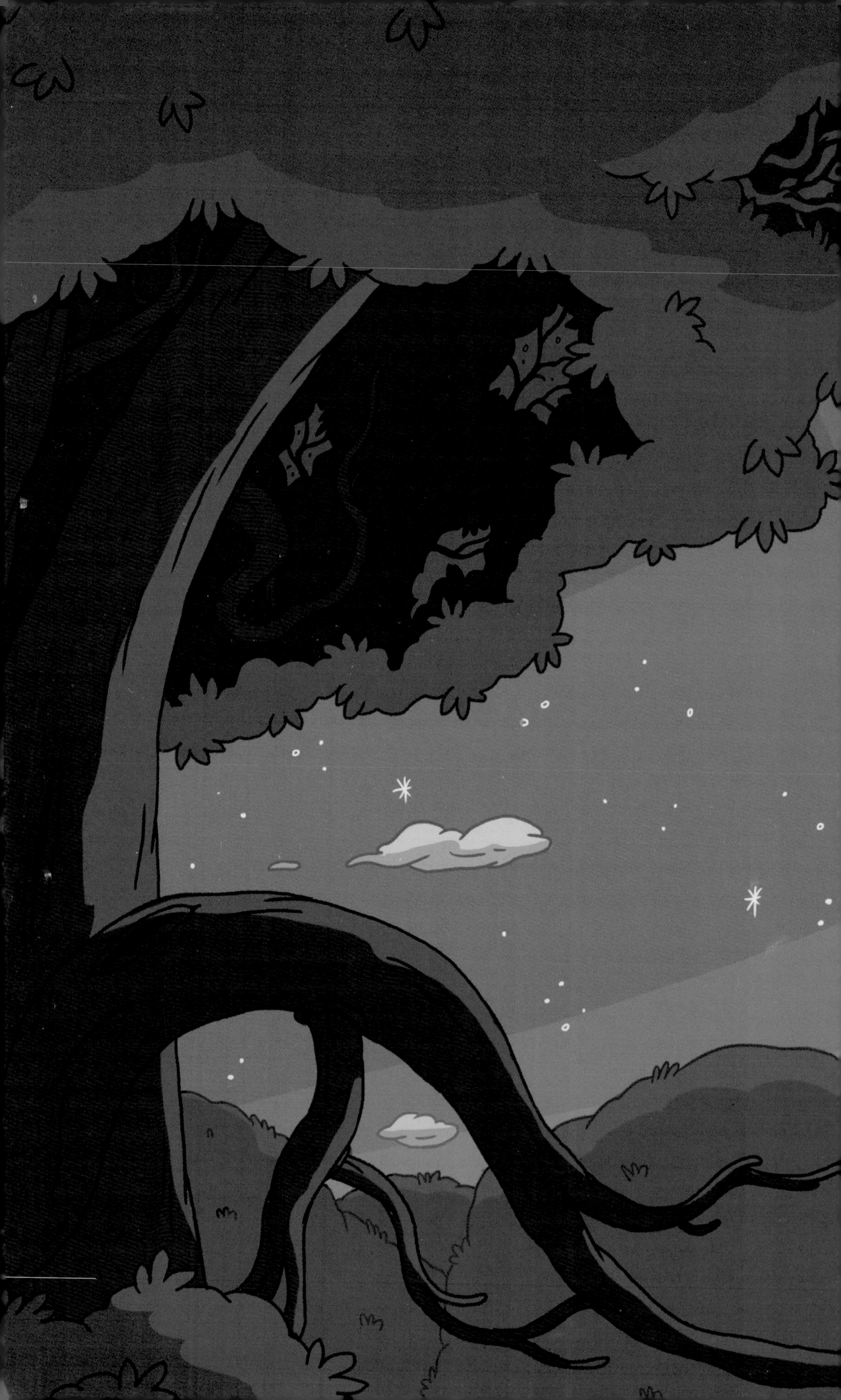

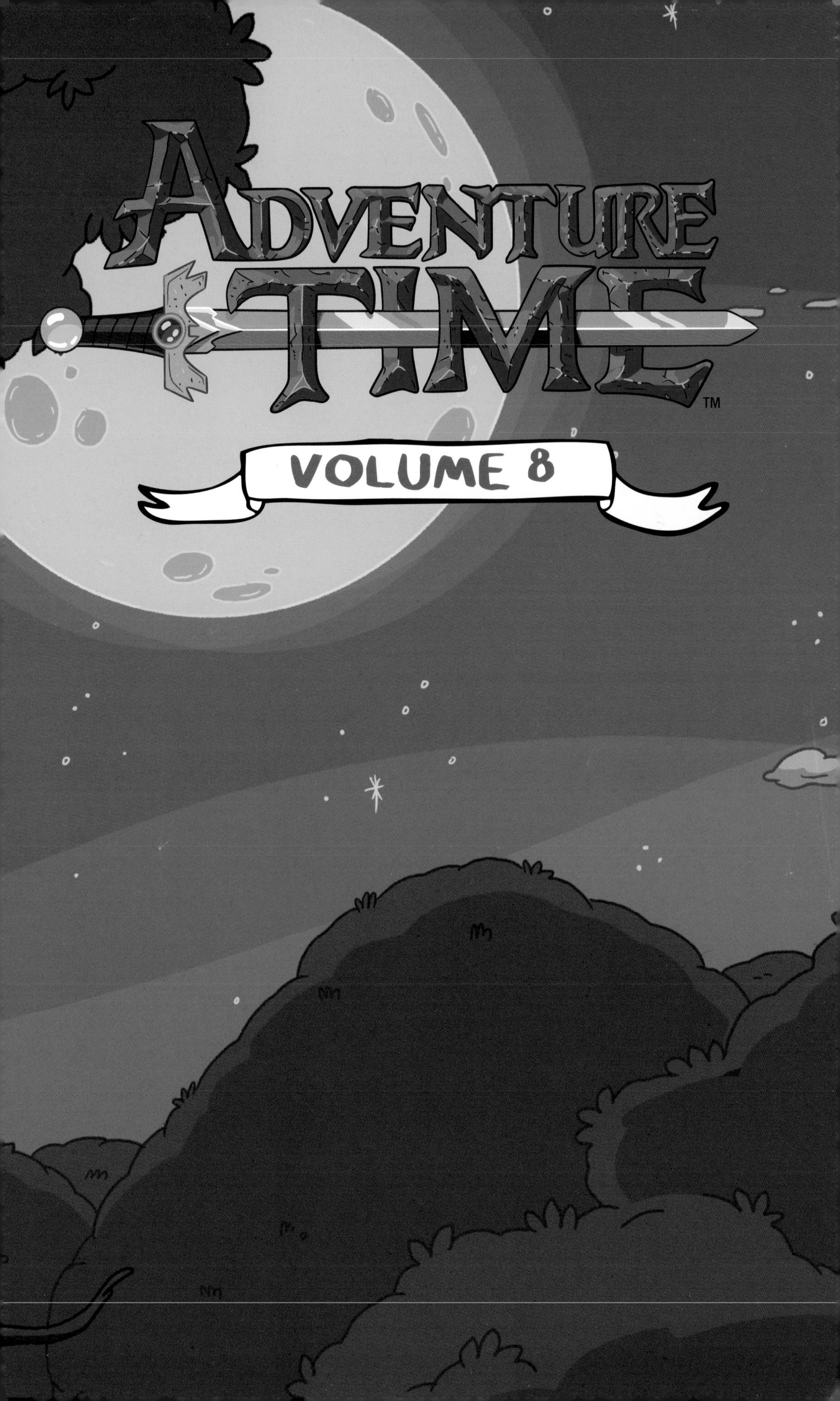
ADVENTURE TIME™
VOLUME 8

ROSS RICHIE CEO & Founder • MATT GAGNON Editor-in-Chief • FILIP SABLIK President of Publishing & Marketing • STEPHEN CHRISTY President of Development • LANCE KREITER VP of Licensing & Merchandising
PHIL BARBARO VP of Finance • BRYCE CARLSON Managing Editor • MEL CAYLO Marketing Manager • SCOTT NEWMAN Production Design Manager • IRENE BRADISH Operations Manager
CHRISTINE DINH Brand Communications Manager • SIERRA HAHN Senior Editor • DAFNA PLEBAN Editor • SHANNON WATTERS Editor • ERIC HARBURN Editor • WHITNEY LEOPARD Associate Editor • JASMINE AMIRI Associate Editor
CHRIS ROSA Associate Editor • ALEX GALER Assistant Editor • CAMERON CHITTOCK Assistant Editor • MARY GUMPORT Assistant Editor • KELSEY DIETERICH Production Designer • JILLIAN CRAB Production Designer
KARA LEOPARD Production Designer • MICHELLE ANKLEY Production Design Assistant • AARON FERRARA Operations Coordinator • ELIZABETH LOUGHRIDGE Accounting Coordinator • JOSÉ MEZA Sales Assistant
JAMES ARRIOLA Mailroom Assistant • STEPHANIE HOCUTT Marketing Assistant • SAM KUSEK Direct Market Representative • HILLARY LEVI Executive Assistant • KATE ALBIN Administrative Assistant

CREATED BY
Pendleton Ward

ISSUE 35
WRITTEN BY
Ryan North

ILLUSTRATED BY
Shelli Paroline & Braden Lamb

ISSUES 36-39
WRITTEN BY
Christopher Hastings

ILLUSTRATED BY
Zachary Sterling

COLORS BY
Maarta Laiho

LETTERS BY
Steve Wands

COVER BY
Shelli Paroline & Braden Lamb

DESIGNER
Kelsey Dieterich

ASSOCIATE EDITOR
Whitney Leopard

EDITOR
Shannon Watters

With special thanks to
Marisa Marionakis, Rick Blanco, Nicole Rivera, Conrad Montgomery, Meghan Bradley,
Curtis Lelash and the wonderful folks at Cartoon Network.

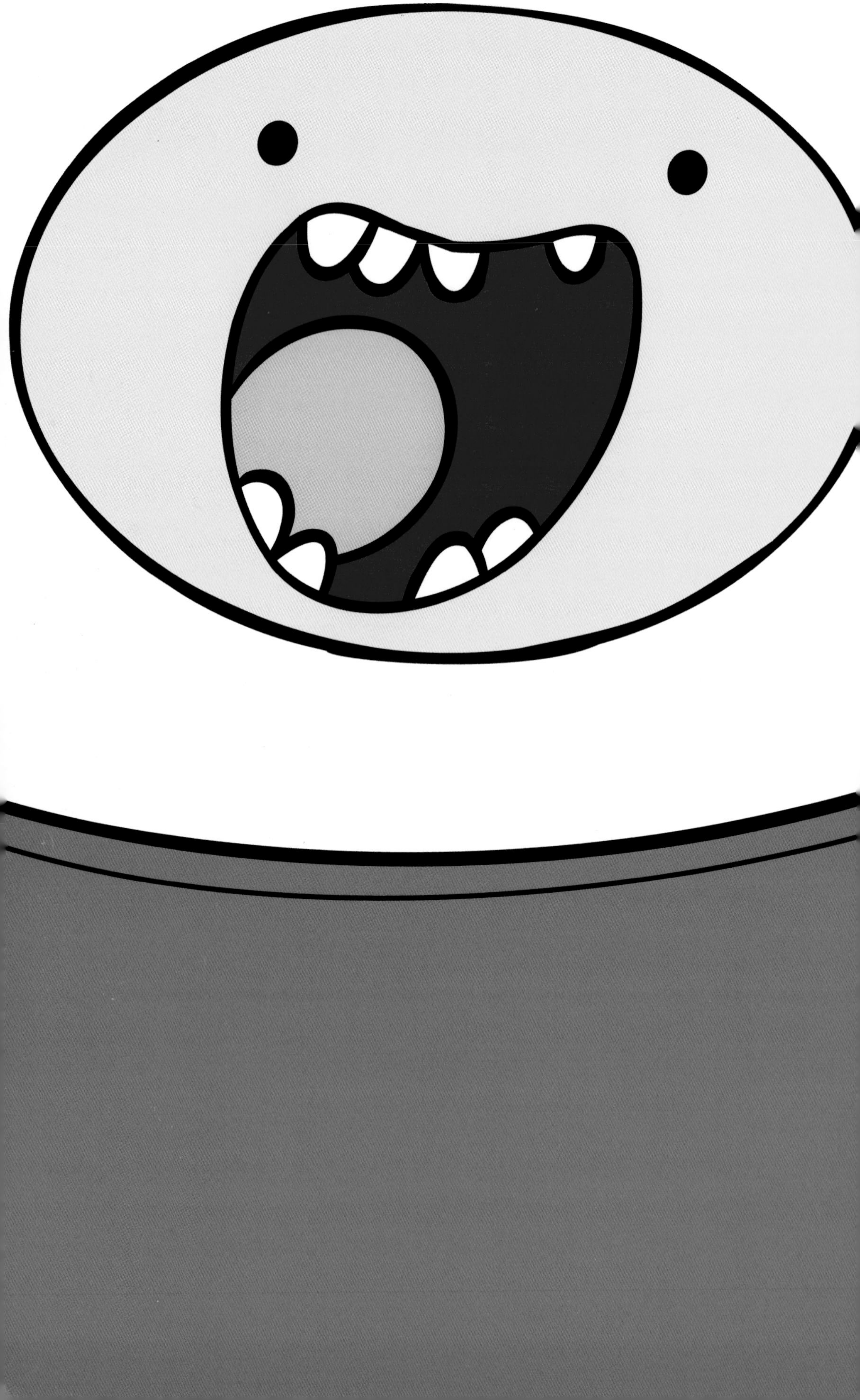

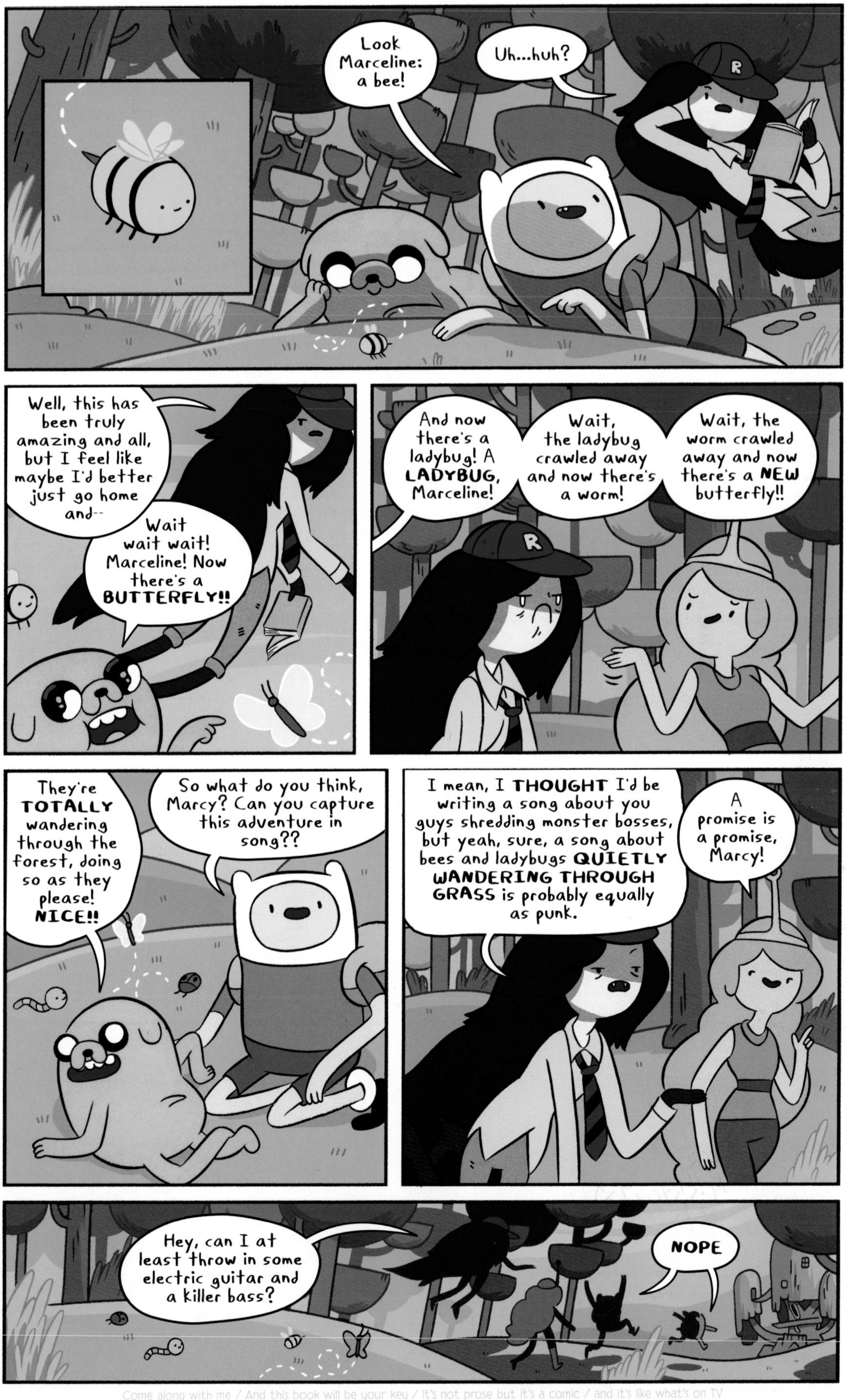

Look Marceline: a bee!
Uh...huh?
Well, this has been truly amazing and all, but I feel like maybe I'd better just go home and--
Wait wait wait! Marceline! Now there's a BUTTERFLY!!
And now there's a ladybug! A LADYBUG, Marceline!
Wait, the ladybug crawled away and now there's a worm!
Wait, the worm crawled away and now there's a NEW butterfly!!
They're TOTALLY wandering through the forest, doing so as they please! NICE!!
So what do you think, Marcy? Can you capture this adventure in song??
I mean, I THOUGHT I'd be writing a song about you guys shredding monster bosses, but yeah, sure, a song about bees and ladybugs QUIETLY WANDERING THROUGH GRASS is probably equally as punk.
A promise is a promise, Marcy!
Hey, can I at least throw in some electric guitar and a killer bass?
NOPE

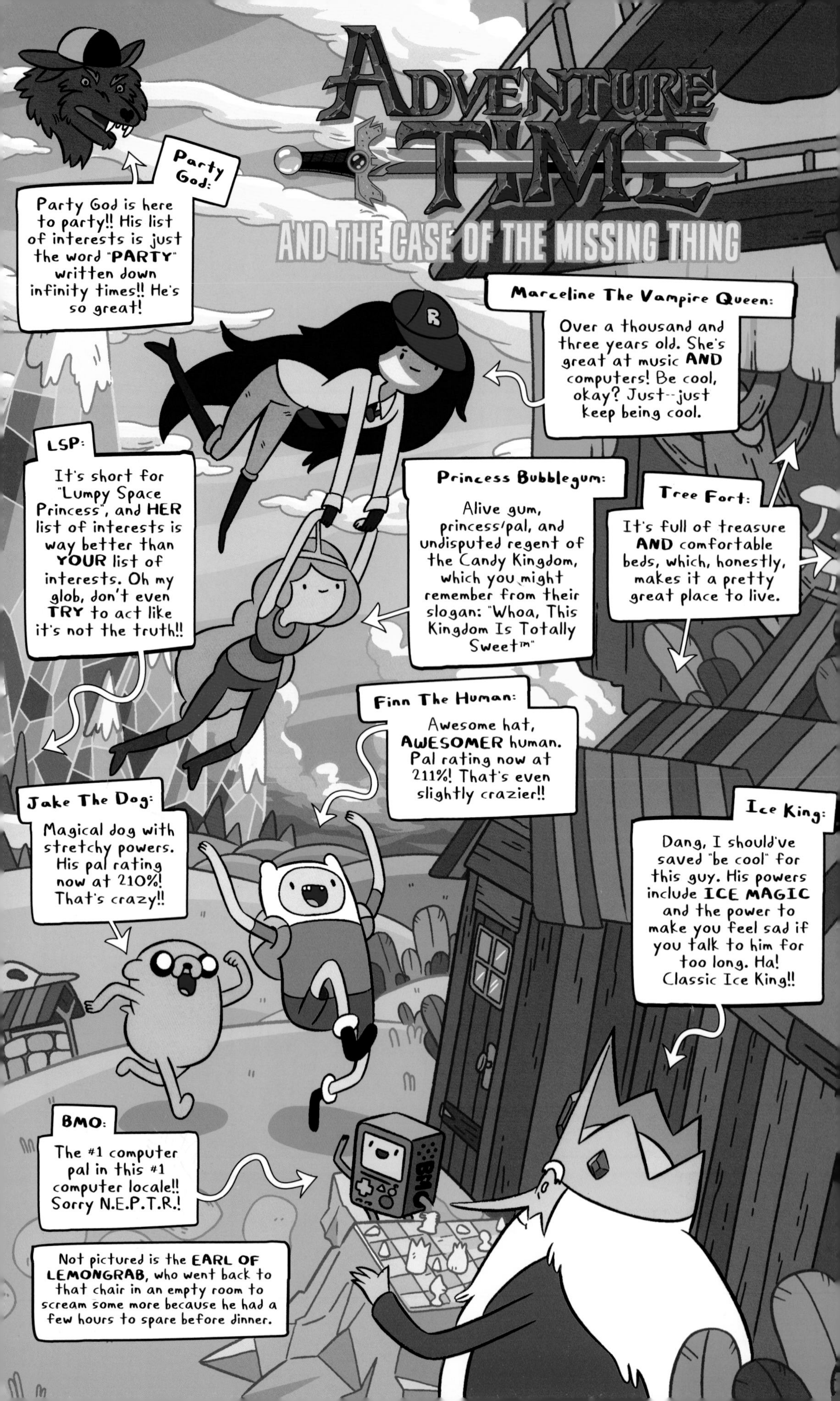
ADVENTURE TIME
AND THE CASE OF THE MISSING THING
Party God:
Party God is here to party!! His list of interests is just the word "PARTY" written down infinity times!! He's so great!
Marceline The Vampire Queen:
Over a thousand and three years old. She's great at music AND computers! Be cool, okay? Just--just keep being cool.
LSP:
It's short for "Lumpy Space Princess", and HER list of interests is way better than YOUR list of interests. Oh my glob, don't even TRY to act like it's not the truth!!
Princess Bubblegum:
Alive gum, princess/pal, and undisputed regent of the Candy Kingdom, which you might remember from their slogan: "Whoa, This Kingdom Is Totally Sweet™"
Tree Fort:
It's full of treasure AND comfortable beds, which, honestly, makes it a pretty great place to live.
Finn The Human:
Awesome hat, AWESOMER human. Pal rating now at 211%! That's even slightly crazier!!
Jake The Dog:
Magical dog with stretchy powers. His pal rating now at 210%! That's crazy!!
Ice King:
Dang, I should've saved "be cool" for this guy. His powers include ICE MAGIC and the power to make you feel sad if you talk to him for too long. Ha! Classic Ice King!!
BMO:
The #1 computer pal in this #1 computer locale!! Sorry N.E.P.T.R.!
BMO
Not pictured is the EARL OF LEMONGRAB, who went back to that chair in an empty room to scream some more because he had a few hours to spare before dinner.

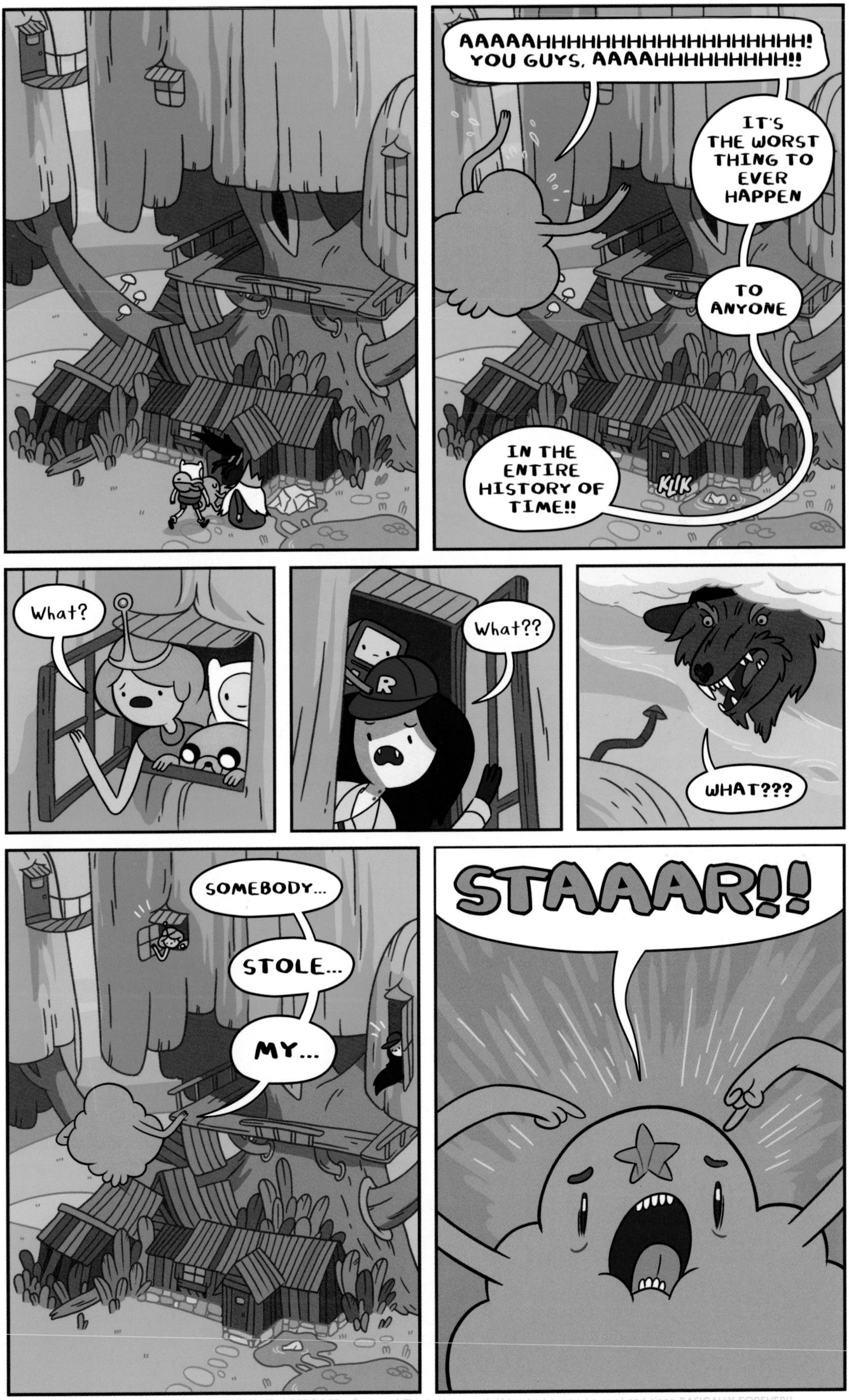
AAAAAHHHHHHHHHHHHHHHHHHH! YOU GUYS, AAAAHHHHHHHHHH!!
IT'S THE WORST THING TO EVER HAPPEN
TO ANYONE
IN THE ENTIRE HISTORY OF TIME!!
KLIK
What?
What??
WHAT???
SOMEBODY...
STOLE...
MY...
STAAAR!!

Now I've got a hole. there and that's the **OPPOSITE** of a lump! This is the worst thing to happen to my head since **BASICALLY FOREVER!!**

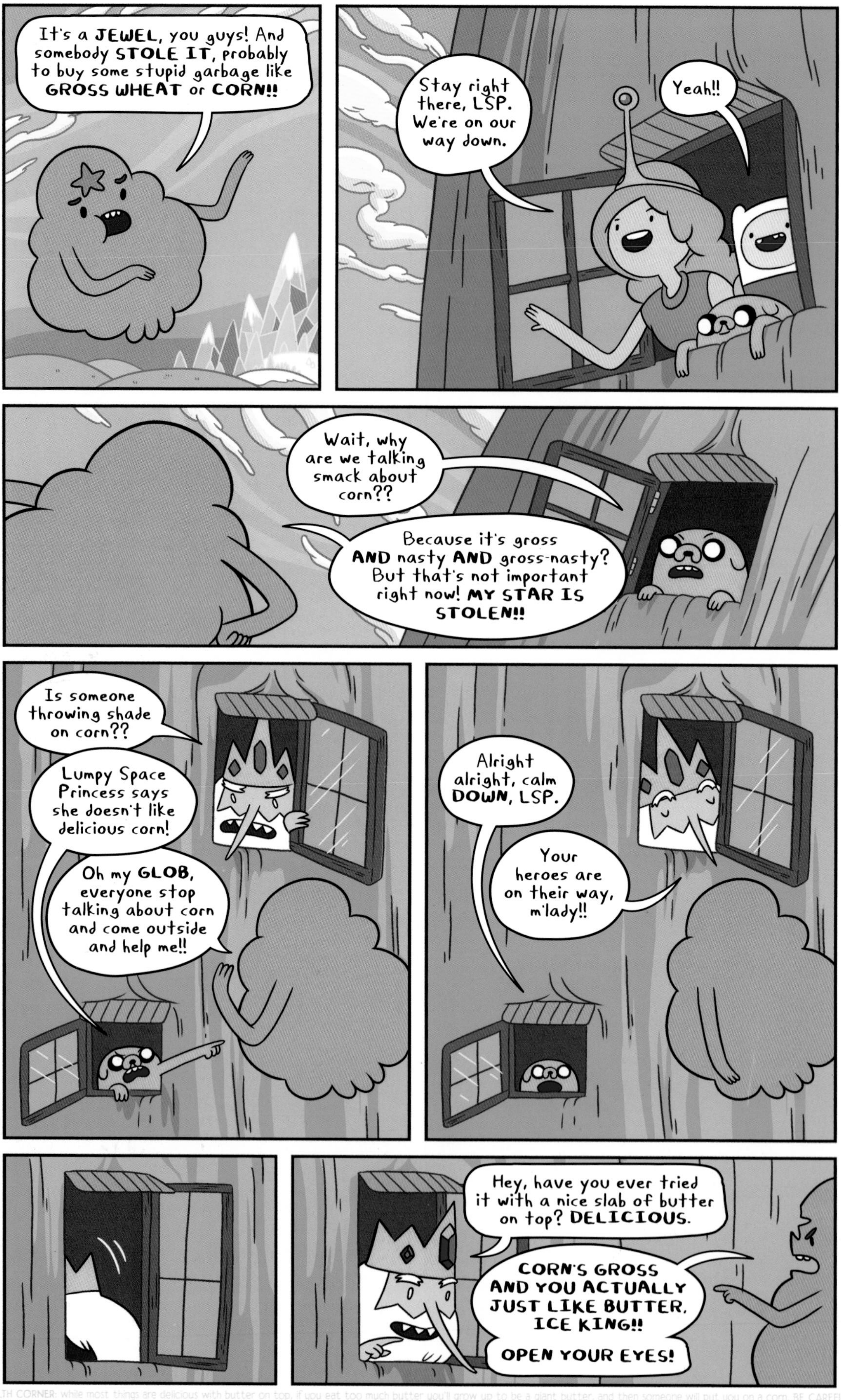
It's a JEWEL, you guys! And somebody STOLE IT, probably to buy some stupid garbage like GROSS WHEAT or CORN!!
Stay right there, LSP. We're on our way down.
Yeah!!
Wait, why are we talking smack about corn??
Because it's gross AND nasty AND gross-nasty? But that's not important right now! MY STAR IS STOLEN!!
Is someone throwing shade on corn??
Lumpy Space Princess says she doesn't like delicious corn!
Oh my GLOB, everyone stop talking about corn and come outside and help me!!
Alright alright, calm DOWN, LSP.
Your heroes are on their way, m'lady!!
Hey, have you ever tried it with a nice slab of butter on top? DELICIOUS.
CORN'S GROSS AND YOU ACTUALLY JUST LIKE BUTTER, ICE KING!!
OPEN YOUR EYES!

HEALTH CORNER: while most things are delicious with butter on top, if you eat too much butter you'll grow up to be a giant butter, and then someone will put you on a corn. BE CAREFUL

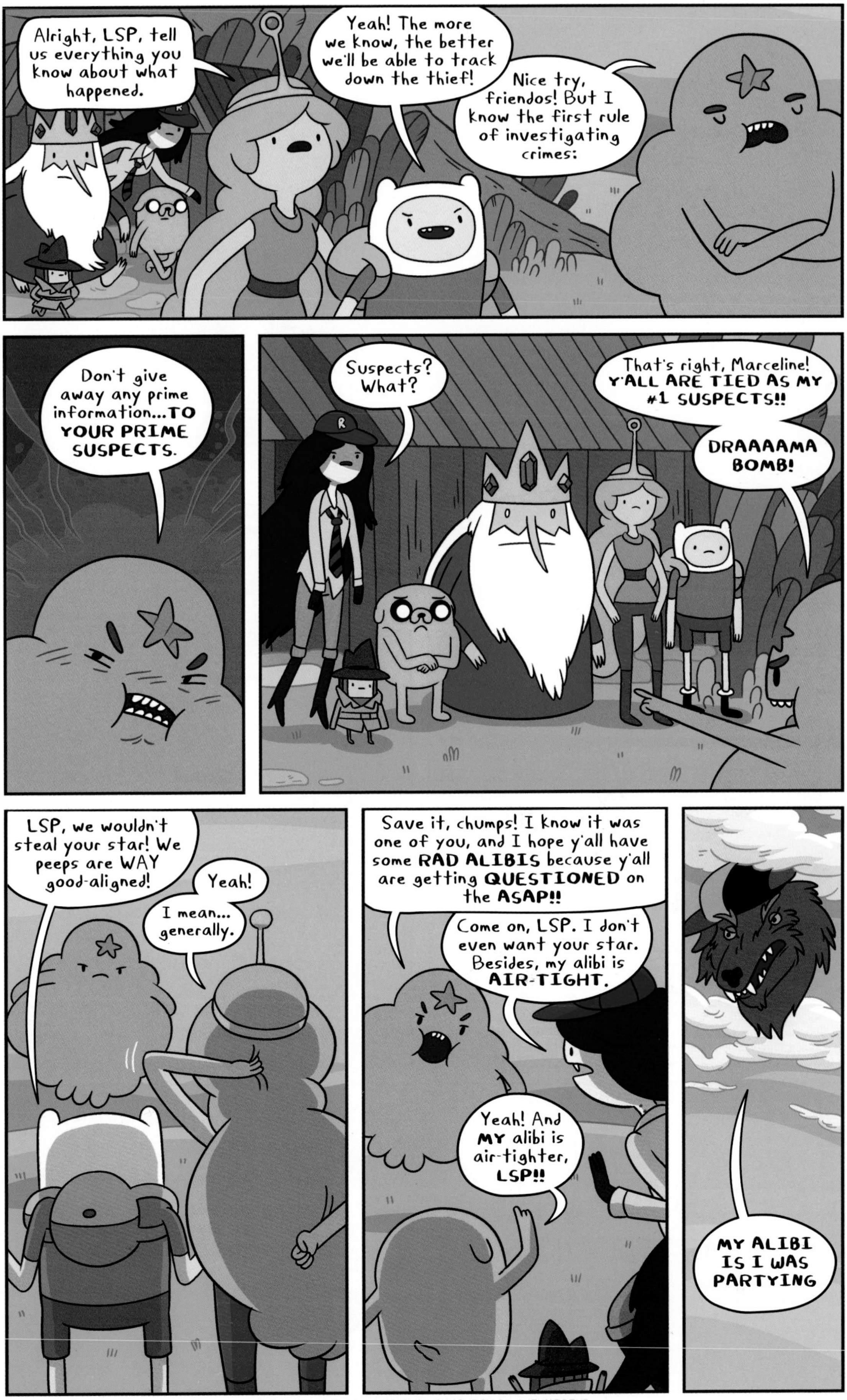
Alright, LSP, tell us everything you know about what happened.
Yeah! The more we know, the better we'll be able to track down the thief!
Nice try, friendos! But I know the first rule of investigating crimes:
Don't give away any prime information...TO YOUR PRIME SUSPECTS.
Suspects? What?
That's right, Marceline! Y'ALL ARE TIED AS MY #1 SUSPECTS!!
DRAAAAMA BOMB!
LSP, we wouldn't steal your star! We peeps are WAY good-aligned!
Yeah!
I mean... generally.
Save it, chumps! I know it was one of you, and I hope y'all have some RAD ALIBIS because y'all are getting QUESTIONED on the ASAP!!
Come on, LSP. I don't even want your star. Besides, my alibi is AIR-TIGHT.
Yeah! And MY alibi is air-tighter, LSP!!
MY ALIBI IS I WAS PARTYING

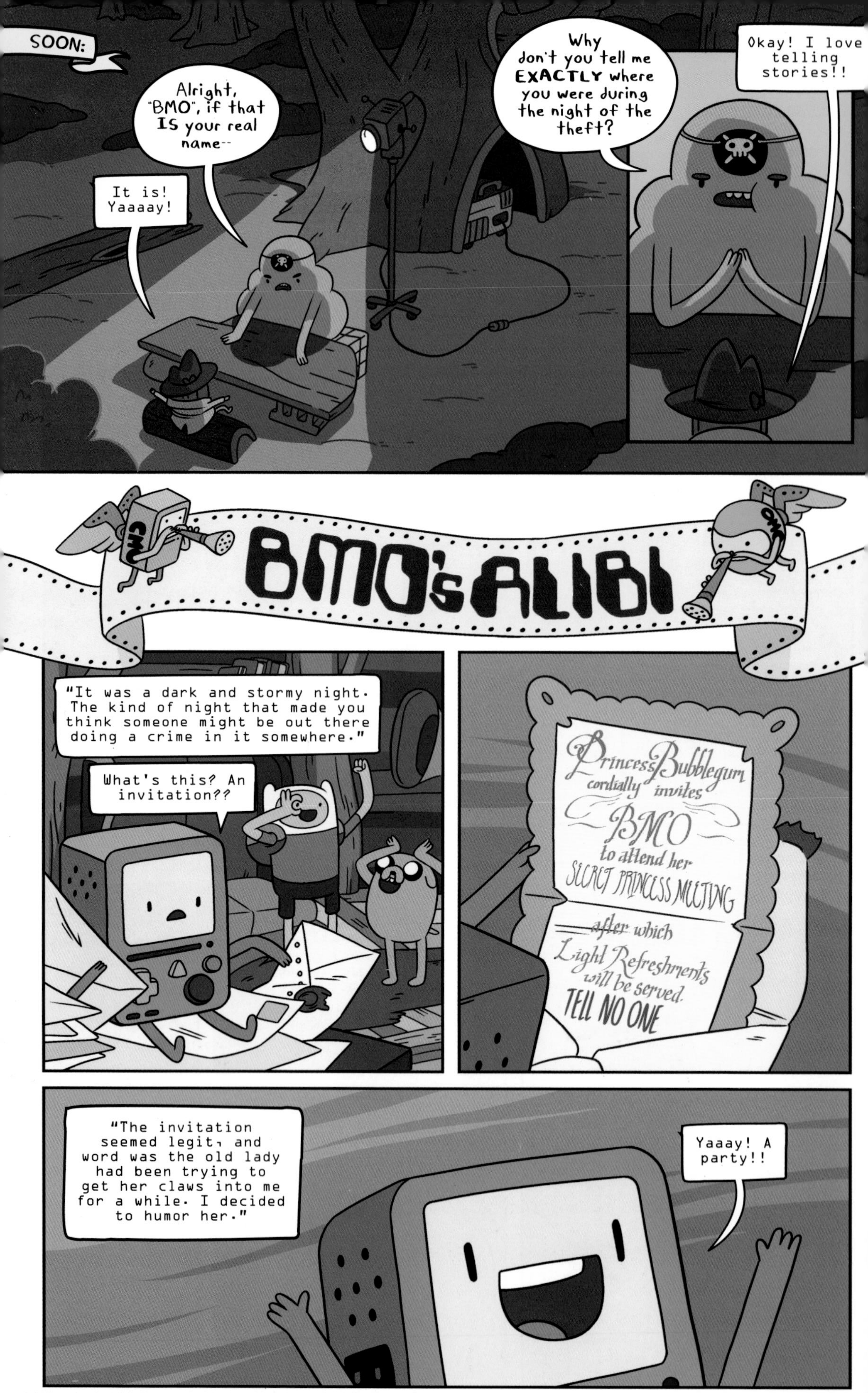
SOON:
Alright, "BMO", if that IS your real name--
It is! Yaaaay!
Why don't you tell me EXACTLY where you were during the night of the theft?
Okay! I love telling stories!!
BMO's ALIBI
"It was a dark and stormy night. The kind of night that made you think someone might be out there doing a crime in it somewhere."
What's this? An invitation??
Princess Bubblegum cordially invites BMO to attend her SECRET PRINCESS MEETING after which Light Refreshments will be served. TELL NO ONE
"The invitation seemed legit, and word was the old lady had been trying to get her claws into me for a while. I decided to humor her."
Yaaay! A party!!

I didn't need my keen detective senses to detect one thing: crime was bad. And BMO stood for one thing: "Best Detective, Yo." Hey: I said I was good at detection. Never said I was good at acronym

"So I showed up. Double checked the invitation, and yeah: I was there in the right place at the right time.

"Couldn't shake the feeling that tomorrow morning, folks'd be saying the opposite.

"Flashed the doorman my credentials and he let me in nice and easy. Seemed to me like he wasn't looking for trouble.

"Seemed to me like that made one of us."

I'm BMO and I'm a good friend!!

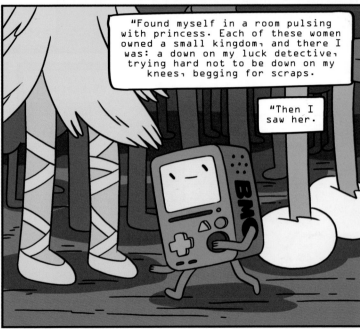

"Found myself in a room pulsing with princess. Each of these women owned a small kingdom, and there I was: a down on my luck detective, trying hard not to be down on my knees, begging for scraps.

"Then I saw her.

"The princess even other princesses call "The Princess". Sweet as candy. Just as bad for my teeth.

"Bubblegum.

"And she had a proposition for us."

Hello, princesses. So glad you could make it. After all...

...the weather outside is KILLER.

She was sweet as candy, sure, but she could be hard like hard candy and sour like sour candy too. She was metaphorically like candy in a whole kingdom's worth of ways.

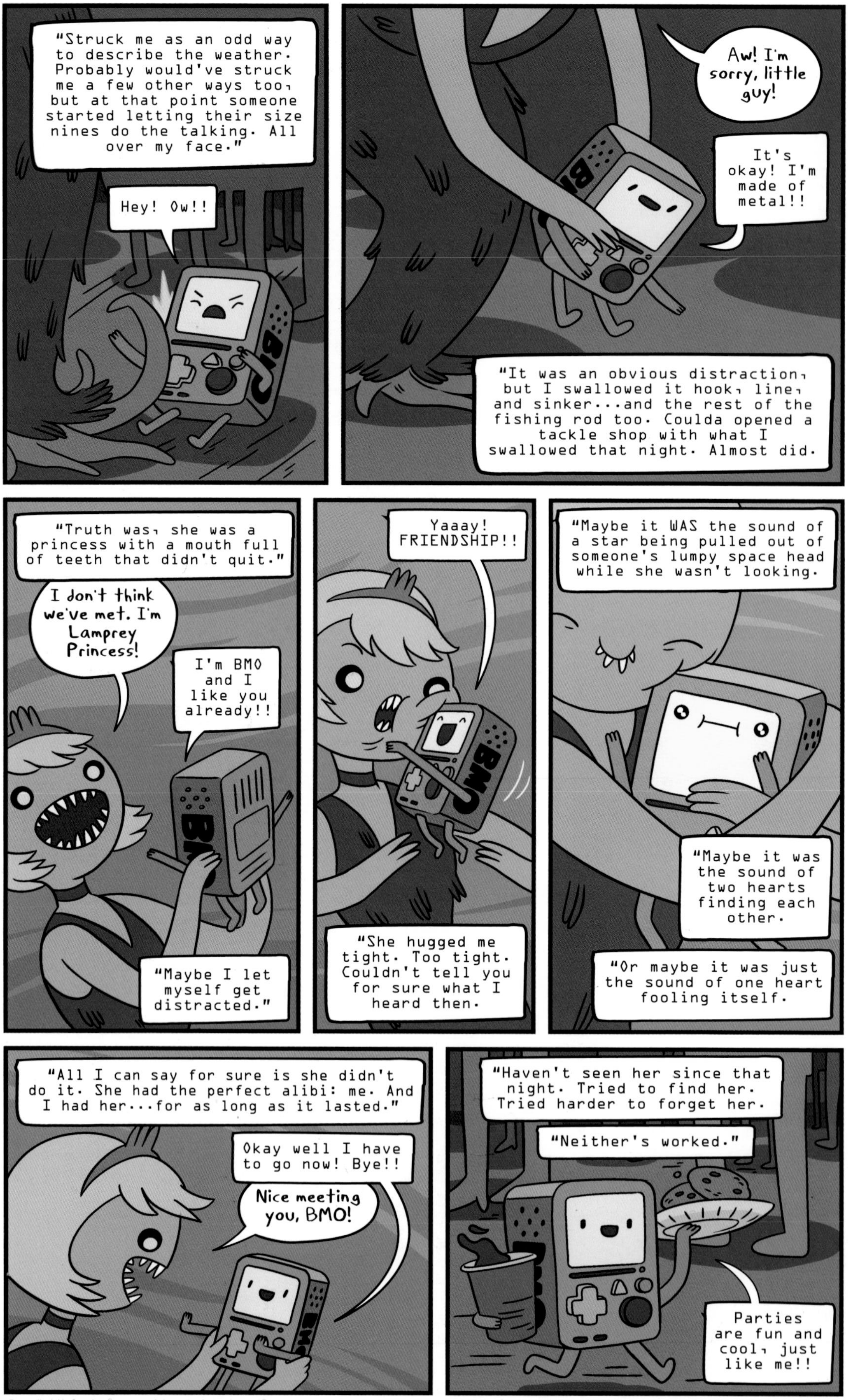
"Struck me as an odd way to describe the weather. Probably would've struck me a few other ways too, but at that point someone started letting their size nines do the talking. All over my face."
Hey! Ow!!
Aw! I'm sorry, little guy!
It's okay! I'm made of metal!!
"It was an obvious distraction, but I swallowed it hook, line, and sinker...and the rest of the fishing rod too. Coulda opened a tackle shop with what I swallowed that night. Almost did.
"Truth was, she was a princess with a mouth full of teeth that didn't quit."
I don't think we've met. I'm Lamprey Princess!
I'm BMO and I like you already!!
"Maybe I let myself get distracted."
Yaaay! FRIENDSHIP!!
"She hugged me tight. Too tight. Couldn't tell you for sure what I heard then.
"Maybe it WAS the sound of a star being pulled out of someone's lumpy space head while she wasn't looking.
"Maybe it was the sound of two hearts finding each other.
"Or maybe it was just the sound of one heart fooling itself.
"All I can say for sure is she didn't do it. She had the perfect alibi: me. And I had her...for as long as it lasted."
Okay well I have to go now! Bye!!
Nice meeting you, BMO!
"Haven't seen her since that night. Tried to find her. Tried harder to forget her.
"Neither's worked."
Parties are fun and cool, just like me!!

Cancelled the rest of my appointments, helped myself to some snacks, and smeared them all over my face. No regrets. Sometimes even detectives have to take a "me" day.

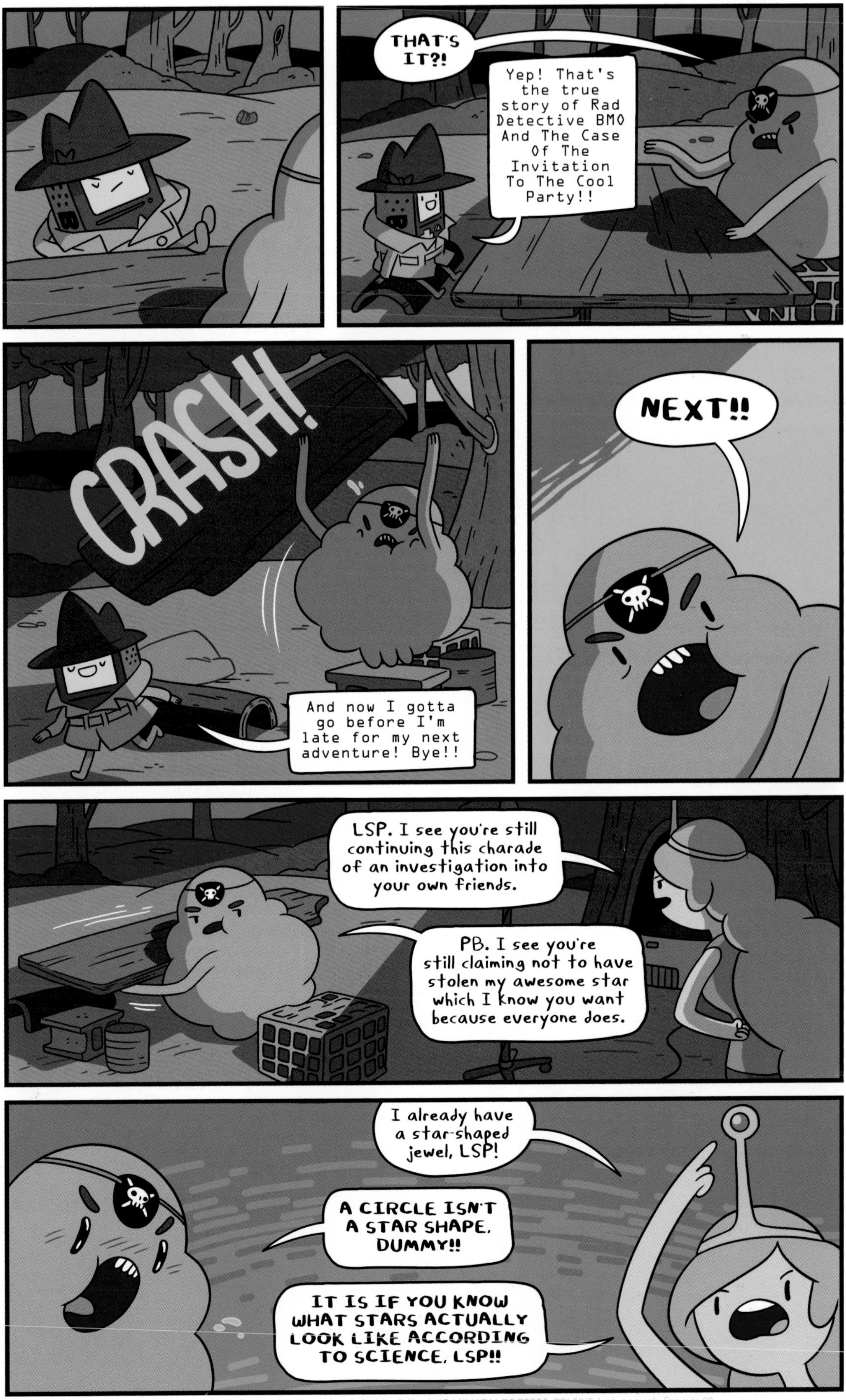
THAT'S IT?!
Yep! That's the true story of Rad Detective BMO And The Case Of The Invitation To The Cool Party!!
CRASH!
And now I gotta go before I'm late for my next adventure! Bye!!
NEXT!!
LSP. I see you're still continuing this charade of an investigation into your own friends.
PB. I see you're still claiming not to have stolen my awesome star which I know you want because everyone does.
I already have a star-shaped jewel, LSP!
A CIRCLE ISN'T A STAR SHAPE, DUMMY!!
IT IS IF YOU KNOW WHAT STARS ACTUALLY LOOK LIKE ACCORDING TO SCIENCE, LSP!!

Oh, you want to talk about whose star is hotter? Um is 15 MILLION DEGREES CELSIUS hot enough for you??

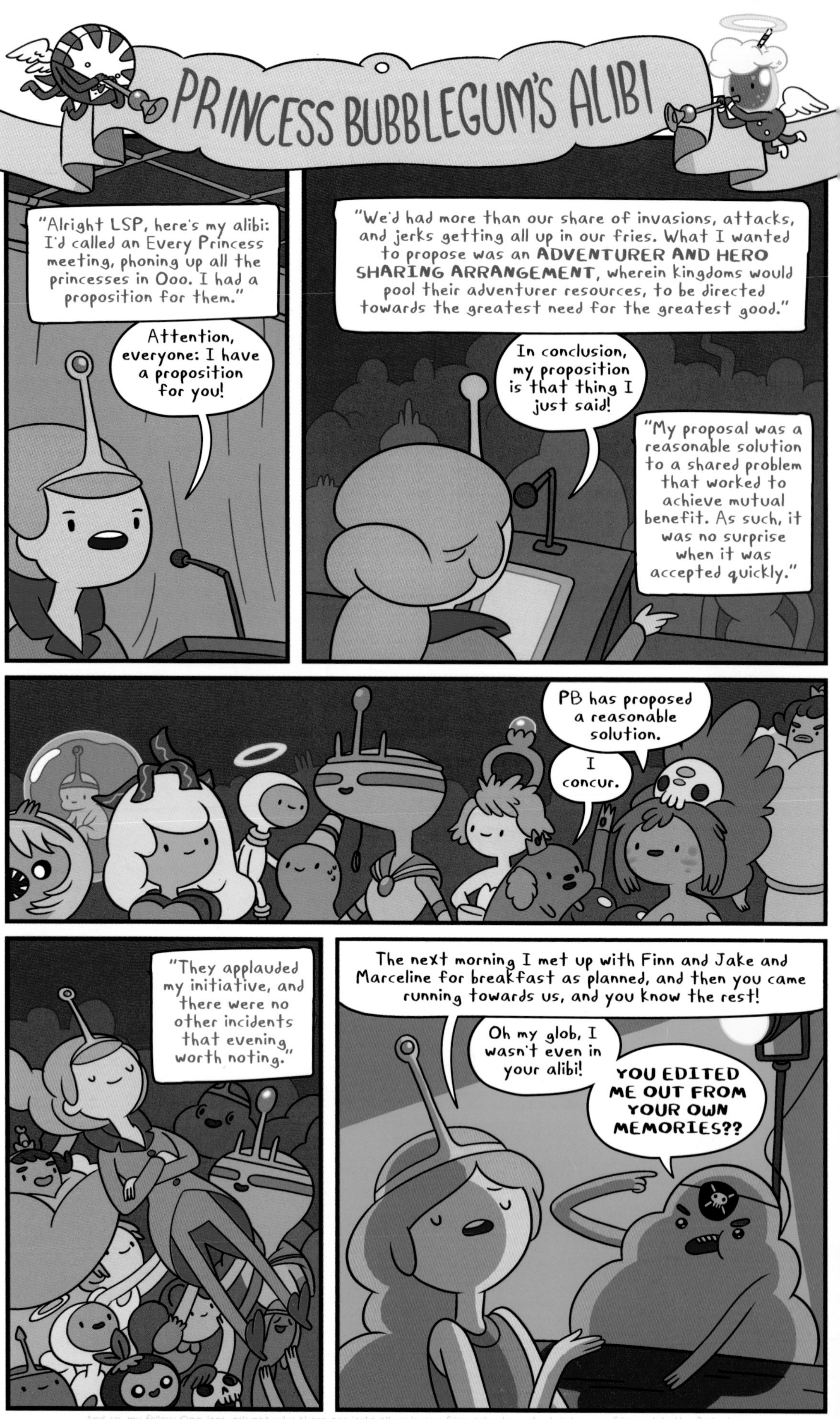
PRINCESS BUBBLEGUM'S ALIBI
"Alright LSP, here's my alibi: I'd called an Every Princess meeting, phoning up all the princesses in Ooo. I had a proposition for them."
Attention, everyone: I have a proposition for you!
"We'd had more than our share of invasions, attacks, and jerks getting all up in our fries. What I wanted to propose was an ADVENTURER AND HERO SHARING ARRANGEMENT, wherein kingdoms would pool their adventurer resources, to be directed towards the greatest need for the greatest good."
In conclusion, my proposition is that thing I just said!
"My proposal was a reasonable solution to a shared problem that worked to achieve mutual benefit. As such, it was no surprise when it was accepted quickly."
PB has proposed a reasonable solution.
I concur.
"They applauded my initiative, and there were no other incidents that evening worth noting."
The next morning I met up with Finn and Jake and Marceline for breakfast as planned, and then you came running towards us, and you know the rest!
Oh my glob, I wasn't even in your alibi!
YOU EDITED ME OUT FROM YOUR OWN MEMORIES??

And so, my fellow Ooo-ians: ask not why there are jerks all up in our fries, ask why we're leaving our fries out in the first place.

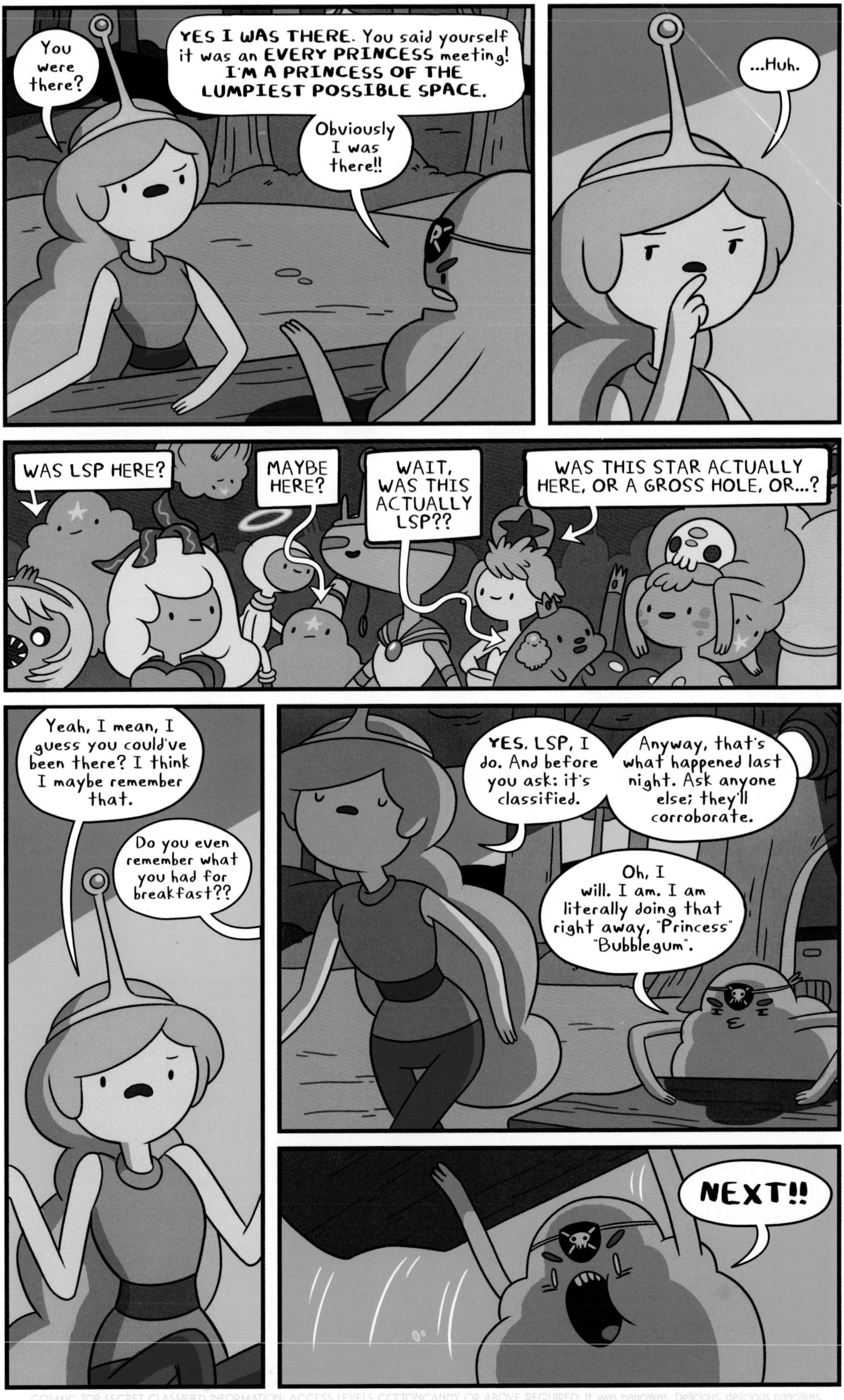
You were there?
YES I WAS THERE. You said yourself it was an EVERY PRINCESS meeting! I'M A PRINCESS OF THE LUMPIEST POSSIBLE SPACE.
Obviously I was there!!
...Huh.
WAS LSP HERE?
MAYBE HERE?
WAIT, WAS THIS ACTUALLY LSP??
WAS THIS STAR ACTUALLY HERE, OR A GROSS HOLE, OR...?
Yeah, I mean, I guess you could've been there? I think I maybe remember that.
Do you even remember what you had for breakfast??
YES, LSP, I do. And before you ask: it's classified.
Anyway, that's what happened last night. Ask anyone else; they'll corroborate.
Oh, I will. I am. I am literally doing that right away, "Princess" "Bubblegum".
NEXT!!

COSMIC TOP SECRET CLASSIFIED INFORMATION: ACCESS LEVELS COTTONCANDY OR ABOVE REQUIRED: it was pancakes. Delicious, delicious pancakes.

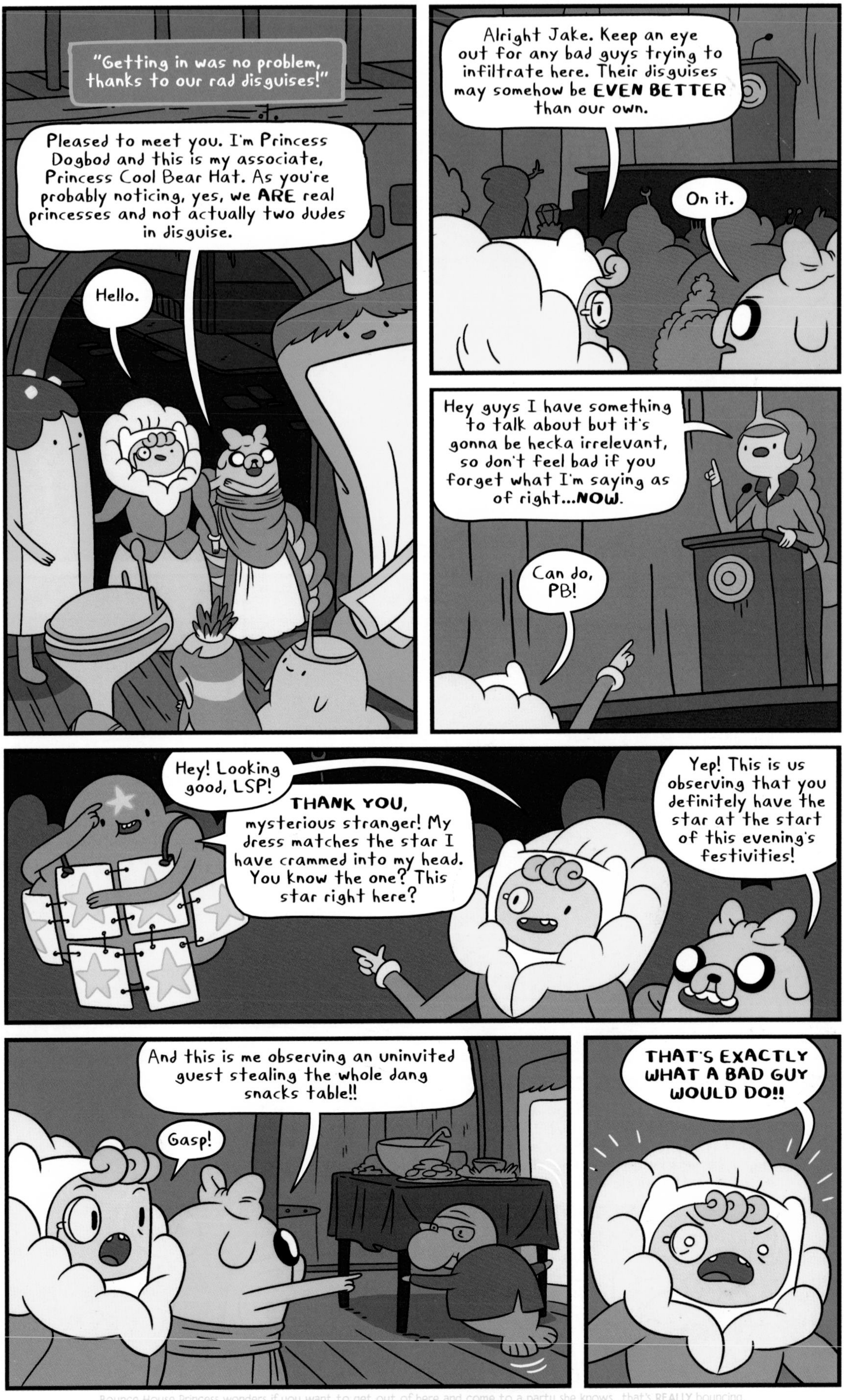
"Getting in was no problem, thanks to our rad disguises!"
Pleased to meet you. I'm Princess Dogbod and this is my associate, Princess Cool Bear Hat. As you're probably noticing, yes, we ARE real princesses and not actually two dudes in disguise.
Hello.
Alright Jake. Keep an eye out for any bad guys trying to infiltrate here. Their disguises may somehow be EVEN BETTER than our own.
On it.
Hey guys I have something to talk about but it's gonna be hecka irrelevant, so don't feel bad if you forget what I'm saying as of right...NOW.
Can do, PB!
Hey! Looking good, LSP!
THANK YOU, mysterious stranger! My dress matches the star I have crammed into my head. You know the one? This star right here?
Yep! This is us observing that you definitely have the star at the start of this evening's festivities!
And this is me observing an uninvited guest stealing the whole dang snacks table!!
Gasp!
THAT'S EXACTLY WHAT A BAD GUY WOULD DO!!

Bounce House Princess wonders if you want to get out of here and come to a party she knows...that's **REALLY** bouncing.

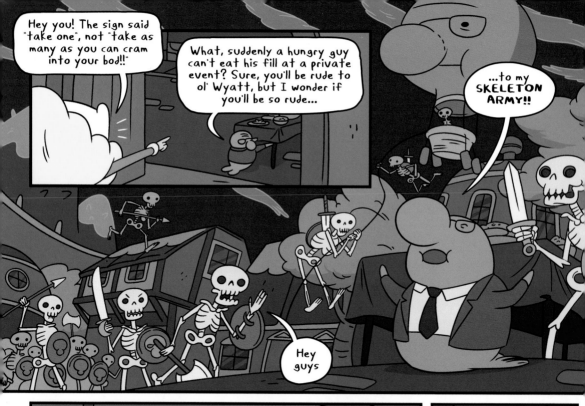

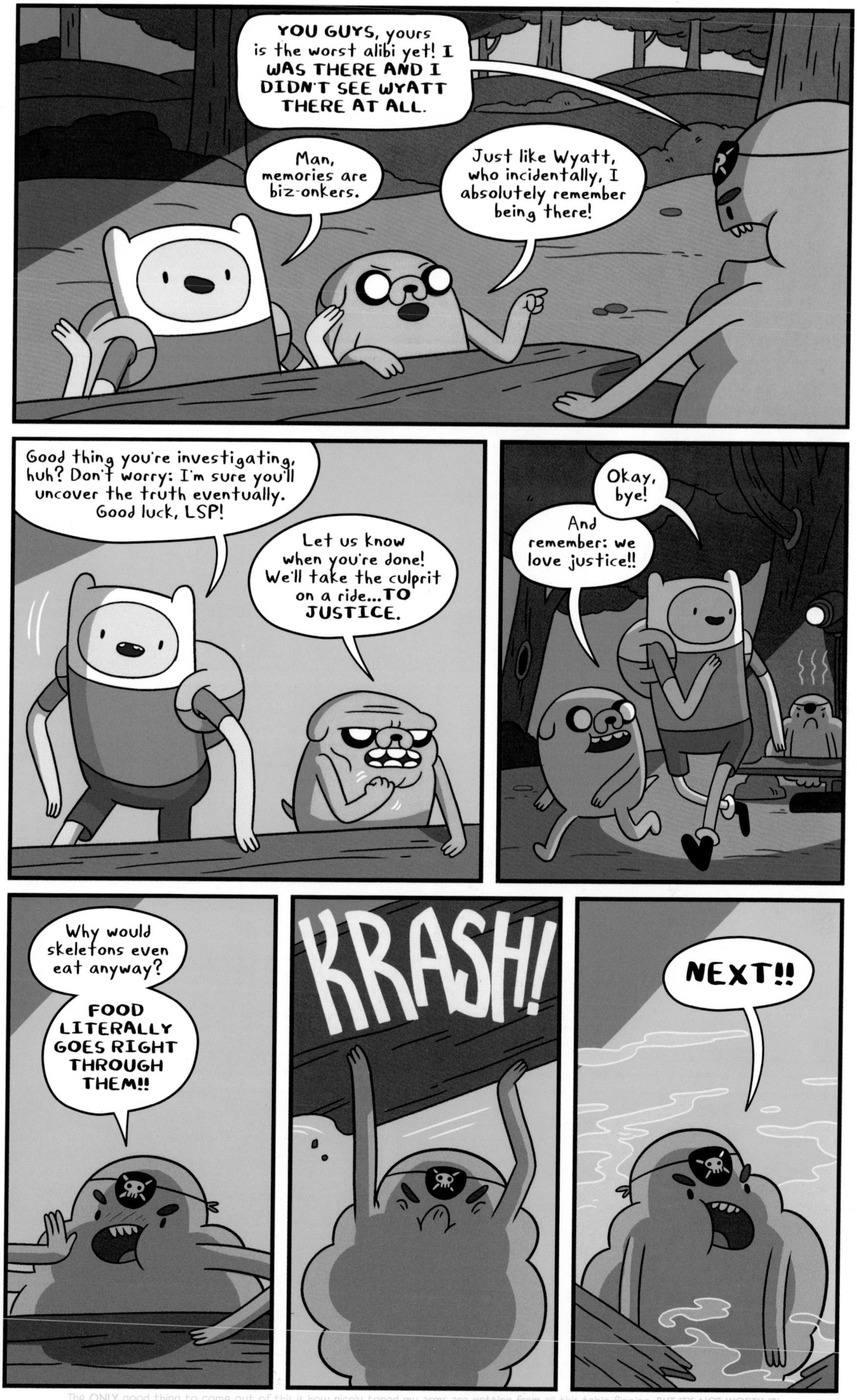

YOU GUYS, yours is the worst alibi yet! I WAS THERE AND I DIDN'T SEE WYATT THERE AT ALL.
Man, memories are biz-onkers.
Just like Wyatt, who incidentally, I absolutely remember being there!
Good thing you're investigating, huh? Don't worry: I'm sure you'll uncover the truth eventually. Good luck, LSP!
Let us know when you're done! We'll take the culprit on a ride...TO JUSTICE.
Okay, bye!
And remember: we love justice!!
Why would skeletons even eat anyway?
FOOD LITERALLY GOES RIGHT THROUGH THEM!!
KRASH!
NEXT!!

The ONLY good thing to come out of this is how nicely toned my arms are getting from all this table flipping. BUT IT'S NOT WORTH IT!

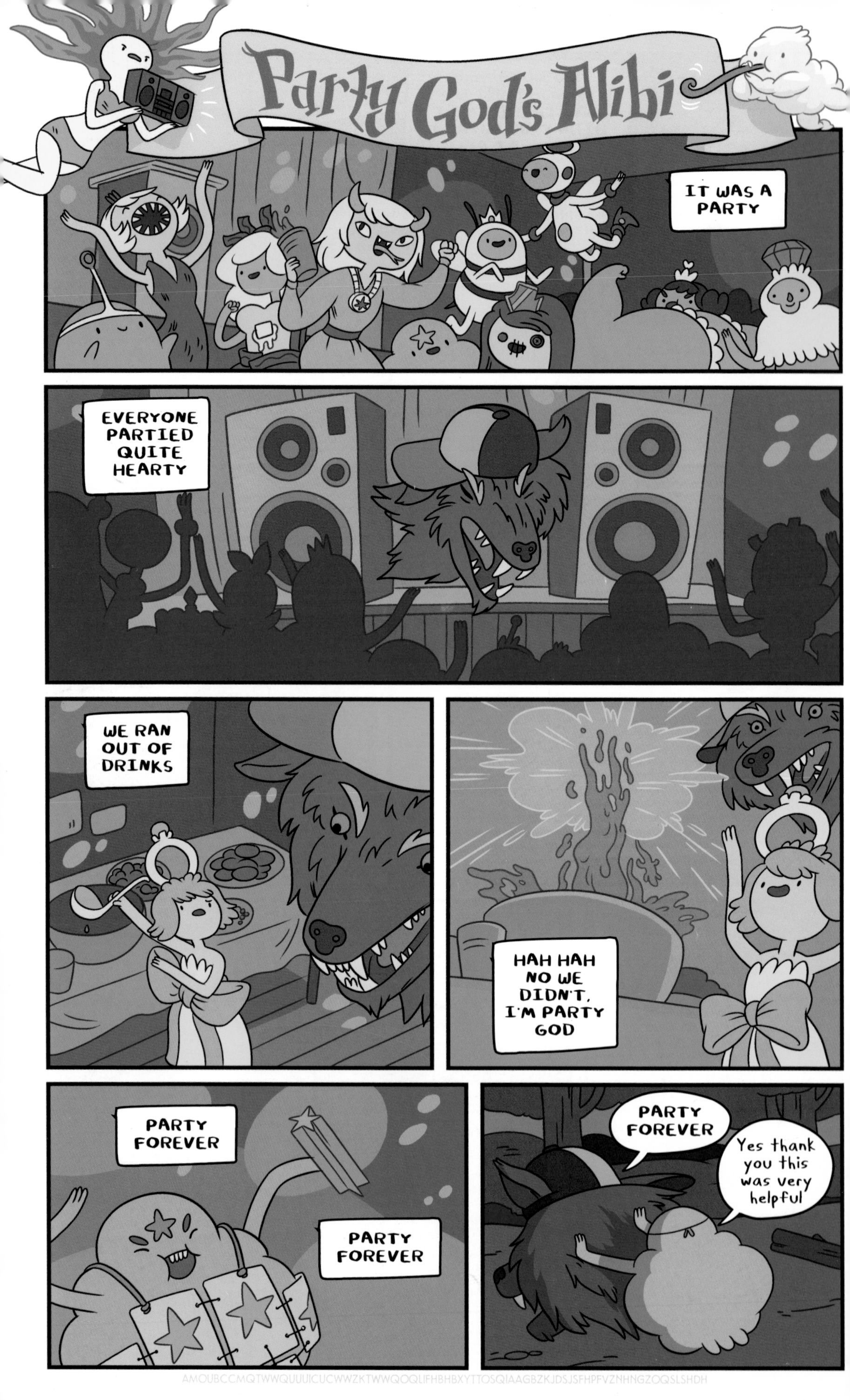

Party God's Alibi
IT WAS A PARTY
EVERYONE PARTIED QUITE HEARTY
WE RAN OUT OF DRINKS
HAH HAH NO WE DIDN'T, I'M PARTY GOD
PARTY FOREVER
PARTY FOREVER
PARTY FOREVER
Yes thank you this was very helpful

AMOUBCCMQTWWQUUUICUCWWZKTWWQOQLIFHBHBXYTTOSQIAAGBZKJDSJSFHPFVZNHNGZOQSLSHDH

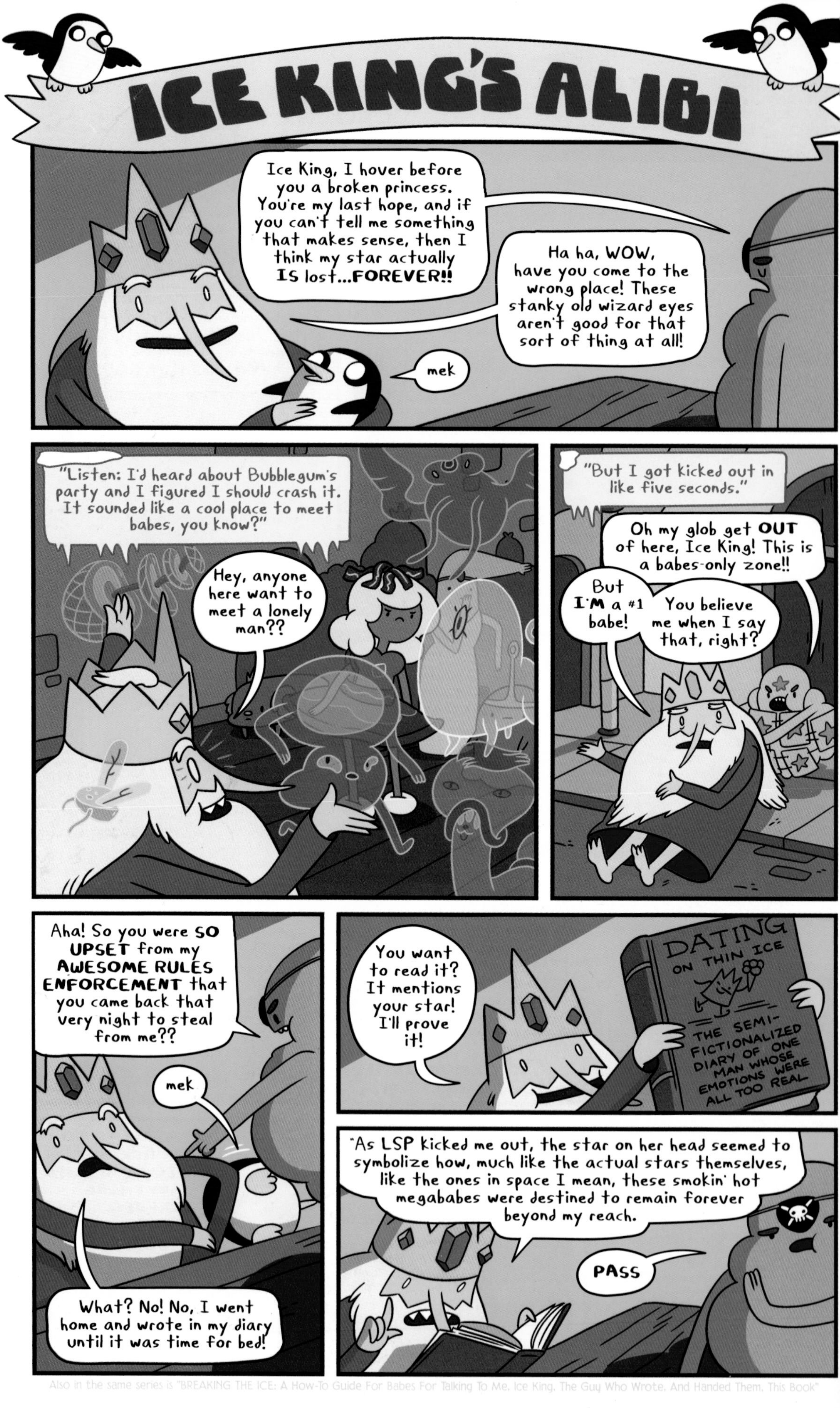
ICE KING'S ALIBI
Ice King, I hover before you a broken princess. You're my last hope, and if you can't tell me something that makes sense, then I think my star actually IS lost...FOREVER!!
Ha ha, WOW, have you come to the wrong place! These stanky old wizard eyes aren't good for that sort of thing at all!
mek
"Listen: I'd heard about Bubblegum's party and I figured I should crash it. It sounded like a cool place to meet babes, you know?"
Hey, anyone here want to meet a lonely man??
"But I got kicked out in like five seconds."
Oh my glob get OUT of here, Ice King! This is a babes-only zone!!
But I'M a #1 babe!
You believe me when I say that, right?
Aha! So you were SO UPSET from my AWESOME RULES ENFORCEMENT that you came back that very night to steal from me??
mek
What? No! No, I went home and wrote in my diary until it was time for bed!
You want to read it? It mentions your star! I'll prove it!
DATING ON THIN ICE
THE SEMI-FICTIONALIZED DIARY OF ONE MAN WHOSE EMOTIONS WERE ALL TOO REAL
"As LSP kicked me out, the star on her head seemed to symbolize how, much like the actual stars themselves, like the ones in space I mean, these smokin' hot megababes were destined to remain forever beyond my reach.
PASS

Also in the same series is "BREAKING THE ICE: A How-To Guide For Babes For Talking To Me, Ice King, The Guy Who Wrote, And Handed Them, This Book"

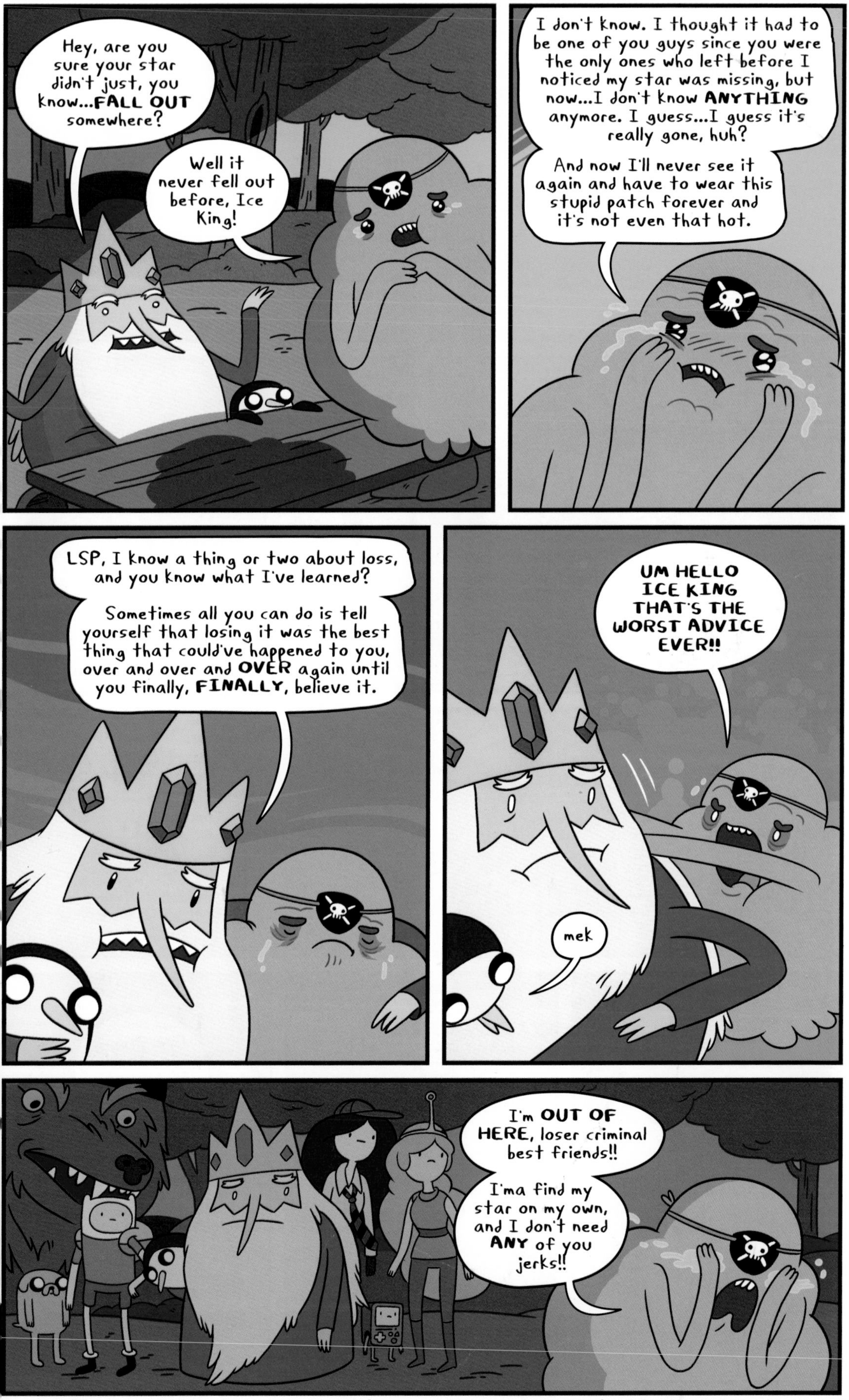
Hey, are you sure your star didn't just, you know...FALL OUT somewhere?
Well it never fell out before, Ice King!
I don't know. I thought it had to be one of you guys since you were the only ones who left before I noticed my star was missing, but now...I don't know ANYTHING anymore. I guess...I guess it's really gone, huh?
And now I'll never see it again and have to wear this stupid patch forever and it's not even that hot.
LSP, I know a thing or two about loss, and you know what I've learned?
Sometimes all you can do is tell yourself that losing it was the best thing that could've happened to you, over and over and OVER again until you finally, FINALLY, believe it.
UM HELLO ICE KING THAT'S THE WORST ADVICE EVER!!
mek
I'm OUT OF HERE, loser criminal best friends!!
I'ma find my star on my own, and I don't need ANY of you jerks!!

Man that was awkward. Are you reading this text down here because you hope to feel less awkward about spying on that raw display of emotion? Well **TOO BAD**, it's awkward down here too!!

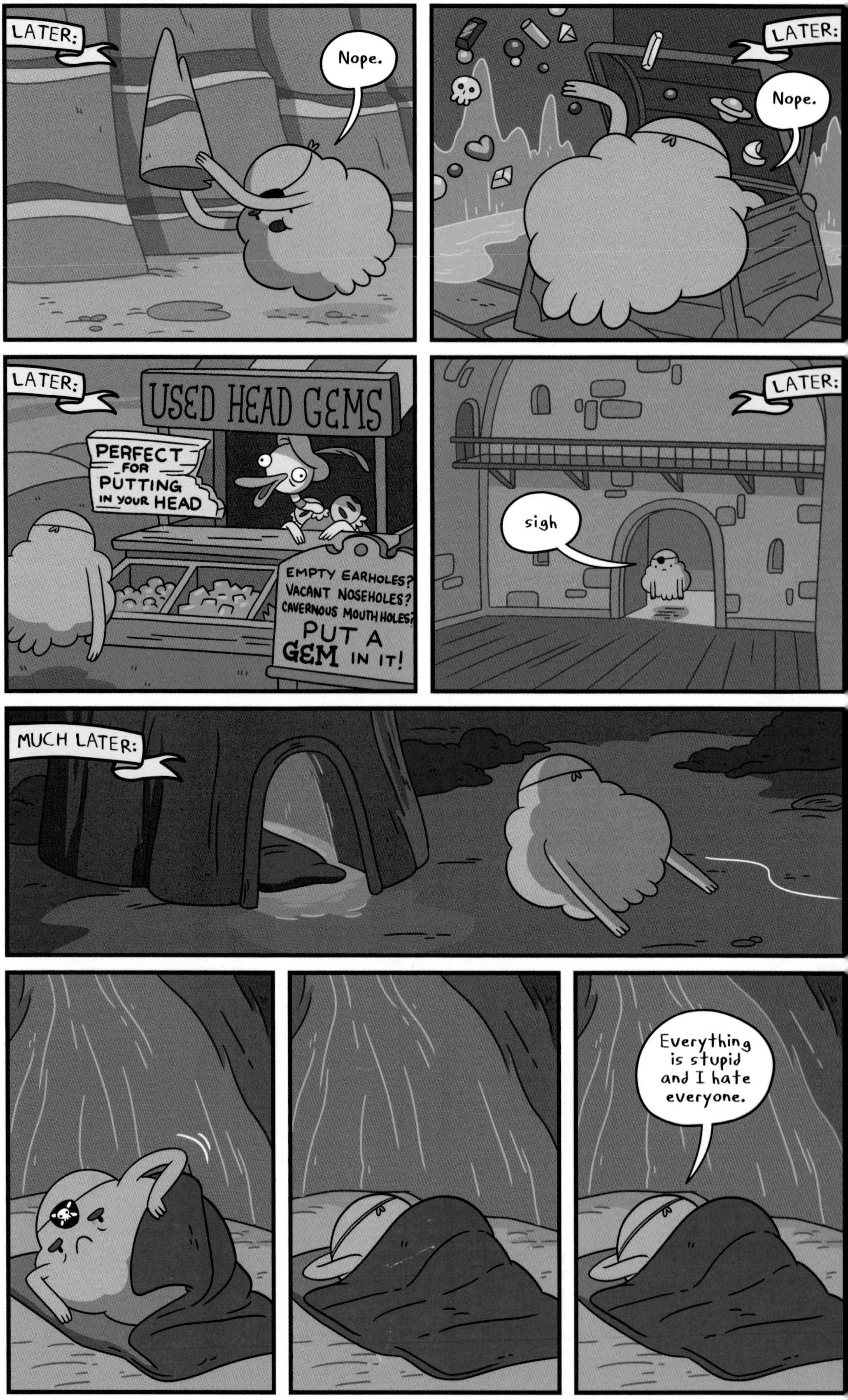
LATER:
Nope.
LATER:
Nope.
LATER:
USED HEAD GEMS
PERFECT FOR PUTTING IN YOUR HEAD
EMPTY EARHOLES? VACANT NOSEHOLES? CAVERNOUS MOUTH HOLES? PUT A GEM IN IT!
LATER:
sigh
MUCH LATER:
Everything is stupid and I hate everyone.

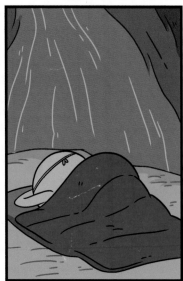

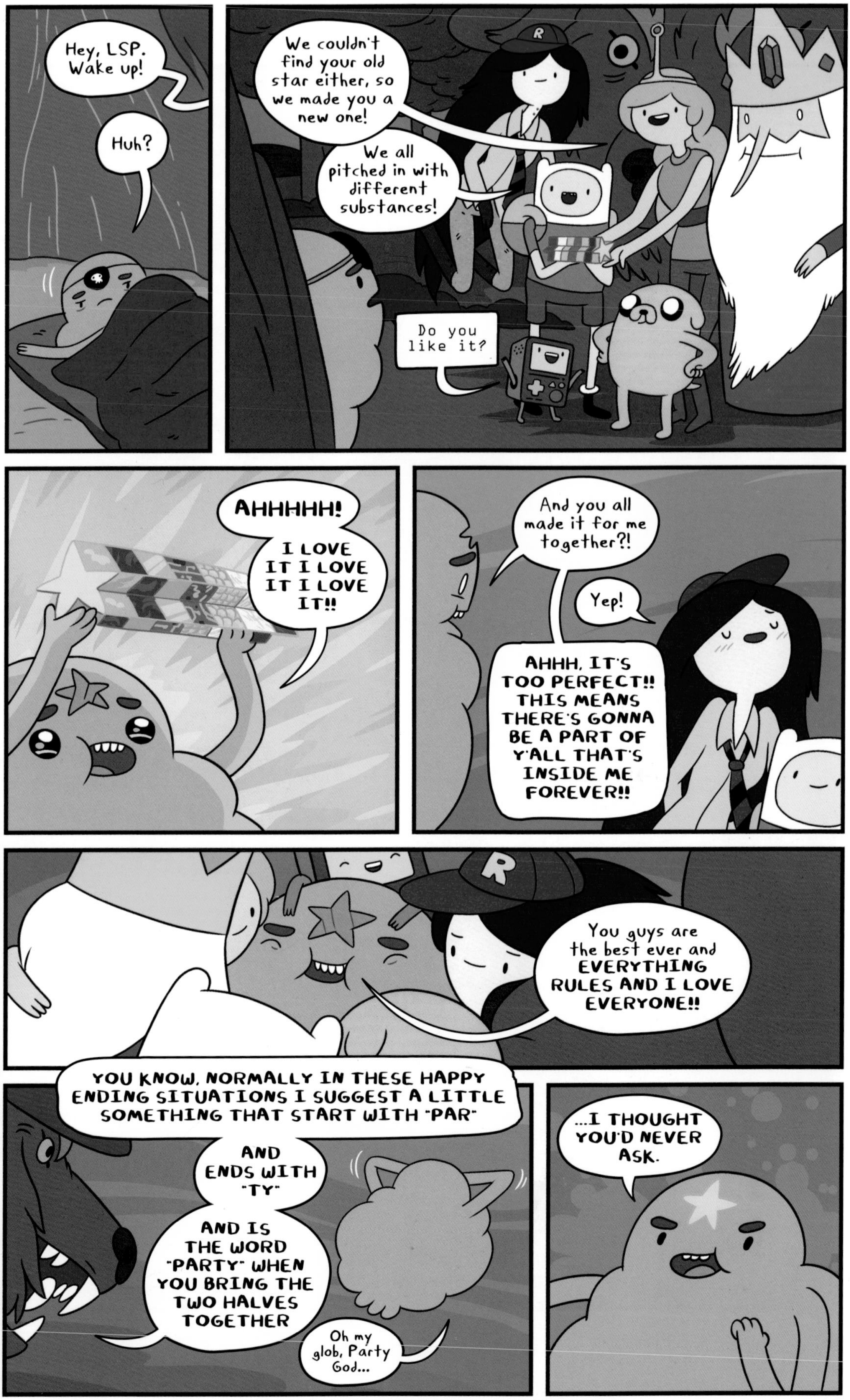
Hey, LSP. Wake up!
Huh?
We couldn't find your old star either, so we made you a new one!
We all pitched in with different substances!
Do you like it?
AHHHHH!
I LOVE IT I LOVE IT I LOVE IT!!
And you all made it for me together?!
Yep!
AHHH, IT'S TOO PERFECT!! THIS MEANS THERE'S GONNA BE A PART OF Y'ALL THAT'S INSIDE ME FOREVER!!
You guys are the best ever and EVERYTHING RULES AND I LOVE EVERYONE!!
YOU KNOW, NORMALLY IN THESE HAPPY ENDING SITUATIONS I SUGGEST A LITTLE SOMETHING THAT START WITH "PAR"
AND ENDS WITH "TY"
AND IS THE WORD "PARTY" WHEN YOU BRING THE TWO HALVES TOGETHER
Oh my glob, Party God...
...I THOUGHT YOU'D NEVER ASK.

LIOQSLSNHOGNSEQSLSOUZUSYTLBDGVWMSYPFCLUBFNGQUAMSXFHUQJZ

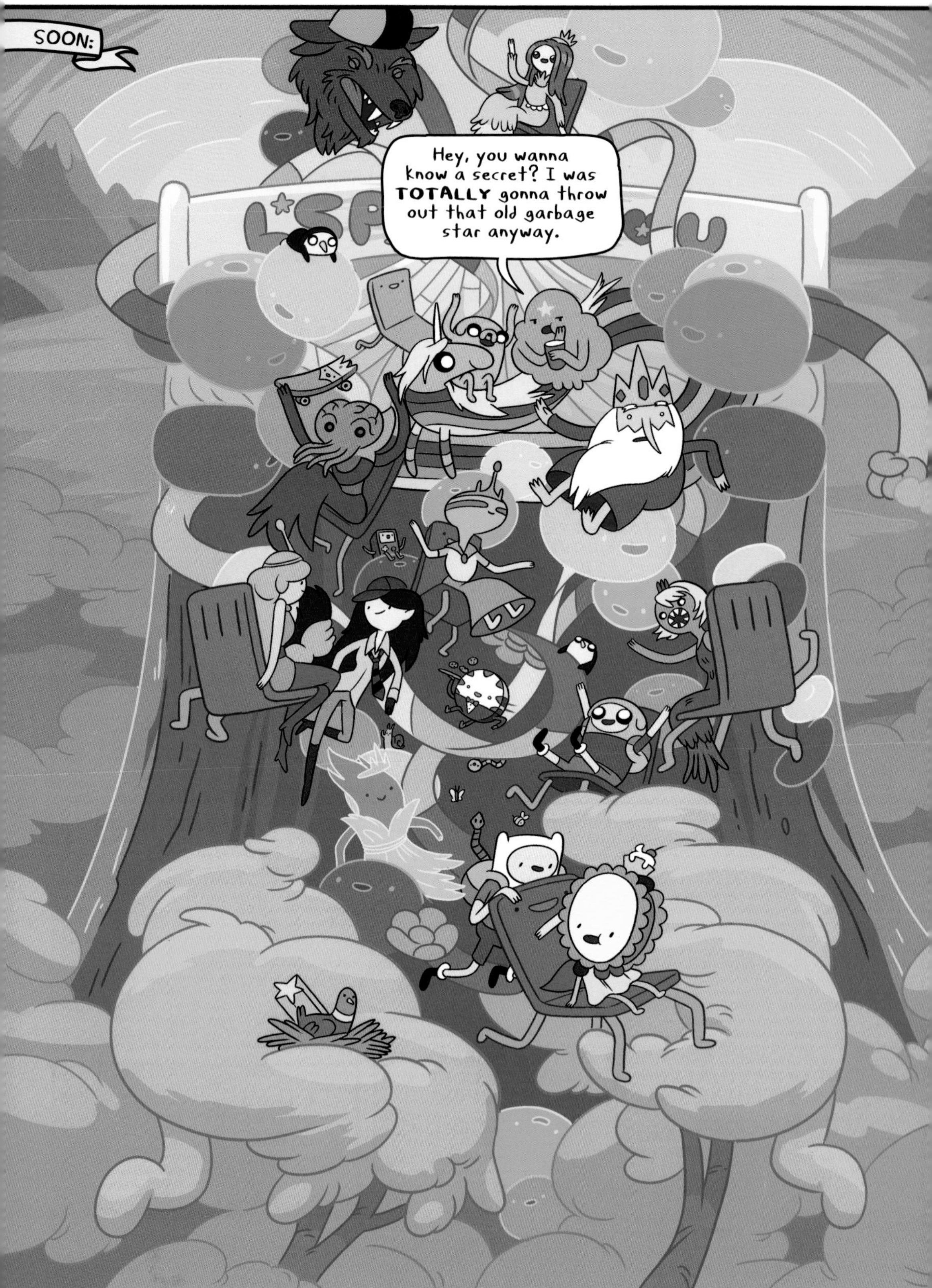
SOON:
Hey, you wanna know a secret? I was **TOTALLY** gonna throw out that old garbage star anyway.

A> <B

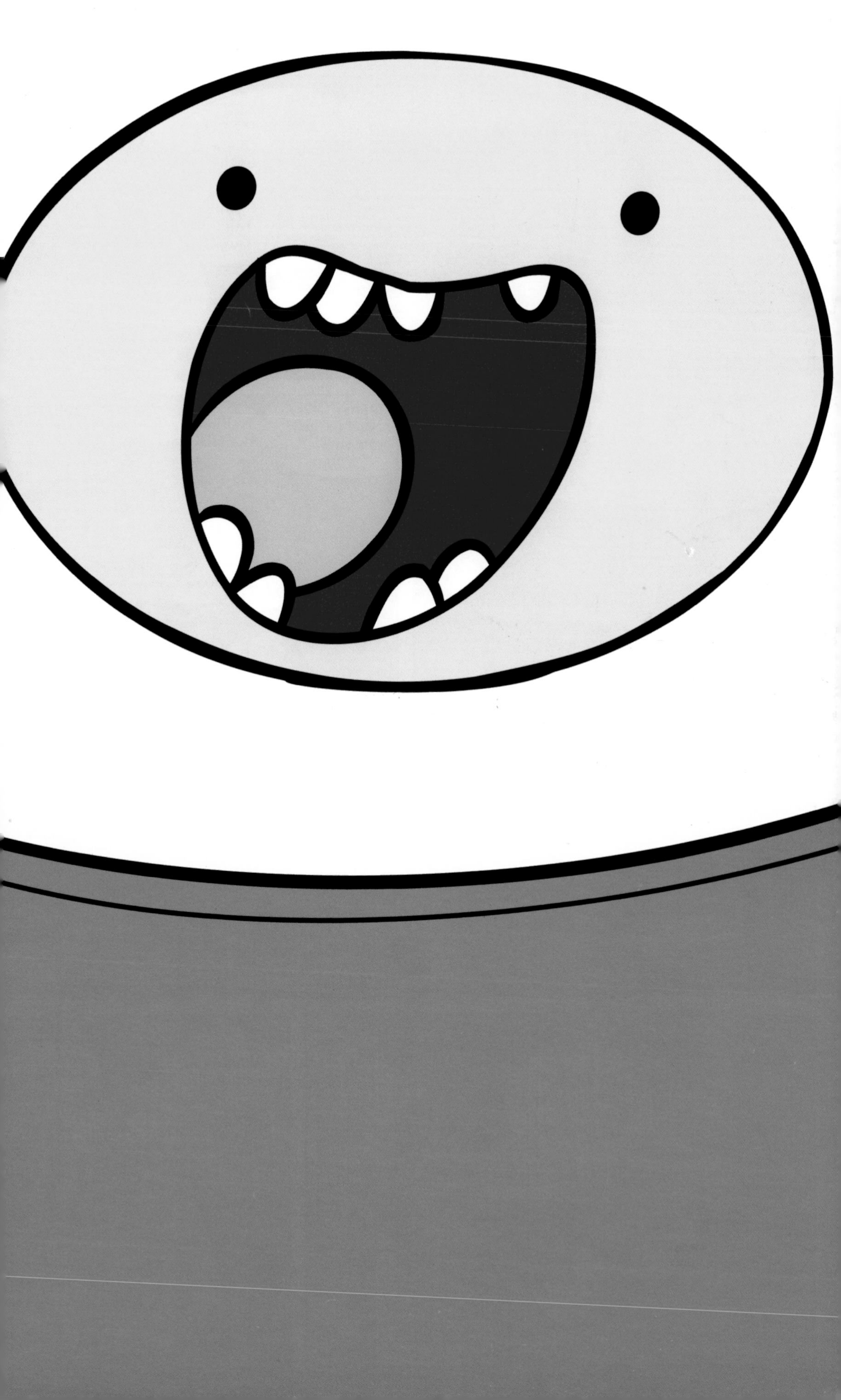

It went in that portal. Are we **ADVENTURERS** not **SURELY TASKED** to **BOLDY FOLLOW**?

I don't know man. **MYSTERIOUS PORTALS** give me the spookie-ookies.

Even if you **ARE** talkin' all knightly.

Afraid of portals? What are you, Jake the **CLOG**?

'Cause like, you're **CLOGGING** my good times?

I'm Jake the **DOG**. The **MAGIC DOG**. Bark bark bark!

Ha ha, I know, buddy. Jay kay. You're not a good times clog.

Bark bark bark!

Ha ha

Okay. Okay. Gotta get you back. Are you...

...Finn the **HU**-- --**MAN**?

Or Fin the huuuuuu....

Reach for it, dude. I believe in you.

...uuuuge **WUSS**?

Nice.

I'm Finn the human, baby! Let's **DO THIS**.

YEAH!

Wait did you trick me into motivating **BOTH** of us to jump in?

I did!

Oh dang. Oh dang oh dang oh dang.

Where **ARE** we?

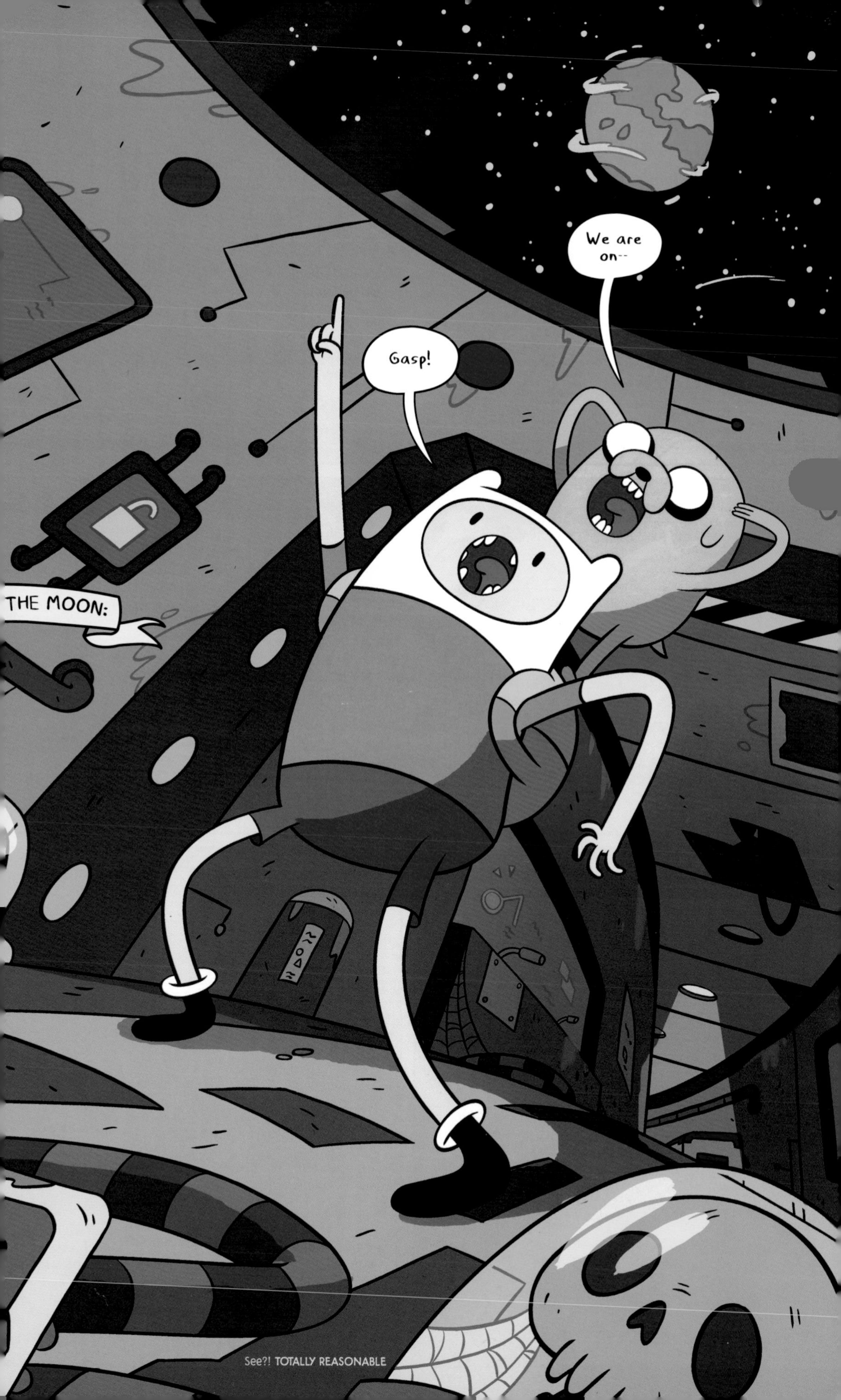
THE MOON:
Gasp!
We are on--
See?! TOTALLY REASONABLE

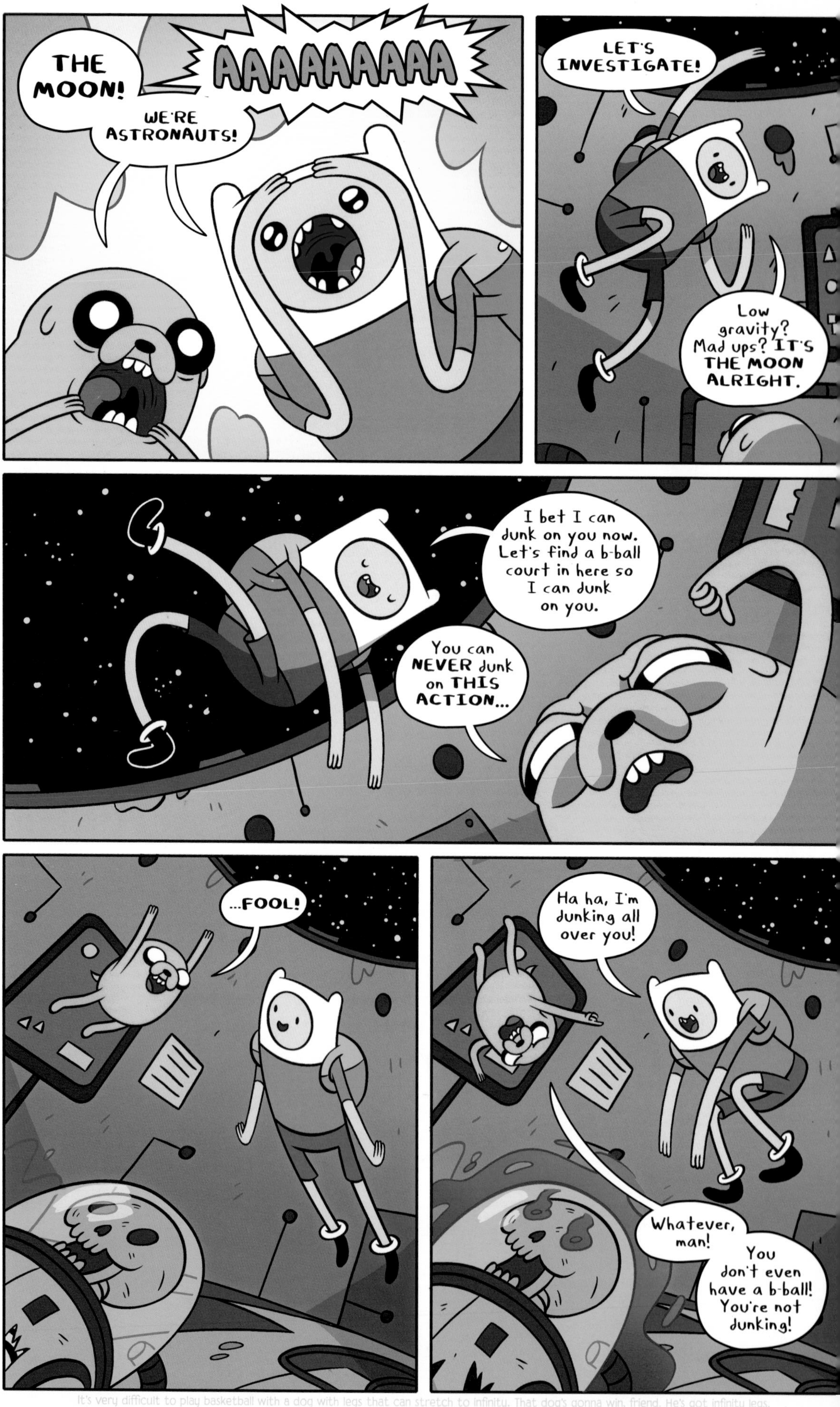
THE MOON!
AAAAAAAAA
WE'RE ASTRONAUTS!
LET'S INVESTIGATE!
Low gravity? Mad ups? IT'S THE MOON ALRIGHT.
I bet I can dunk on you now. Let's find a b-ball court in here so I can dunk on you.
You can NEVER dunk on THIS ACTION...
...FOOL!
Ha ha, I'm dunking all over you!
Whatever, man!
You don't even have a b-ball! You're not dunking!

It's very difficult to play basketball with a dog with legs that can stretch to infinity. That dog's gonna win, friend. He's got infinity legs.

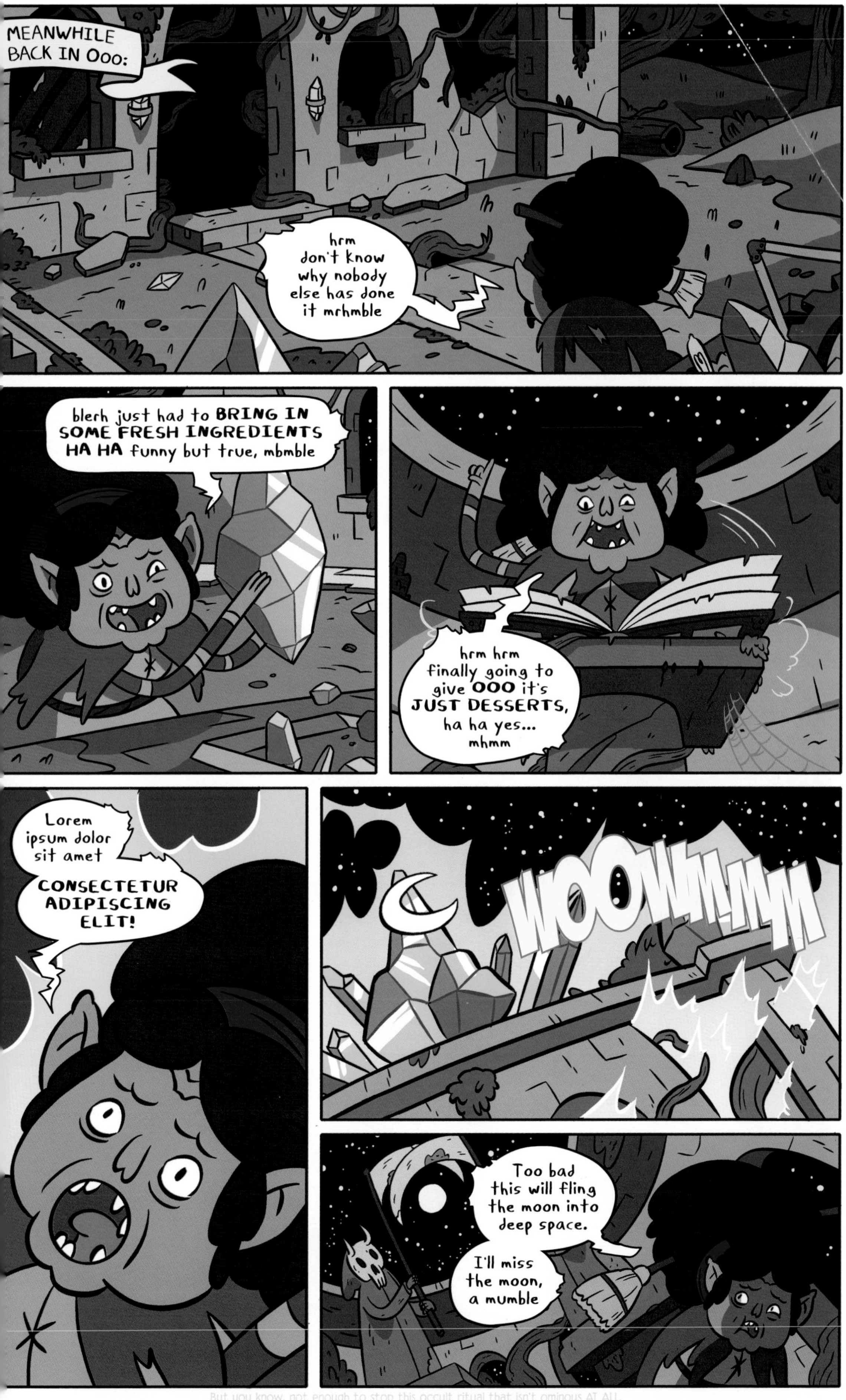

MEANWHILE BACK IN Ooo:
hrm don't know why nobody else has done it mrhmble
blerh just had to BRING IN SOME FRESH INGREDIENTS HA HA funny but true, mbmble
hrm hrm finally going to give OOO it's JUST DESSERTS, ha ha yes... mhmm
Lorem ipsum dolor sit amet
CONSECTETUR ADIPISCING ELIT!
WOOMMMM
Too bad this will fling the moon into deep space.
I'll miss the moon, a mumble

But you know, not enough to stop this occult ritual that isn't ominous AT ALL.

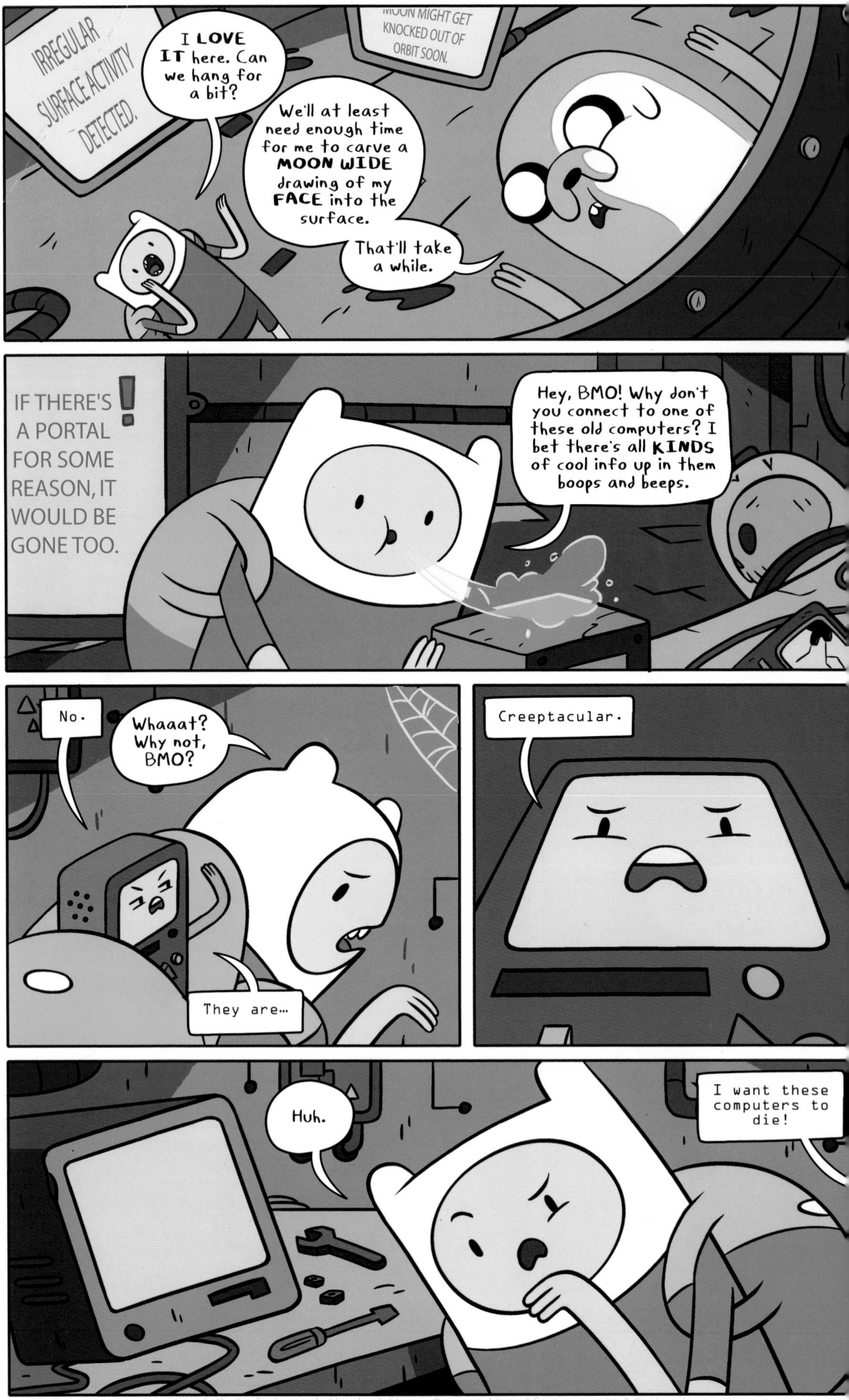

IRREGULAR SURFACE ACTIVITY DETECTED.
MOON MIGHT GET KNOCKED OUT OF ORBIT SOON.
I LOVE IT here. Can we hang for a bit?
We'll at least need enough time for me to carve a MOON WIDE drawing of my FACE into the surface.
That'll take a while.
IF THERE'S A PORTAL FOR SOME REASON, IT WOULD BE GONE TOO.
Hey, BMO! Why don't you connect to one of these old computers? I bet there's all KINDS of cool info up in them boops and beeps.
No.
Whaaat? Why not, BMO?
They are...
Creeptacular.
Huh.
I want these computers to die!

Let's all refer to our desktop hard drives as "boops and beeps" from now on, kay? Cool.

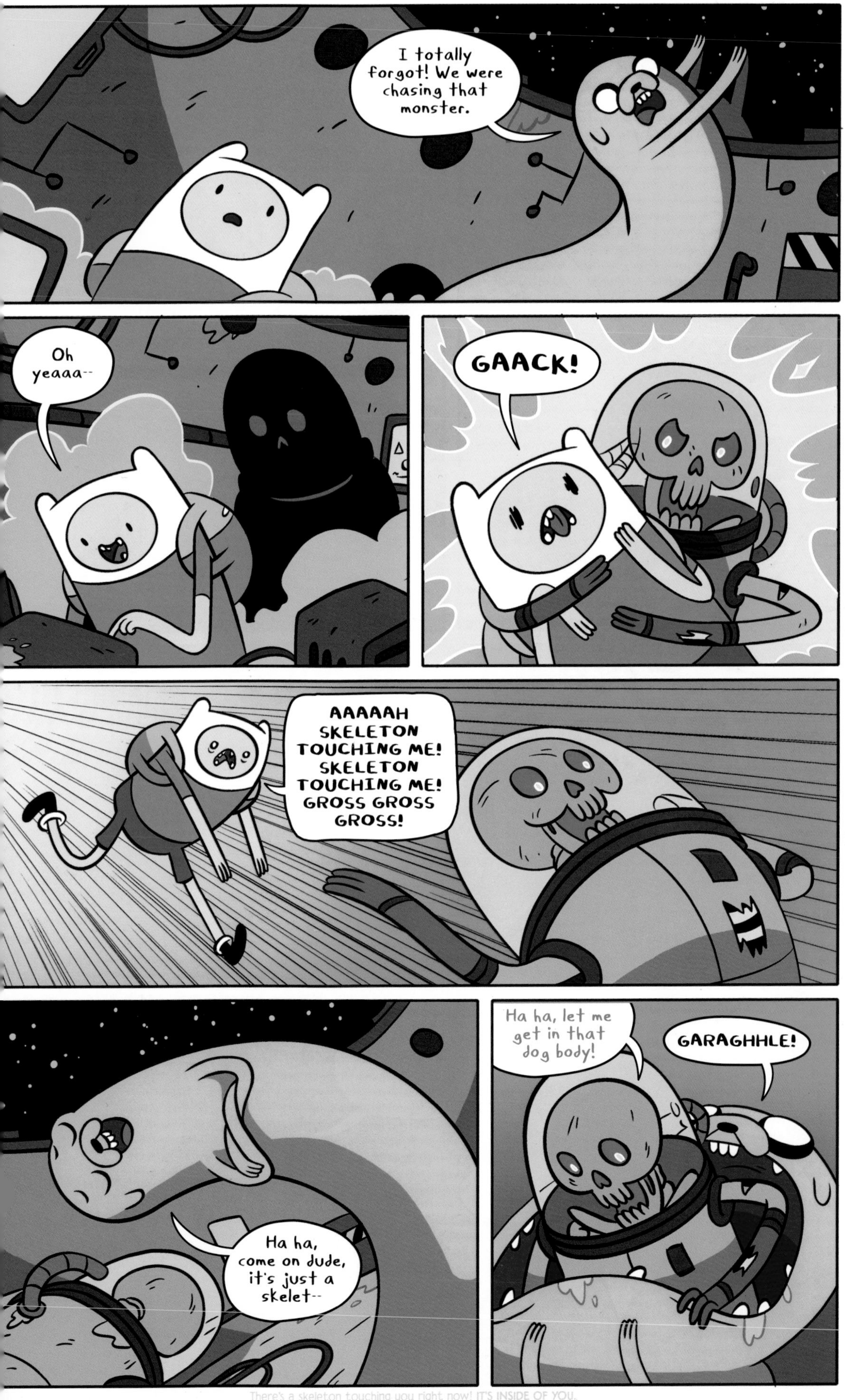
I totally forgot! We were chasing that monster.
Oh yeaaa--
GAACK!
AAAAAH SKELETON TOUCHING ME! SKELETON TOUCHING ME! GROSS GROSS GROSS!
Ha ha, come on dude, it's just a skelet--
Ha ha, let me get in that dog body!
GARAGHHLE!

There's a skeleton touching you right now! IT'S INSIDE OF YOU.

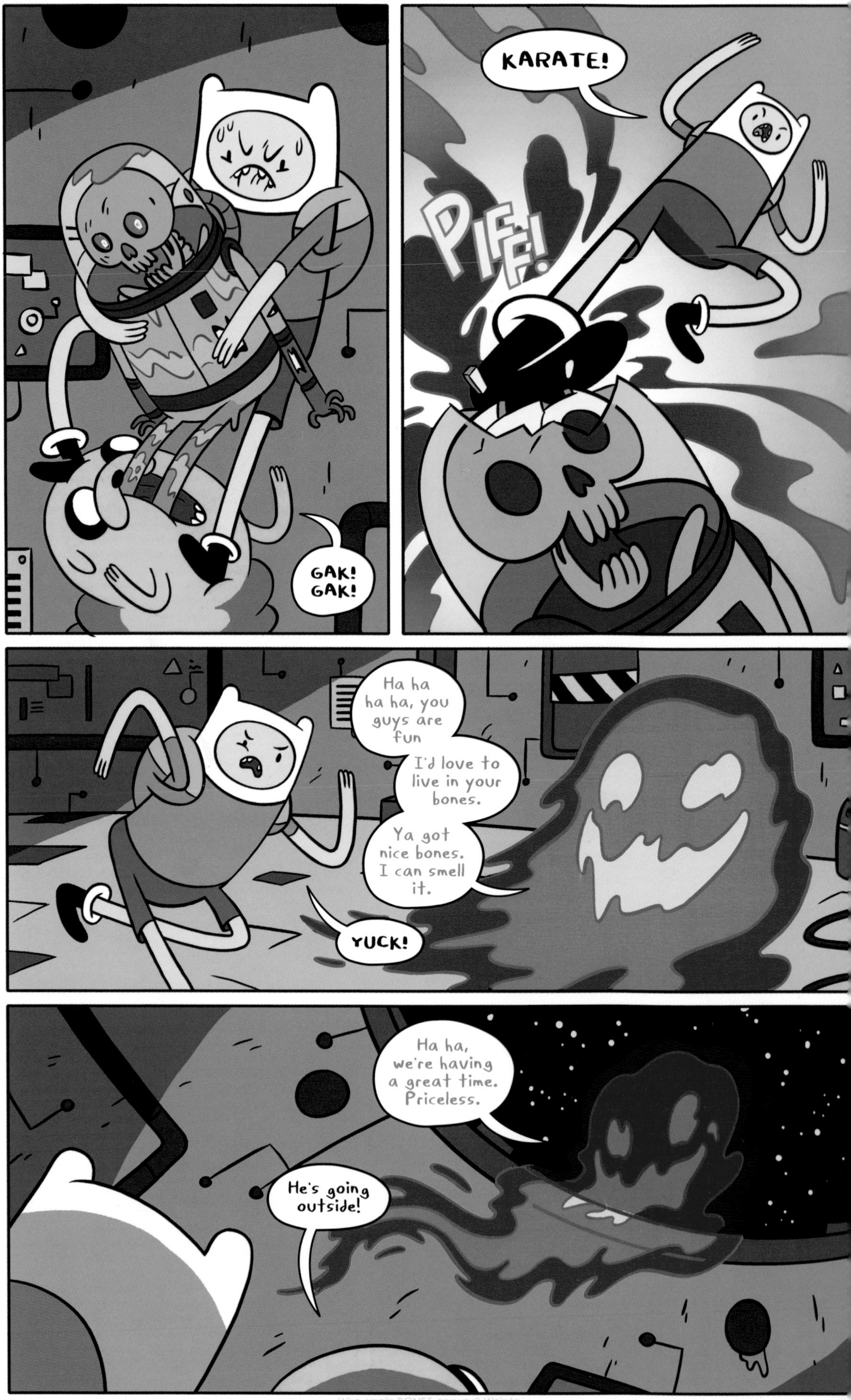
GAK!
GAK!
KARATE!
PIFF!
Ha ha
ha ha, you
guys are
fun
I'd love to
live in your
bones.
Ya got
nice bones.
I can smell
it.
YUCK!
Ha ha,
we're having
a great time.
Priceless.
He's going
outside!

Who smells BONES anyway? Weirdo.

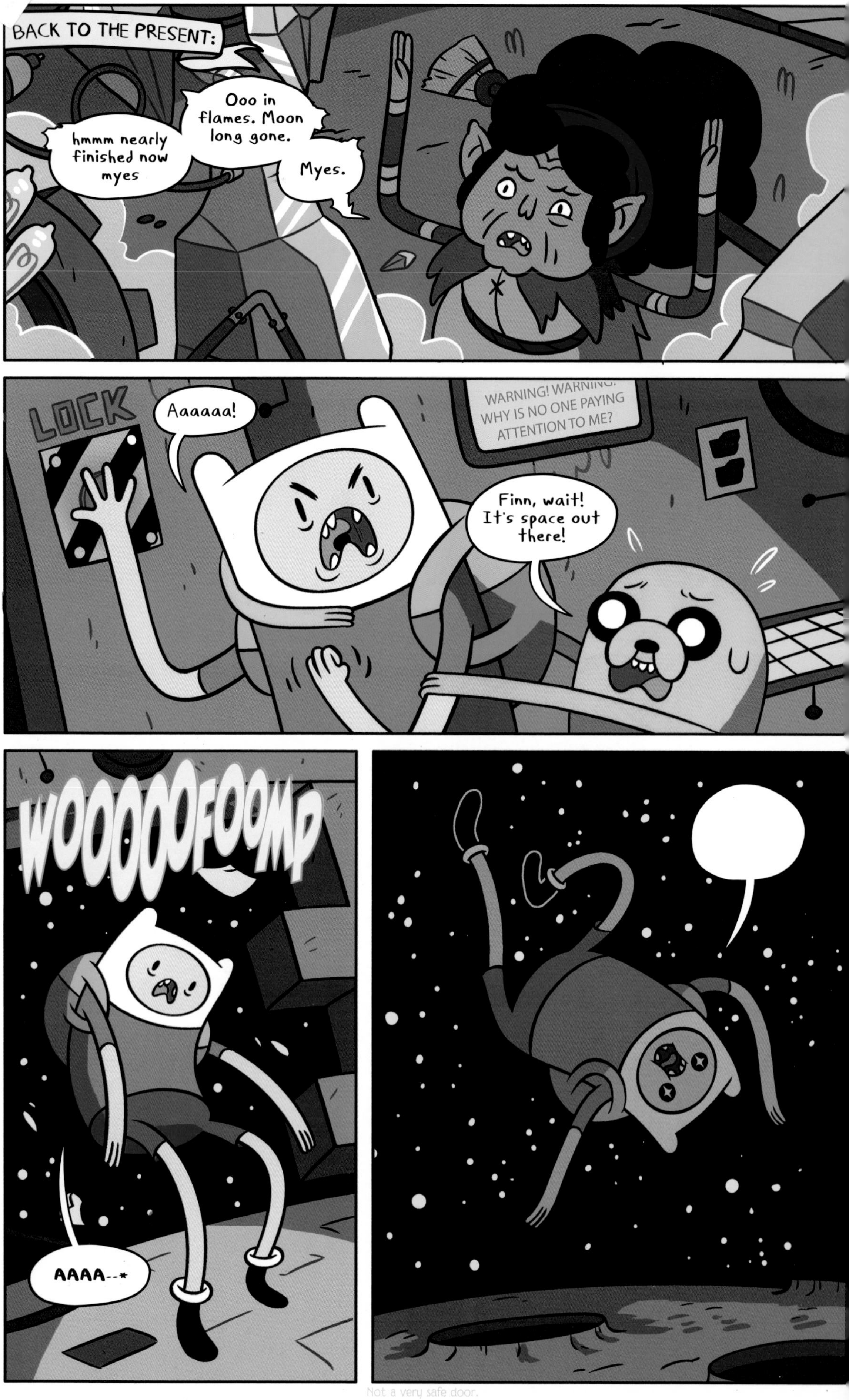
BACK TO THE PRESENT:
hmmm nearly finished now myes
Ooo in flames. Moon long gone.
Myes.
LOCK
Aaaaaa!
WARNING! WARNING! WHY IS NO ONE PAYING ATTENTION TO ME?
Finn, wait! It's space out there!
WOOOOOFOOMP
AAAA--*

Not a very safe door.

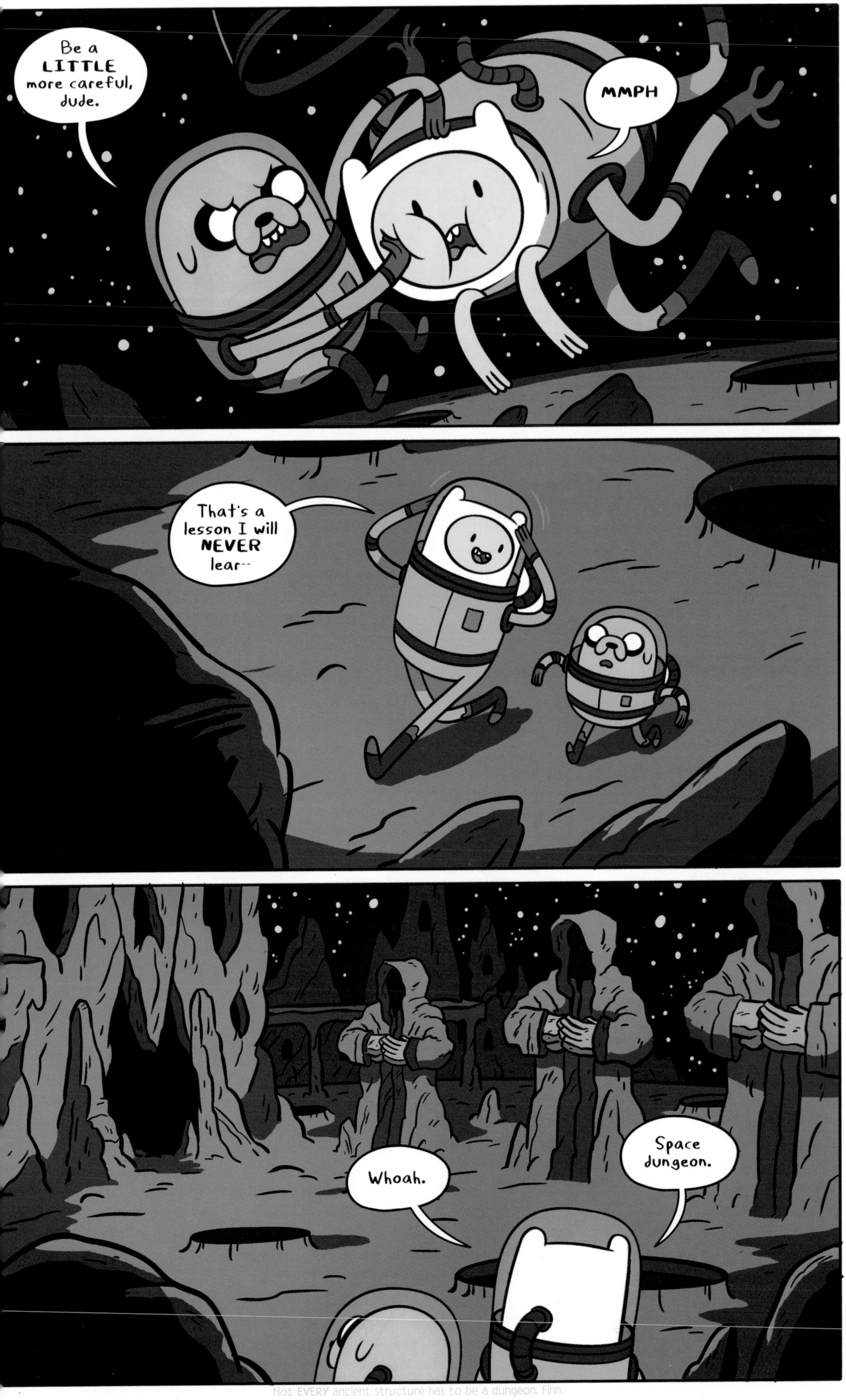
Be a LITTLE more careful, dude.
MMPH
That's a lesson I will NEVER lear--
Whoah.
Space dungeon.

Not EVERY ancient structure has to be a dungeon, Finn.

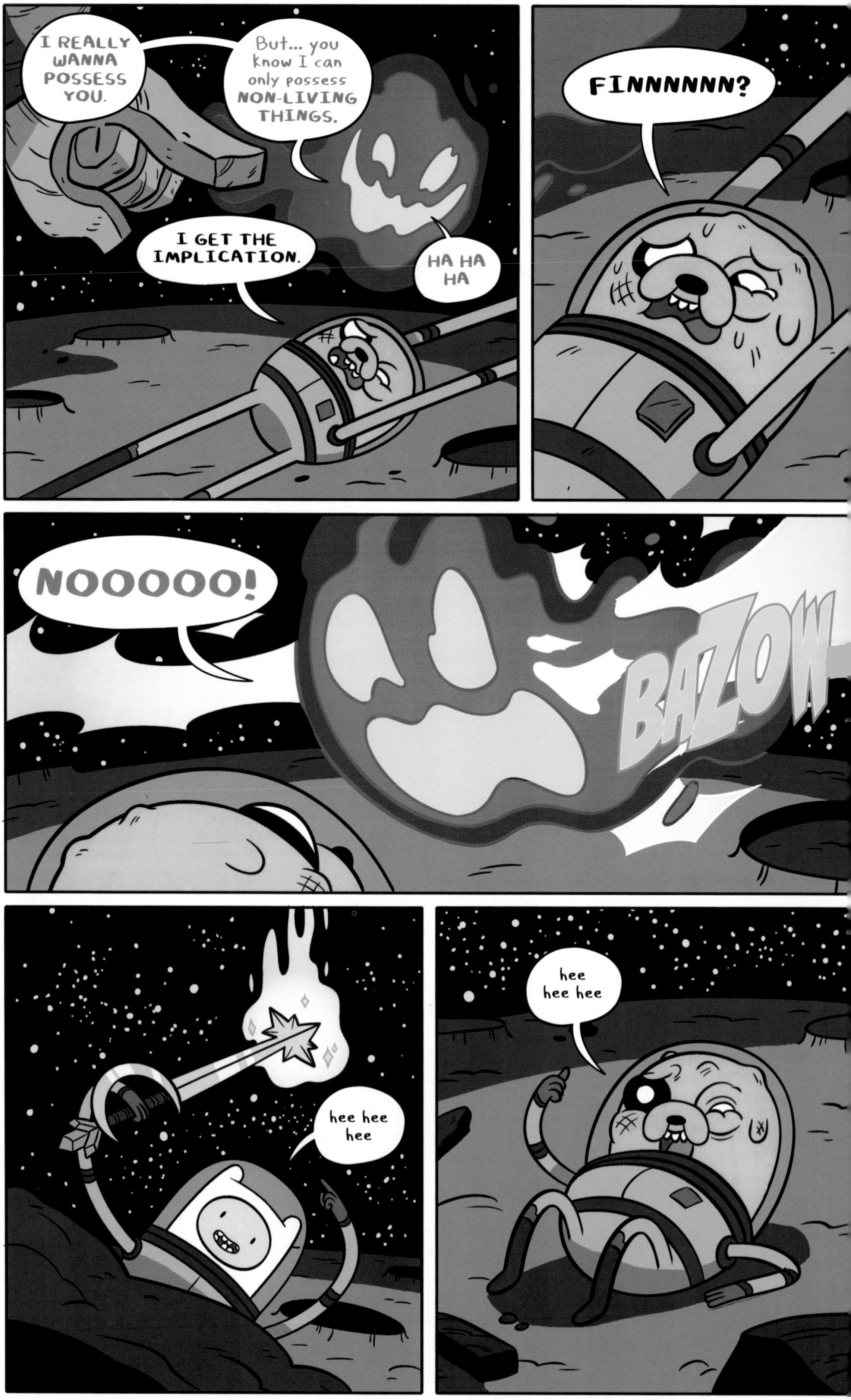
I REALLY WANNA POSSESS YOU.
But... you know I can only possess NON-LIVING THINGS.
I GET THE IMPLICATION.
HA HA HA
FINNNNNN?
NOOOOO!
BAZOW
hee hee hee
hee hee hee

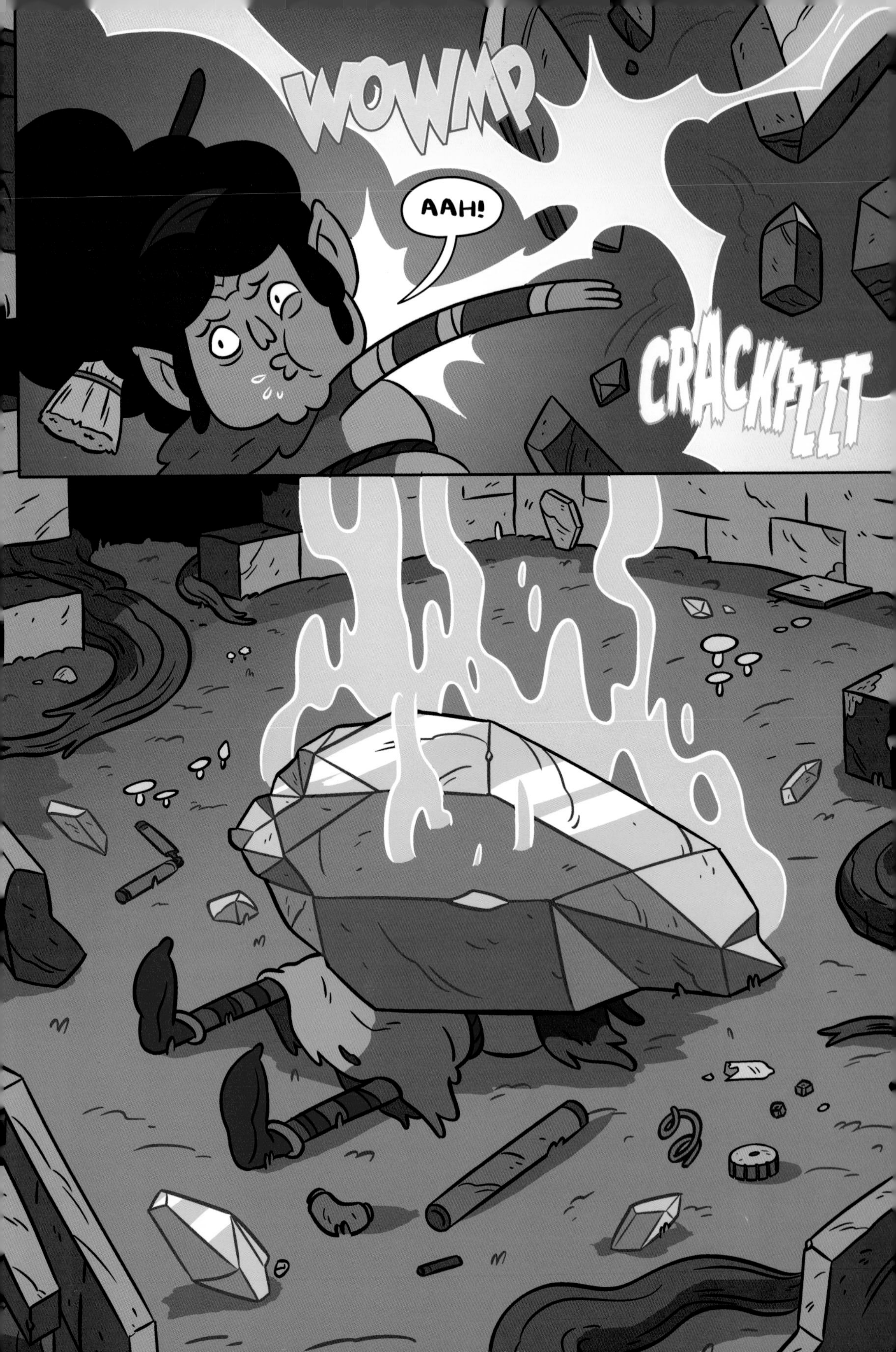
WOWMP
AAH!
CRACKFZZT

She's just sleeping. Probably.

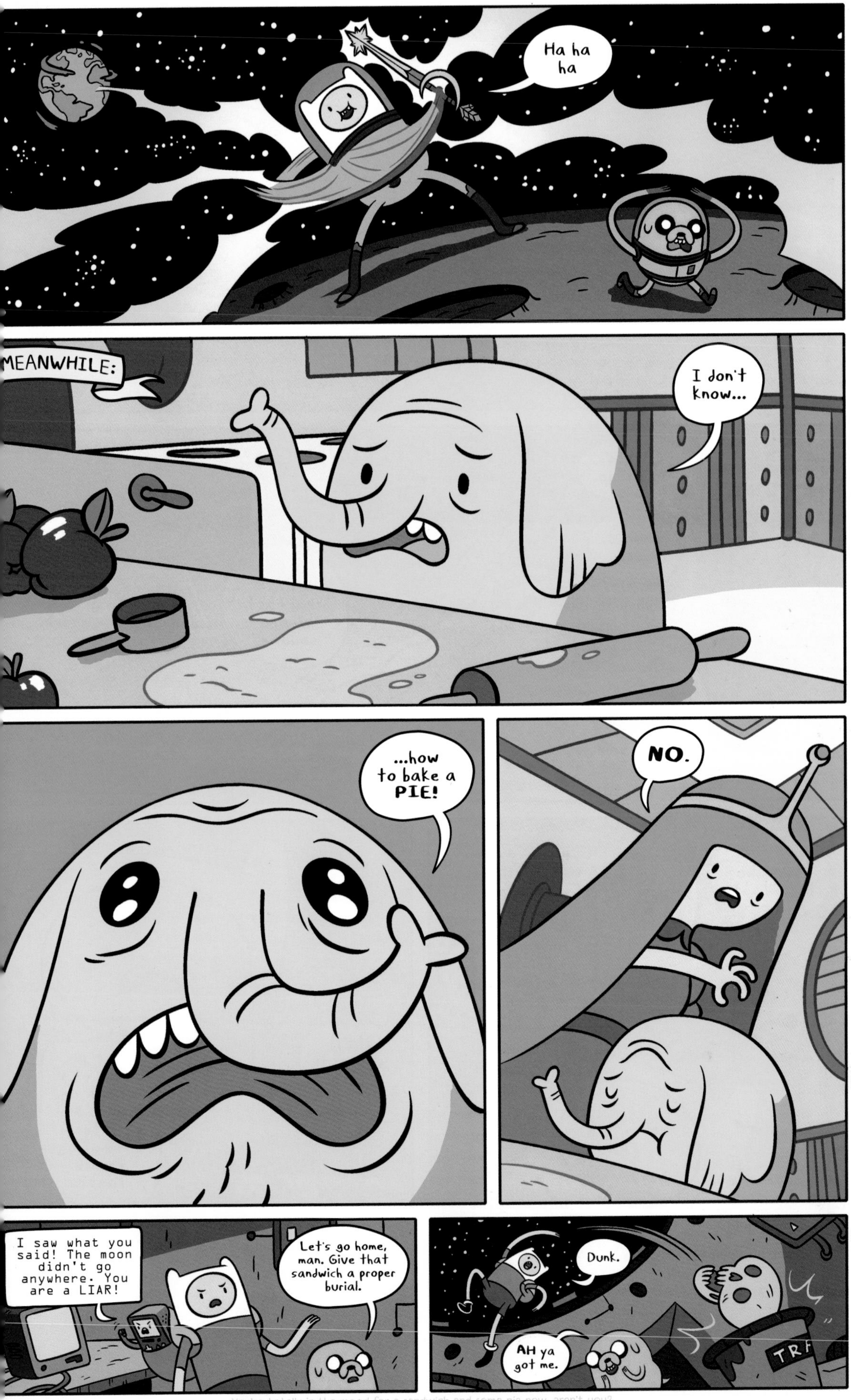
Ha ha ha
MEANWHILE:
I don't know...
...how to bake a PIE!
NO.
I saw what you said! The moon didn't go anywhere. You are a LIAR!
Let's go home, man. Give that sandwich a proper burial.
Dunk.
AH ya got me.

You're totally in the mood for a sandwich and some pie now, aren't you?

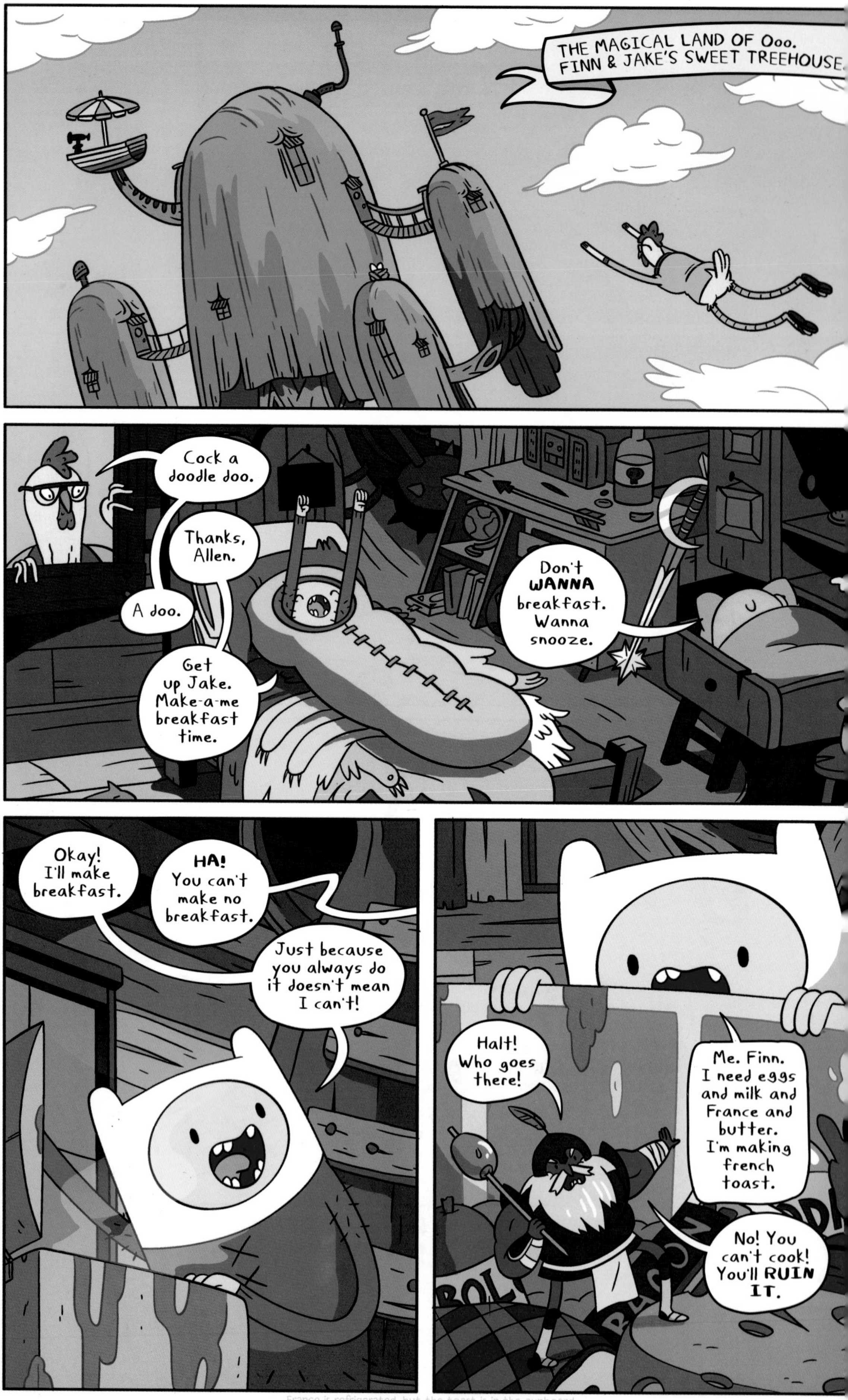
THE MAGICAL LAND OF Ooo. FINN & JAKE'S SWEET TREEHOUSE.
Cock a doodle doo.
Thanks, Allen.
A doo.
Get up Jake. Make-a-me breakfast time.
Don't WANNA breakfast. Wanna snooze.
Okay! I'll make breakfast.
HA! You can't make no breakfast.
Just because you always do it doesn't mean I can't!
Halt! Who goes there!
Me. Finn. I need eggs and milk and France and butter. I'm making french toast.
No! You can't cook! You'll RUIN IT.

France is refrigerated, but the toast is in the cupboard.

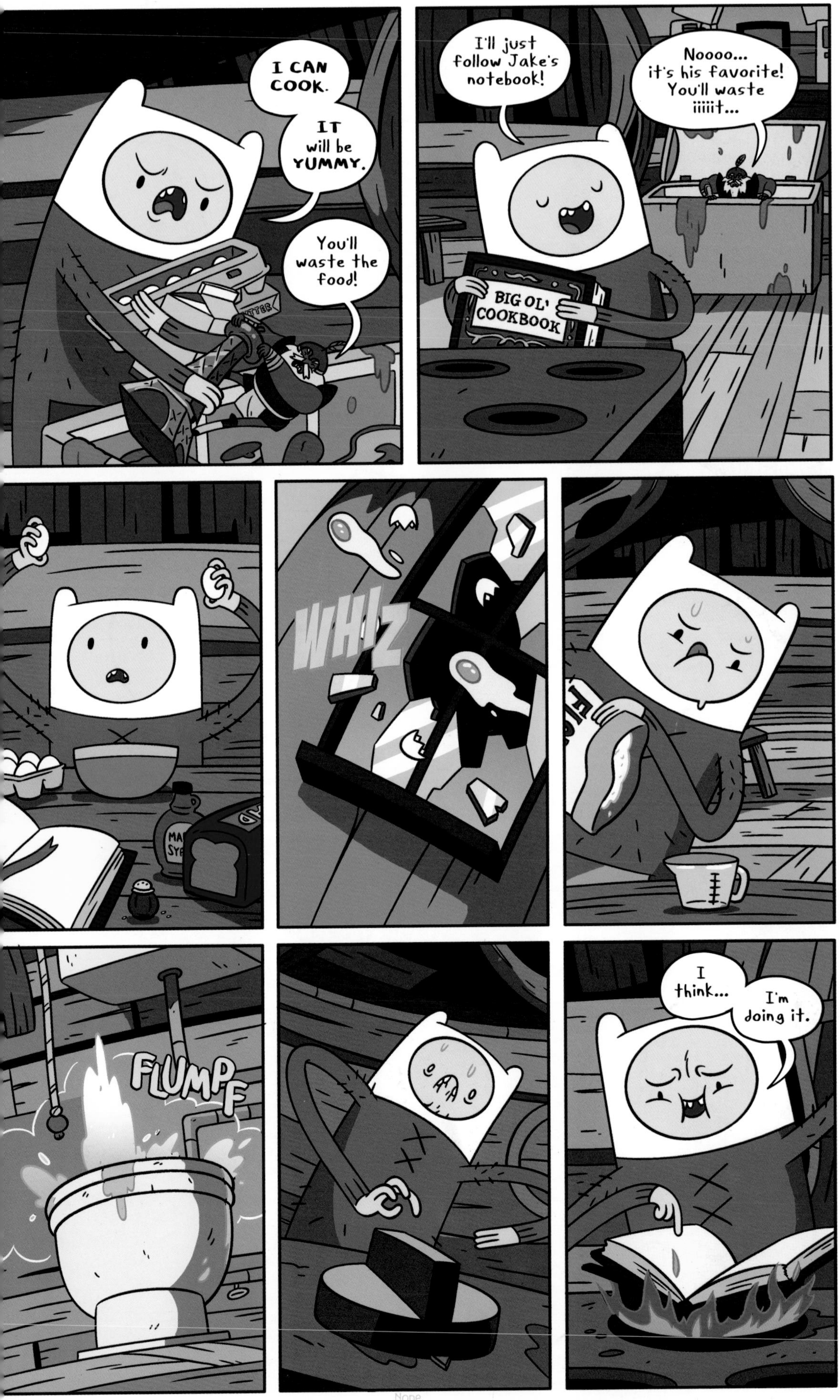
I CAN COOK.
IT will be YUMMY.
You'll waste the food!
BUTTER
I'll just follow Jake's notebook!
Noooo... it's his favorite! You'll waste iiiiit...
BIG OL' COOKBOOK
WHIZ
FLUMPF
I think...
I'm doing it.
Nope.

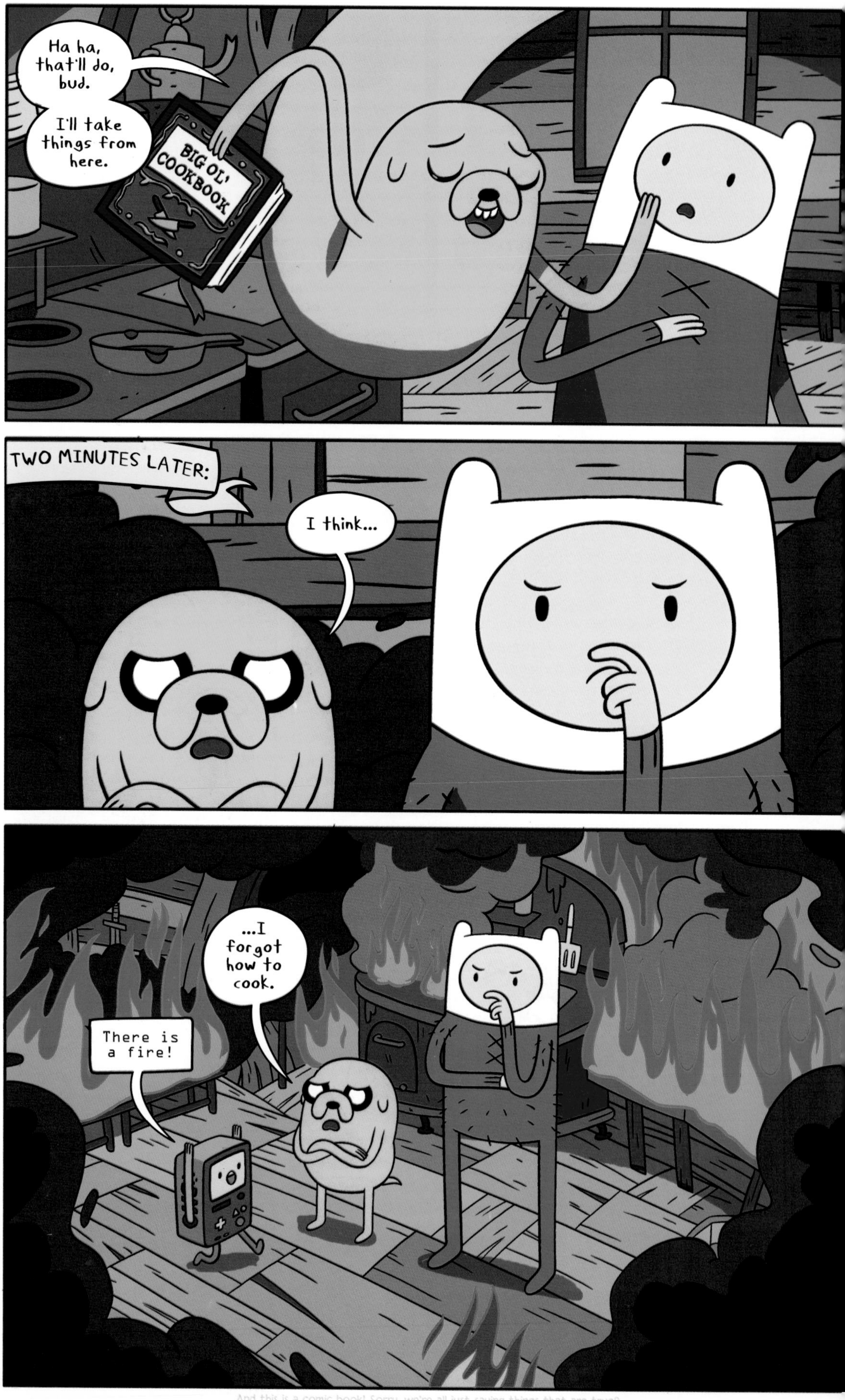
Ha ha, that'll do, bud.
I'll take things from here.
BIG OL' COOKBOOK
TWO MINUTES LATER:
I think...
...I forgot how to cook.
There is a fire!

And this is a comic book! Sorry, we're all just saying things that are true?

Lazers = Maturity. Put it on a t-shirt. Tattoo it on my body.

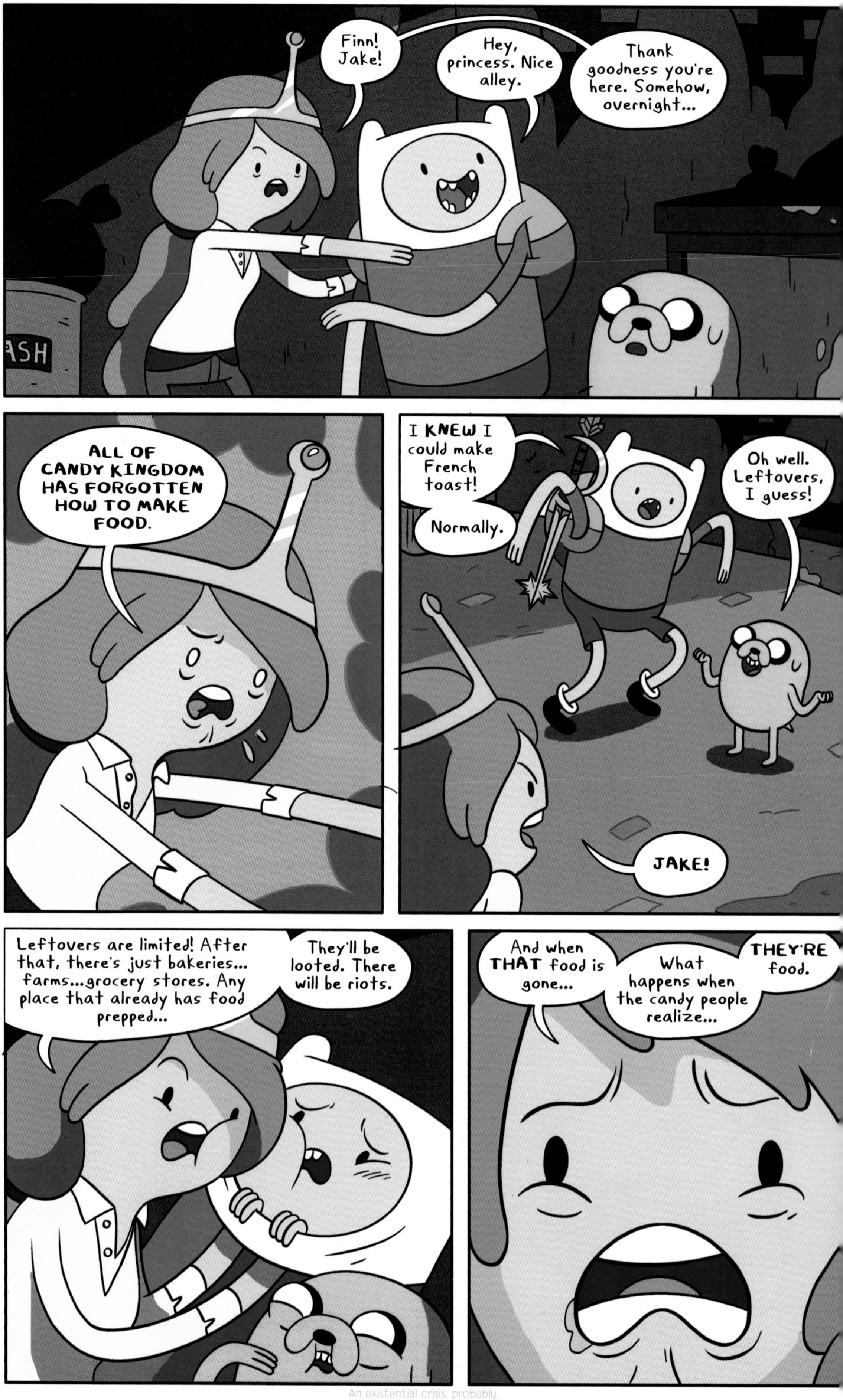
Finn! Jake!
Hey, princess. Nice alley.
Thank goodness you're here. Somehow, overnight...
ASH
ALL OF CANDY KINGDOM HAS FORGOTTEN HOW TO MAKE FOOD.
I KNEW I could make French toast!
Normally.
Oh well. Leftovers, I guess!
JAKE!
Leftovers are limited! After that, there's just bakeries... farms...grocery stores. Any place that already has food prepped...
They'll be looted. There will be riots.
And when THAT food is gone...
What happens when the candy people realize...
THEY'RE food.

An existential crisis, probably.

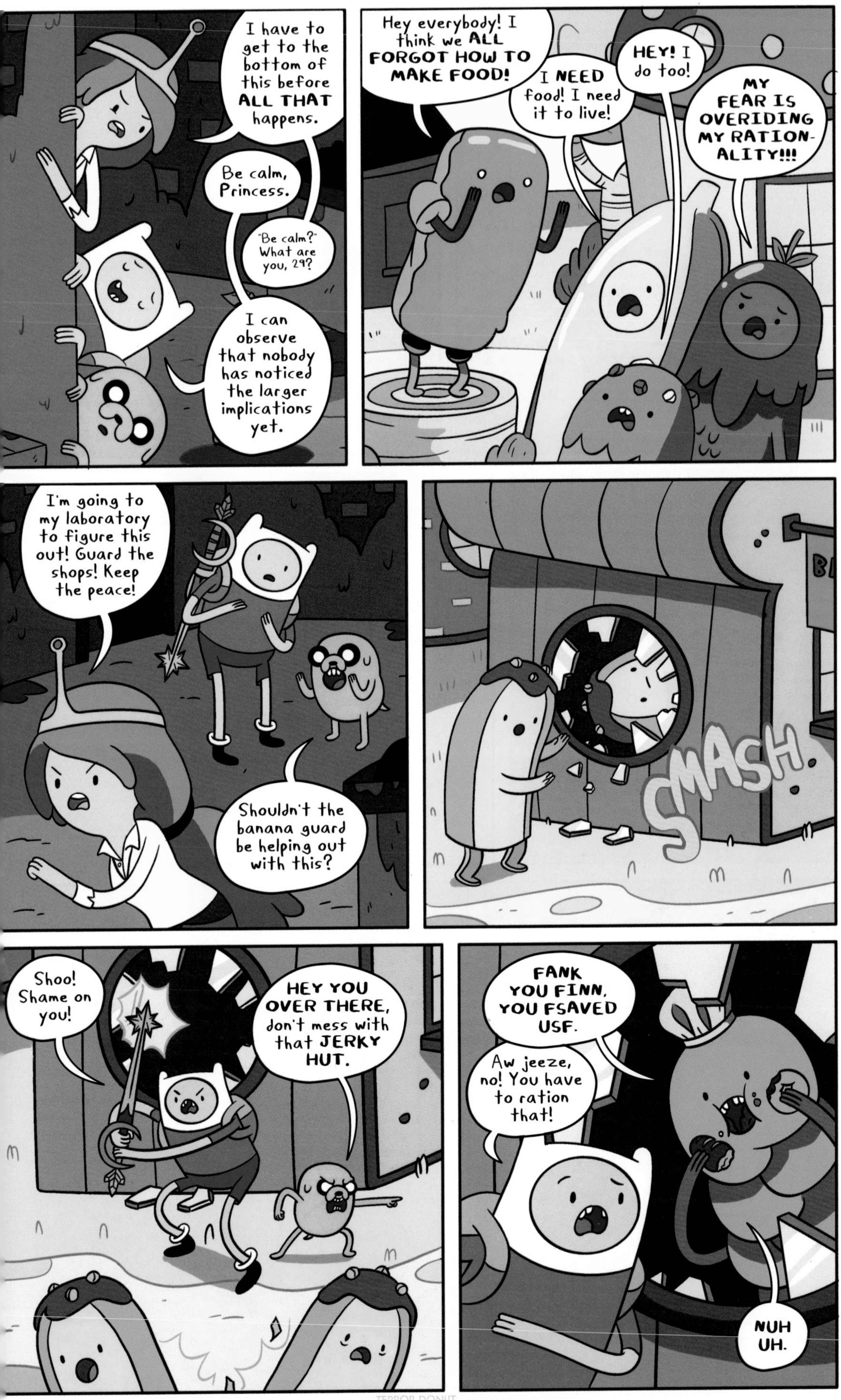

I have to get to the bottom of this before ALL THAT happens.
Be calm, Princess.
"Be calm?" What are you, 29?
I can observe that nobody has noticed the larger implications yet.
Hey everybody! I think we ALL FORGOT HOW TO MAKE FOOD!
I NEED food! I need it to live!
HEY! I do too!
MY FEAR IS OVERIDING MY RATION-ALITY!!!
I'm going to my laboratory to figure this out! Guard the shops! Keep the peace!
Shouldn't the banana guard be helping out with this?
SMASH.
Shoo! Shame on you!
HEY YOU OVER THERE, don't mess with that JERKY HUT.
FANK YOU FINN, YOU FSAVED USF.
Aw jeeze, no! You have to ration that!
NUH UH.

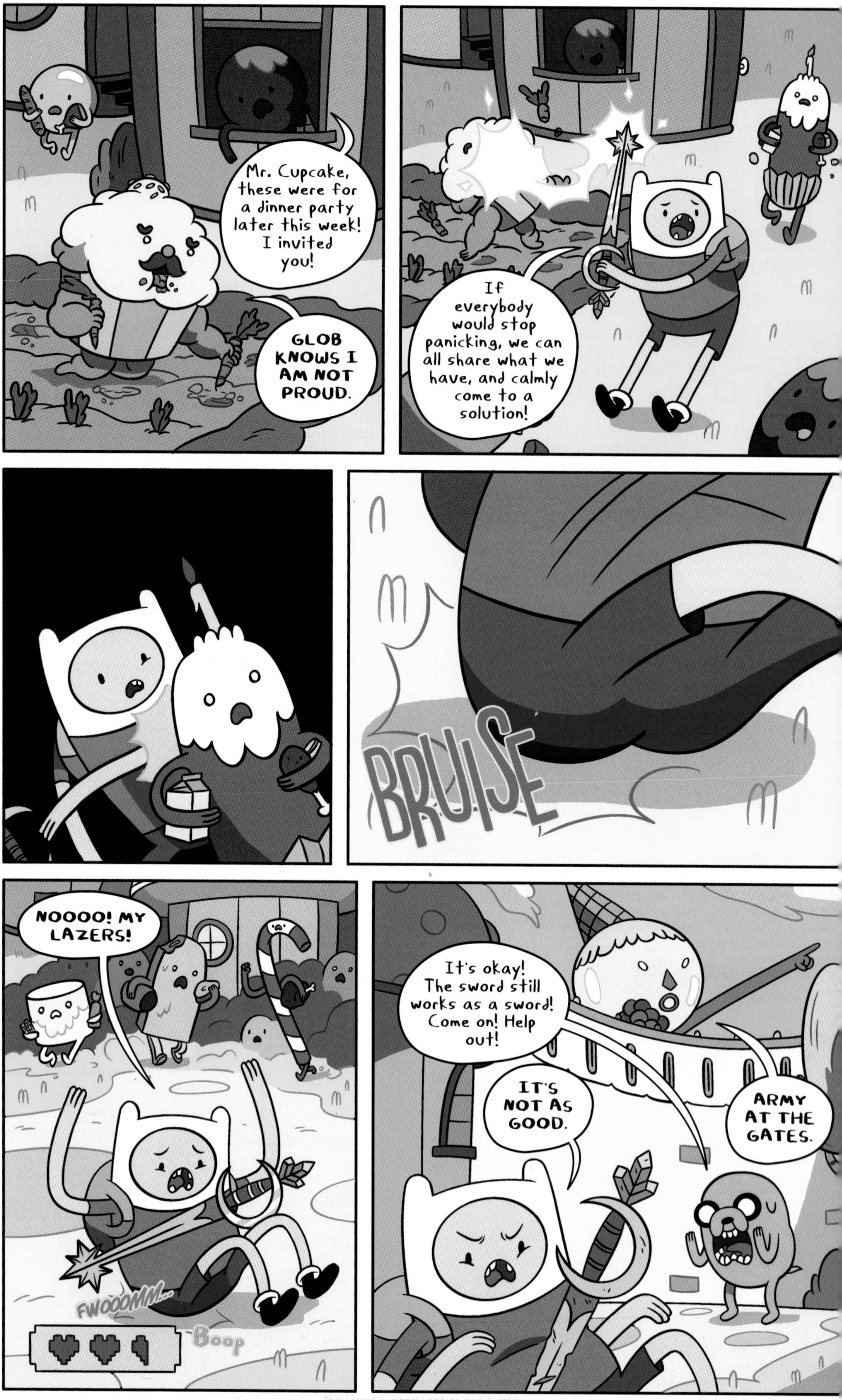
Mr. Cupcake, these were for a dinner party later this week! I invited you!
GLOB KNOWS I AM NOT PROUD.
If everybody would stop panicking, we can all share what we have, and calmly come to a solution!
BRUISE
NOOOO! MY LAZERS!
FWOOOMM...
Boop
It's okay! The sword still works as a sword! Come on! Help out!
IT'S NOT AS GOOD.
ARMY AT THE GATES.

The sword is clearly not as good, Jake.

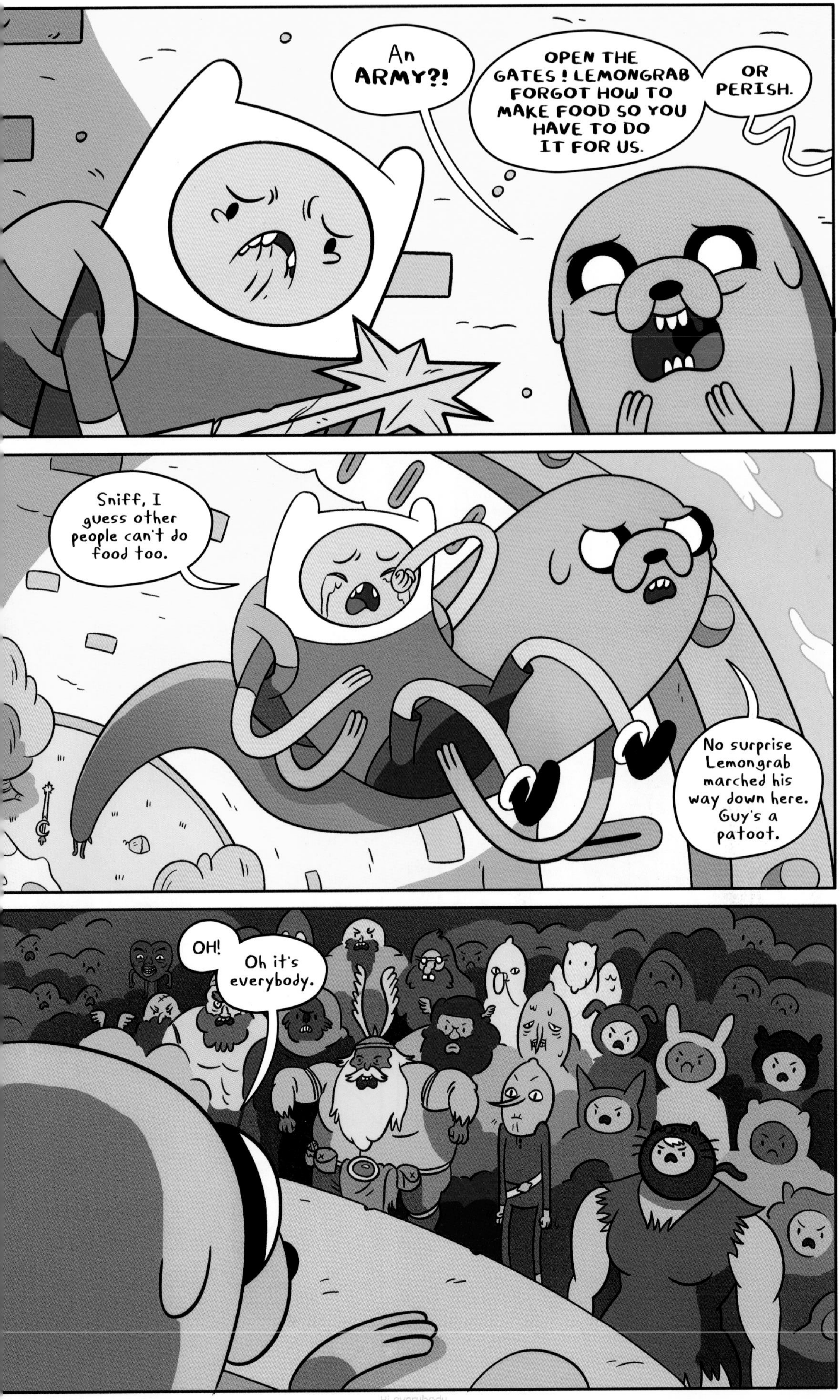

An ARMY?!
OPEN THE GATES! LEMONGRAB FORGOT HOW TO MAKE FOOD SO YOU HAVE TO DO IT FOR US.
OR PERISH.
Sniff, I guess other people can't do food too.
No surprise Lemongrab marched his way down here. Guy's a patoot.
OH!
Oh it's everybody.

Hi everybody.

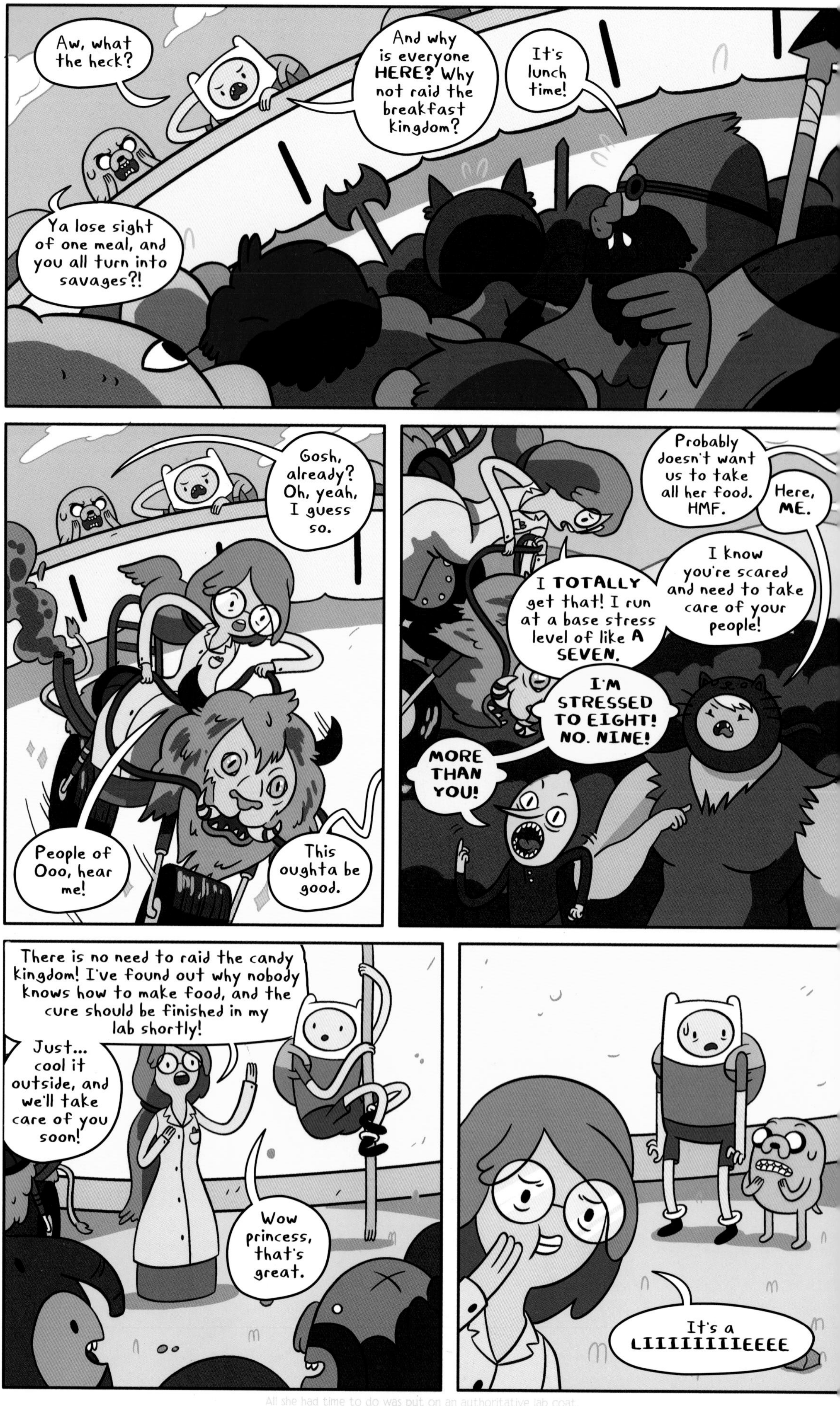
Aw, what the heck?
And why is everyone HERE? Why not raid the breakfast kingdom?
It's lunch time!
Ya lose sight of one meal, and you all turn into savages?!
Gosh, already? Oh, yeah, I guess so.
People of Ooo, hear me!
This oughta be good.
Probably doesn't want us to take all her food. HMF.
Here, ME.
I know you're scared and need to take care of your people!
I TOTALLY get that! I run at a base stress level of like A SEVEN.
I'M STRESSED TO EIGHT! NO. NINE!
MORE THAN YOU!
There is no need to raid the candy kingdom! I've found out why nobody knows how to make food, and the cure should be finished in my lab shortly!
Just... cool it outside, and we'll take care of you soon!
Wow princess, that's great.
It's a LIIIIIIIIEEEE

All she had time to do was put on an authoritative lab coat.

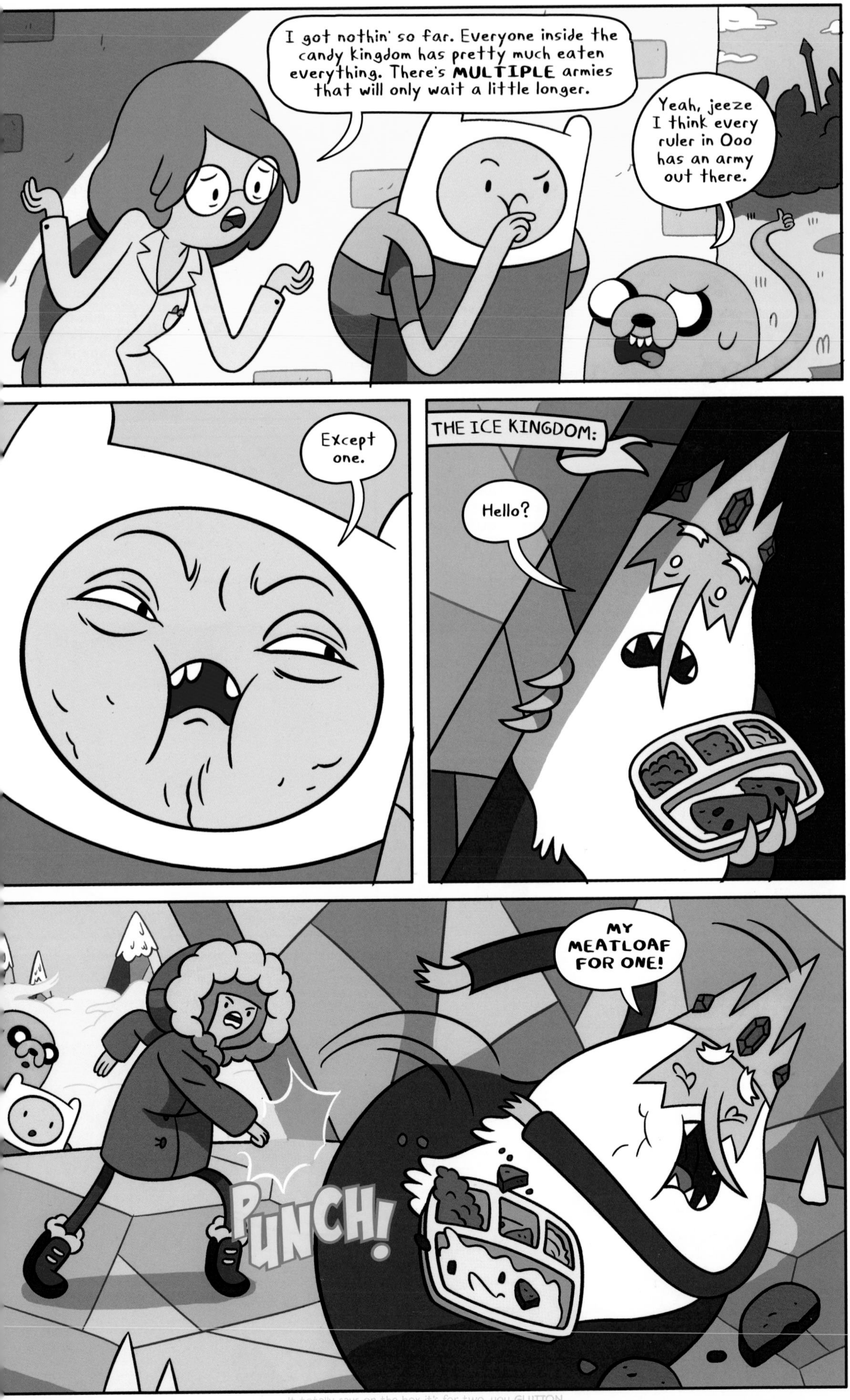
I got nothin' so far. Everyone inside the candy kingdom has pretty much eaten everything. There's MULTIPLE armies that will only wait a little longer.
Yeah, jeeze I think every ruler in Ooo has an army out there.
Except one.
THE ICE KINGDOM:
Hello?
MY MEATLOAF FOR ONE!
PUNCH!

it totally says on the box it's for two, you GLUTTON.

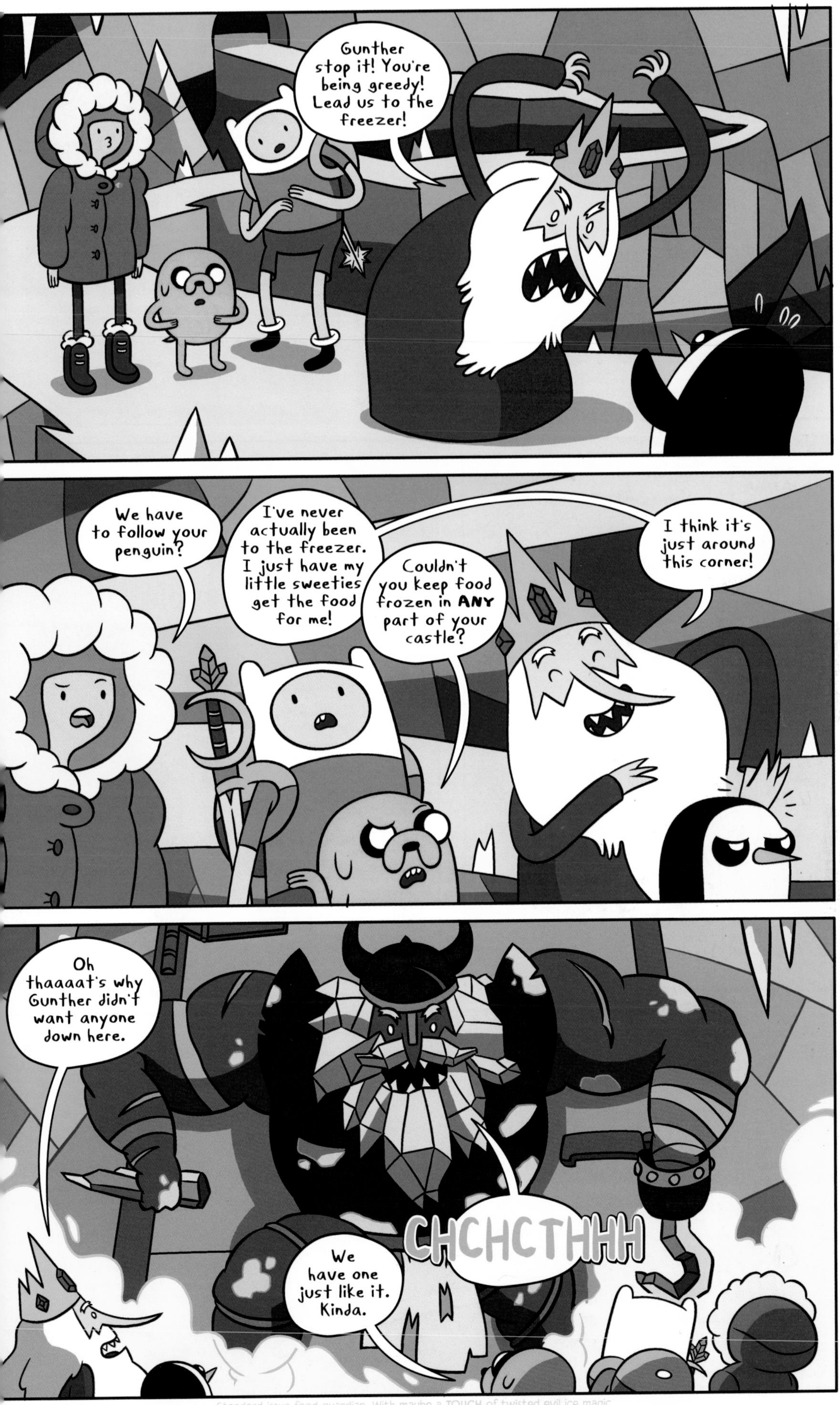
Gunther stop it! You're being greedy! Lead us to the freezer!
We have to follow your penguin?
I've never actually been to the freezer. I just have my little sweeties get the food for me!
Couldn't you keep food frozen in ANY part of your castle?
I think it's just around this corner!
Oh thaaaat's why Gunther didn't want anyone down here.
CHCHCTHHH
We have one just like it. Kinda.

Standard issue food guardian. With maybe a TOUCH of twisted evil ice magic.

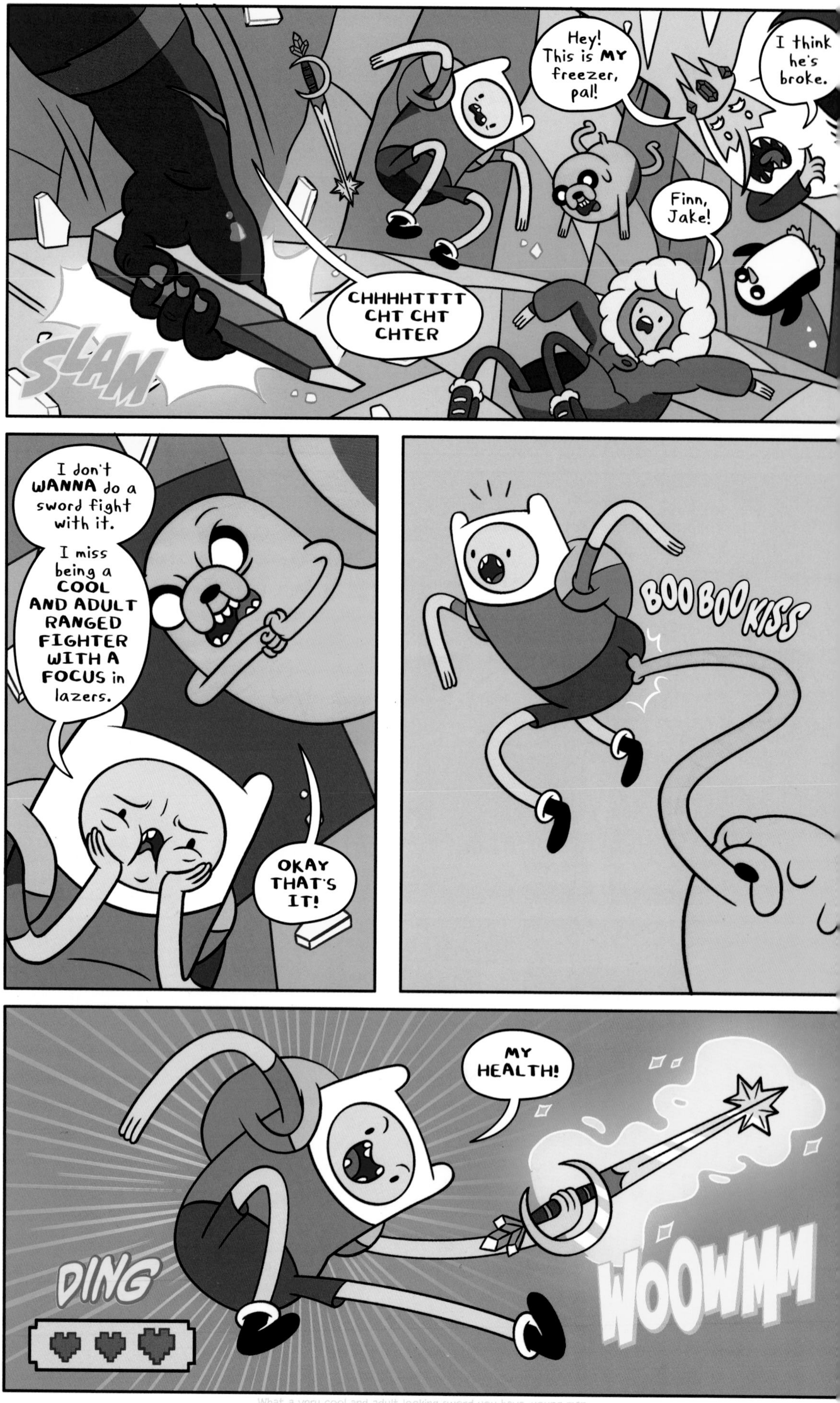
Hey! This is MY freezer, pal!
I think he's broke.
Finn, Jake!
CHHHHTTTT CHT CHT CHTER
SLAM
I don't WANNA do a sword fight with it.
I miss being a COOL AND ADULT RANGED FIGHTER WITH A FOCUS in lazers.
OKAY THAT'S IT!
BOO BOO KISS
MY HEALTH!
DING
WOOWMM

What a very cool and adult looking sword you have, young man.

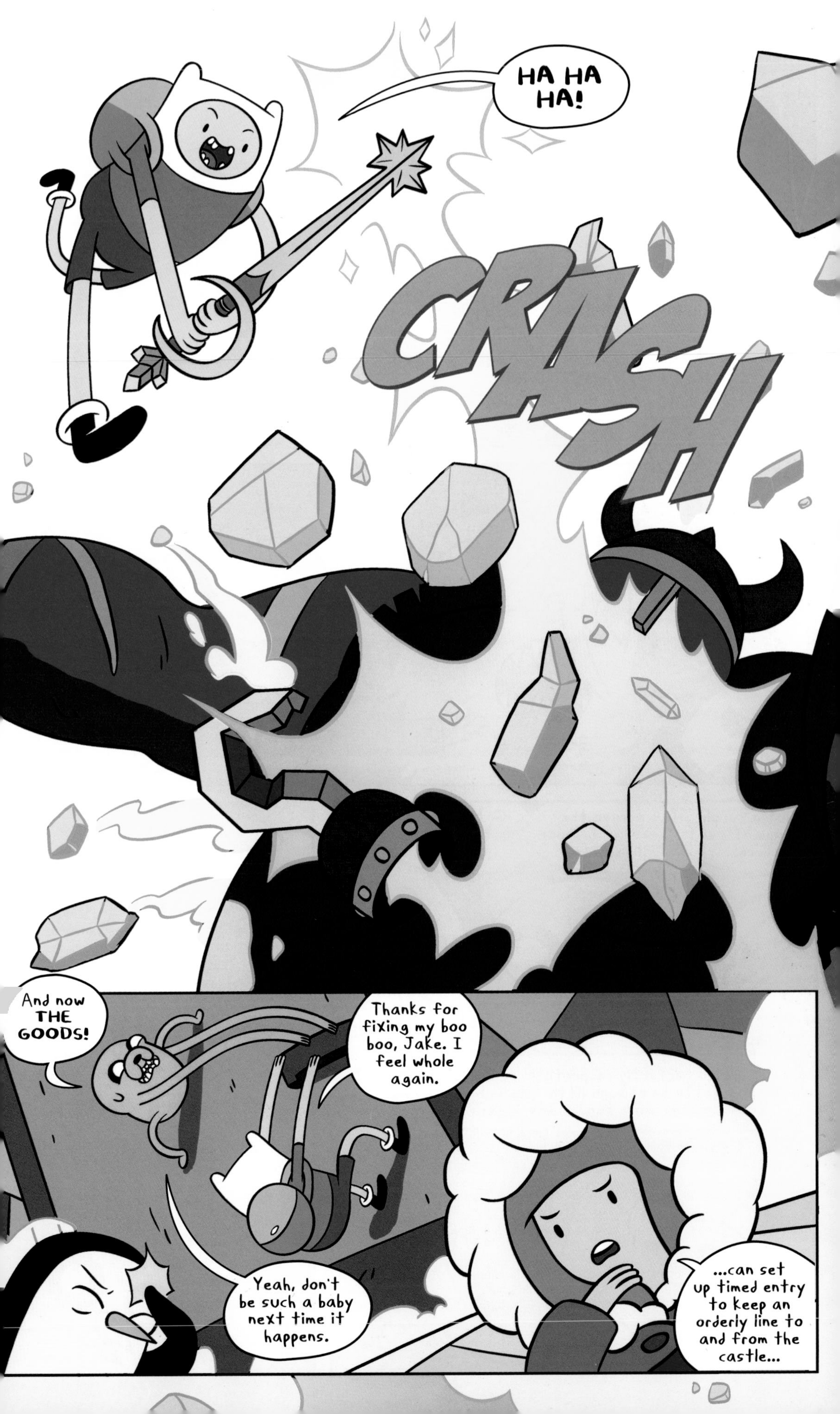
HA HA HA!
CRASH
And now THE GOODS!
Thanks for fixing my boo boo, Jake. I feel whole again.
Yeah, don't be such a baby next time it happens.
...can set up timed entry to keep an orderly line to and from the castle...

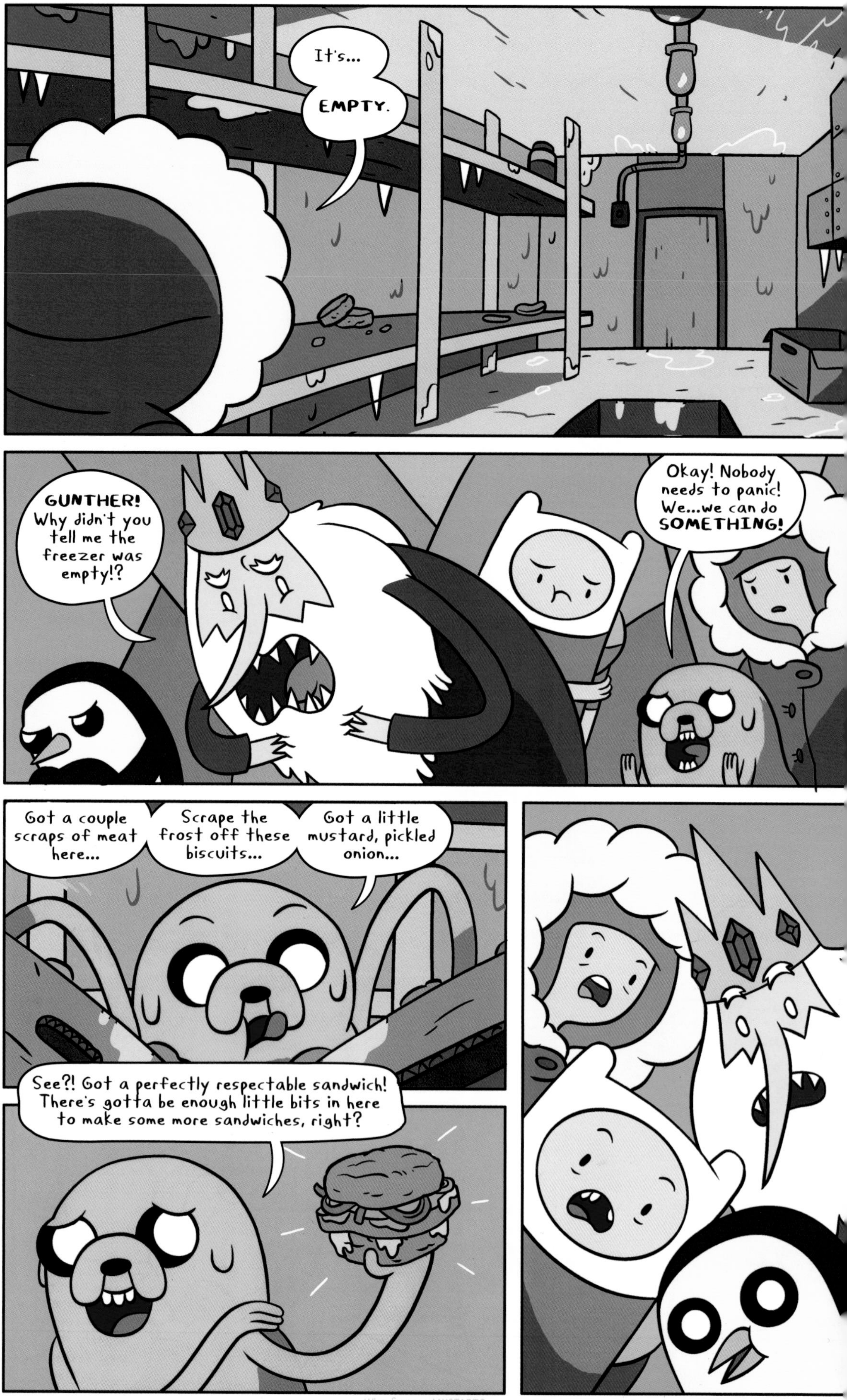
It's...
EMPTY.
GUNTHER! Why didn't you tell me the freezer was empty!?
Okay! Nobody needs to panic! We...we can do SOMETHING!
Got a couple scraps of meat here...
Scrape the frost off these biscuits...
Got a little mustard, pickled onion...
See?! Got a perfectly respectable sandwich! There's gotta be enough little bits in here to make some more sandwiches, right?

Who freezes MUSTARD?

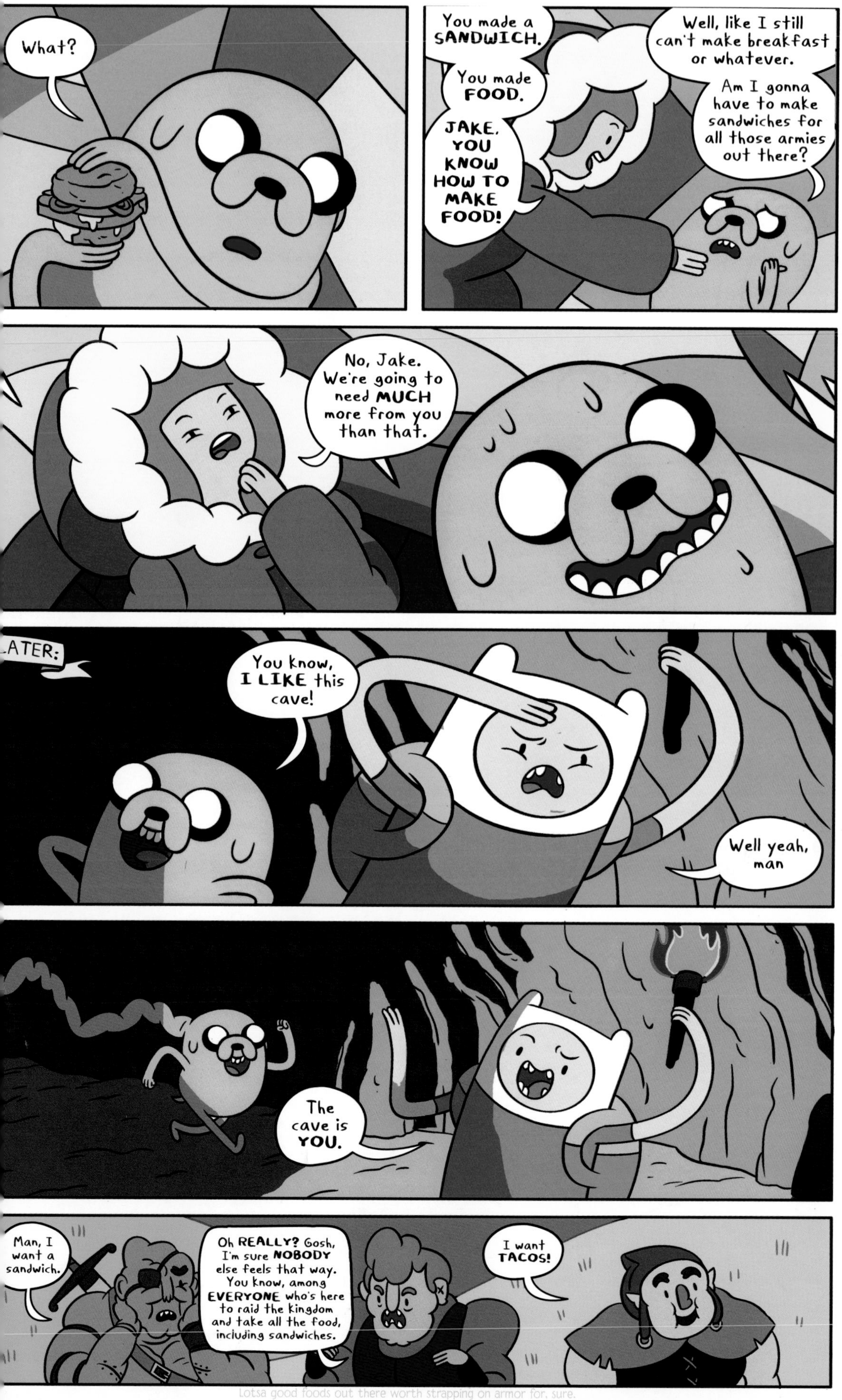
What?
You made a SANDWICH.
You made FOOD.
JAKE, YOU KNOW HOW TO MAKE FOOD!
Well, like I still can't make breakfast or whatever.
Am I gonna have to make sandwiches for all those armies out there?
No, Jake. We're going to need MUCH more from you than that.
LATER:
You know, I LIKE this cave!
Well yeah, man
The cave is YOU.
Man, I want a sandwich.
Oh REALLY? Gosh, I'm sure NOBODY else feels that way. You know, among EVERYONE who's here to raid the kingdom and take all the food, including sandwiches.
I want TACOS!
Lotsa good foods out there worth strapping on armor for, sure.

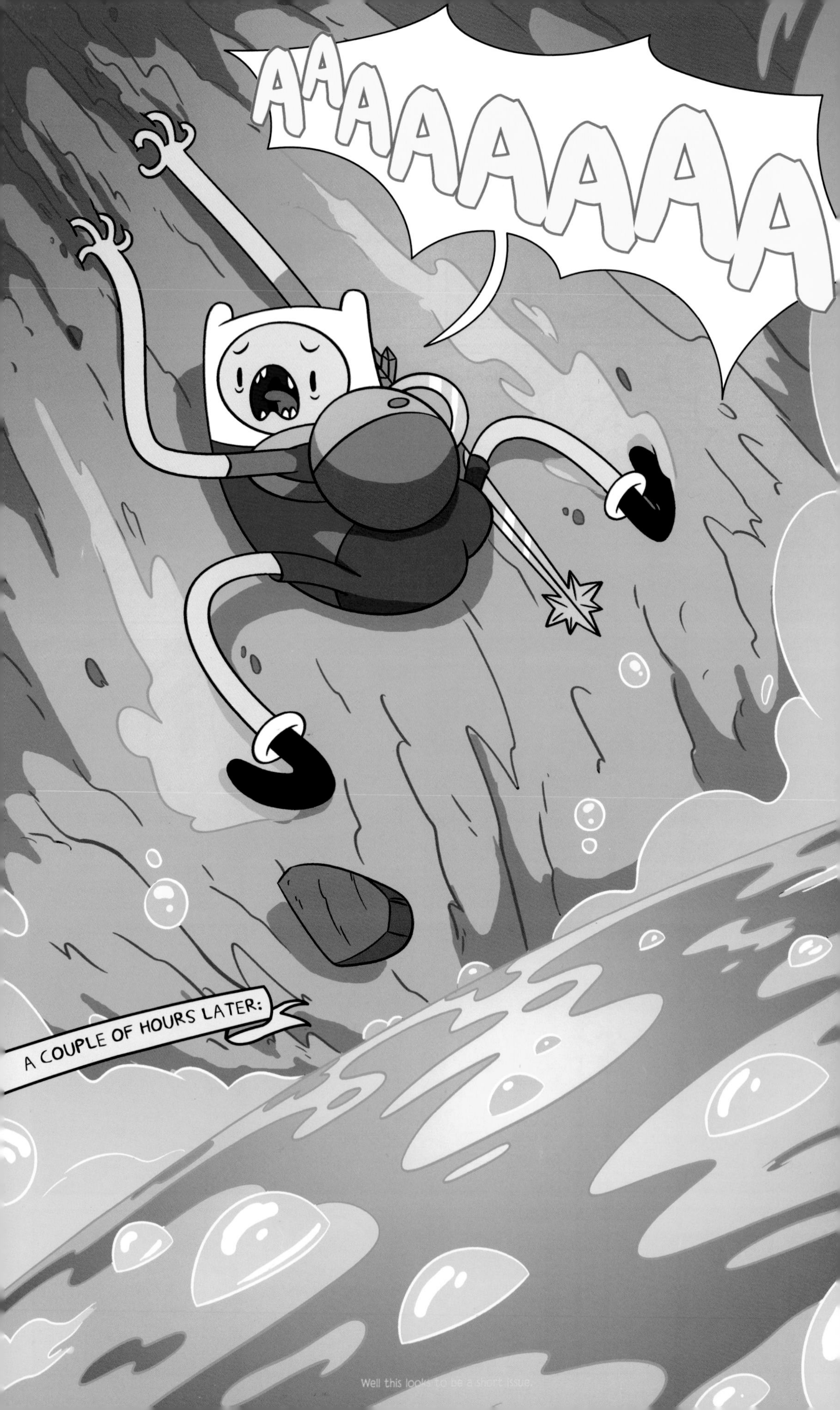
AAAAAAAA
A COUPLE OF HOURS LATER:
Well this looks to be a short issue.

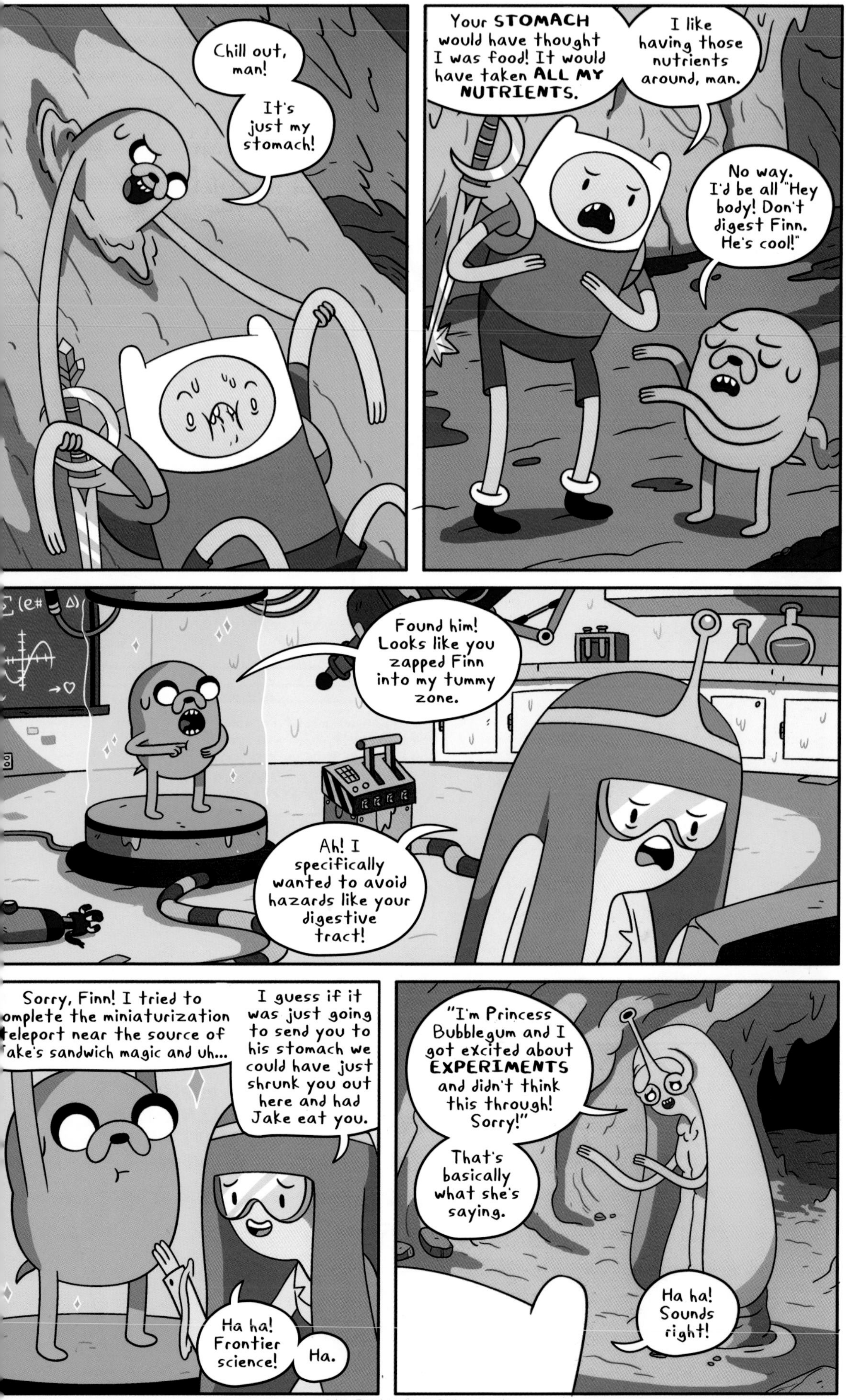
Chill out, man!
It's just my stomach!
Your STOMACH would have thought I was food! It would have taken ALL MY NUTRIENTS.
I like having those nutrients around, man.
No way. I'd be all "Hey body! Don't digest Finn. He's cool!"
Found him! Looks like you zapped Finn into my tummy zone.
Ah! I specifically wanted to avoid hazards like your digestive tract!
Sorry, Finn! I tried to complete the miniaturization teleport near the source of Jake's sandwich magic and uh...
I guess if it was just going to send you to his stomach we could have just shrunk you out here and had Jake eat you.
Ha ha! Frontier science!
Ha.
"I'm Princess Bubblegum and I got excited about EXPERIMENTS and didn't think this through! Sorry!"
That's basically what she's saying.
Ha ha! Sounds right!

Jake: Good on faces. Bad on words.

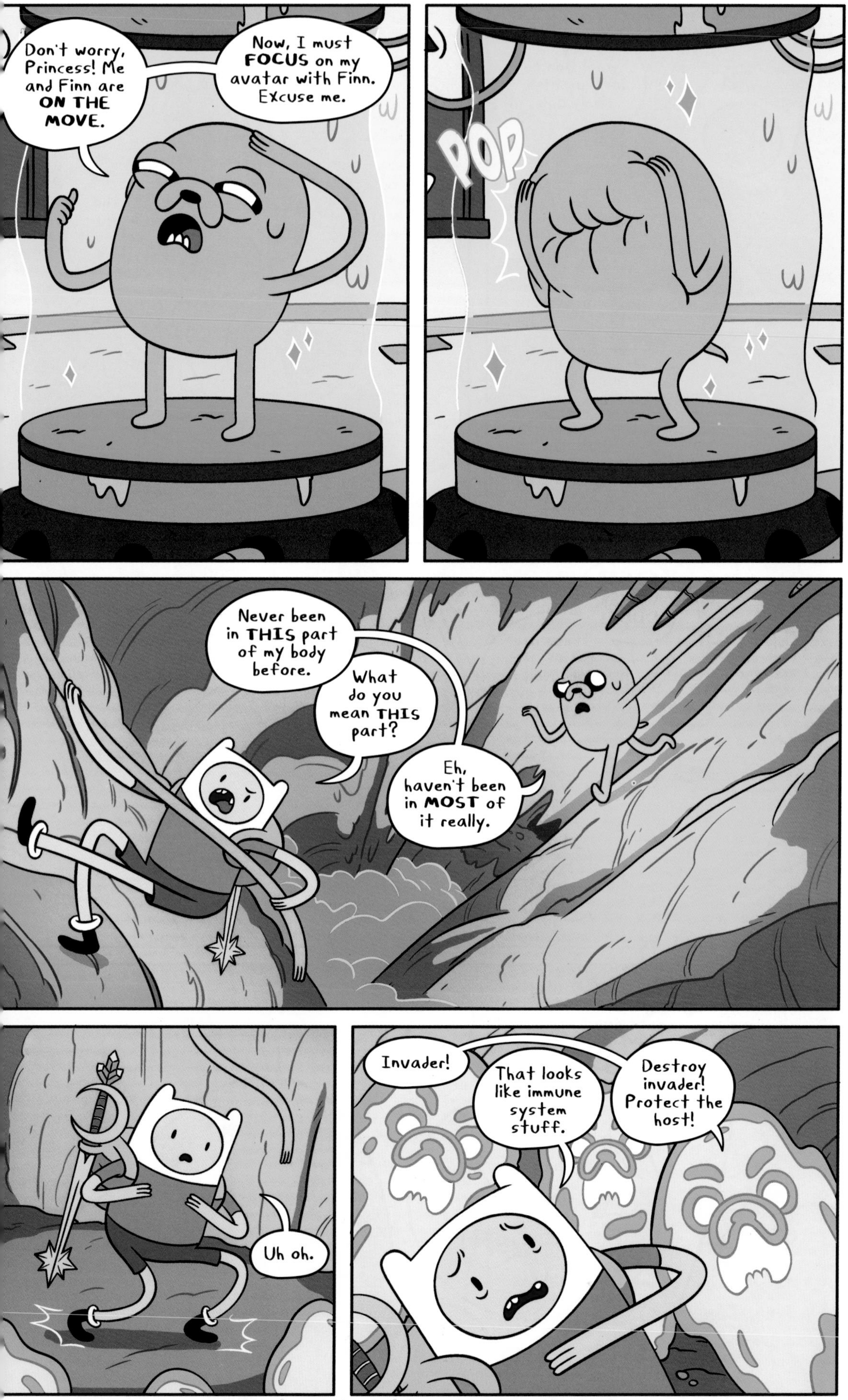
Don't worry, Princess! Me and Finn are **ON THE MOVE.**
Now, I must **FOCUS** on my avatar with Finn. Excuse me.
POP
Never been in **THIS** part of my body before.
What do you mean **THIS** part?
Eh, haven't been in **MOST** of it really.
Uh oh.
Invader!
That looks like immune system stuff.
Destroy invader! Protect the host!

Does your face go inside yourself when you dream? How would you know?

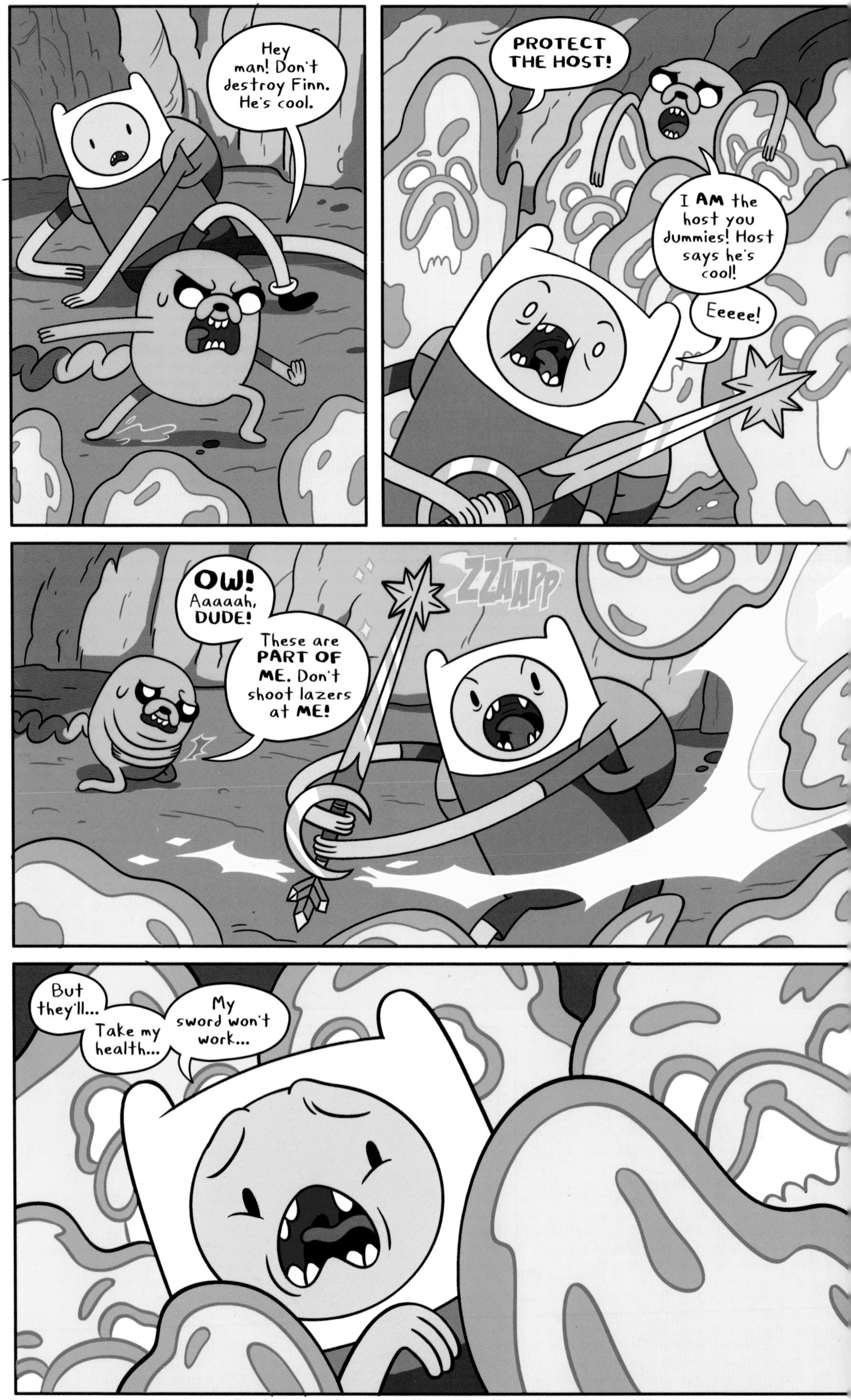
Hey man! Don't destroy Finn. He's cool.
PROTECT THE HOST!
I AM the host you dummies! Host says he's cool!
Eeeee!
OW! Aaaaah, DUDE!
These are PART OF ME. Don't shoot lazers at ME!
ZZAAPP
But they'll...
Take my health...
My sword won't work...

Though, a very precise zapping to the cornea could really improve your eyesight.

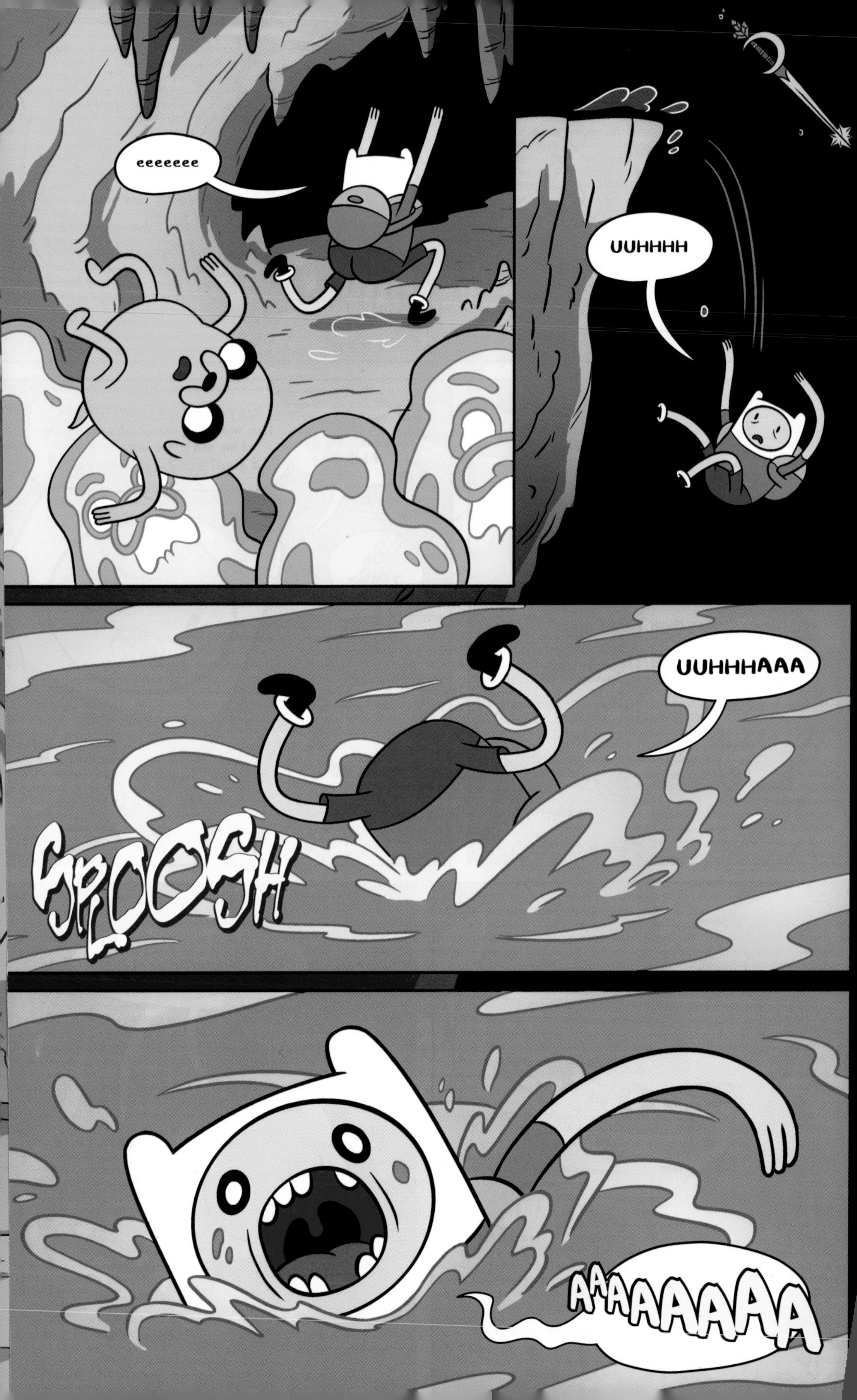
eeeeeee
UUHHHH
UUHHHAAA
SPLOOSH
AAAAAAAA

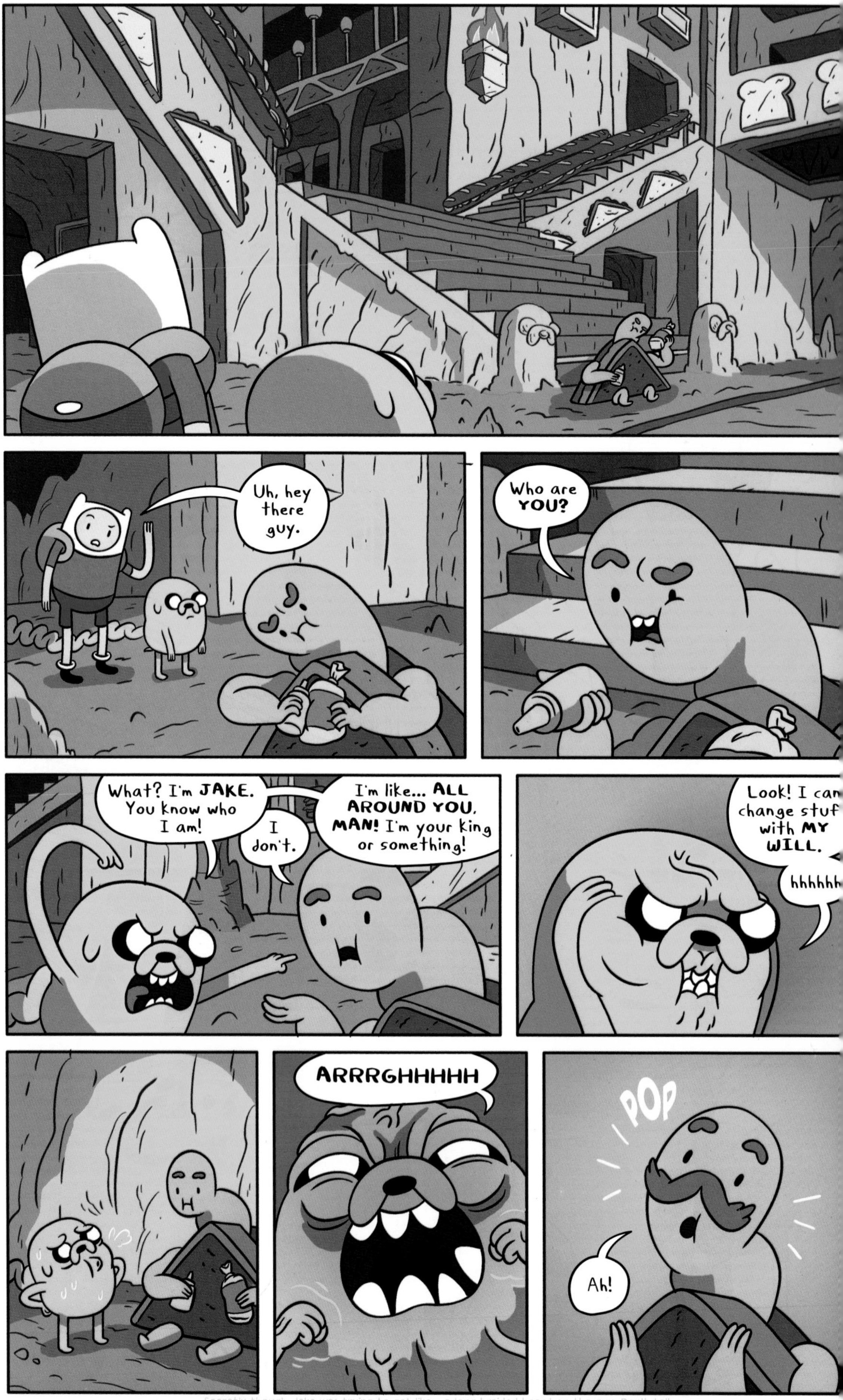
Uh, hey there guy.
Who are YOU?
What? I'm JAKE. You know who I am!
I don't.
I'm like... ALL AROUND YOU, MAN! I'm your king or something!
Look! I can change stuf with MY WILL.
hhhhhh
ARRRGHHHHH
POP
Ah!

Secretly though, Jake was trying to get like... a long braided beard on the guy. Don't tell.

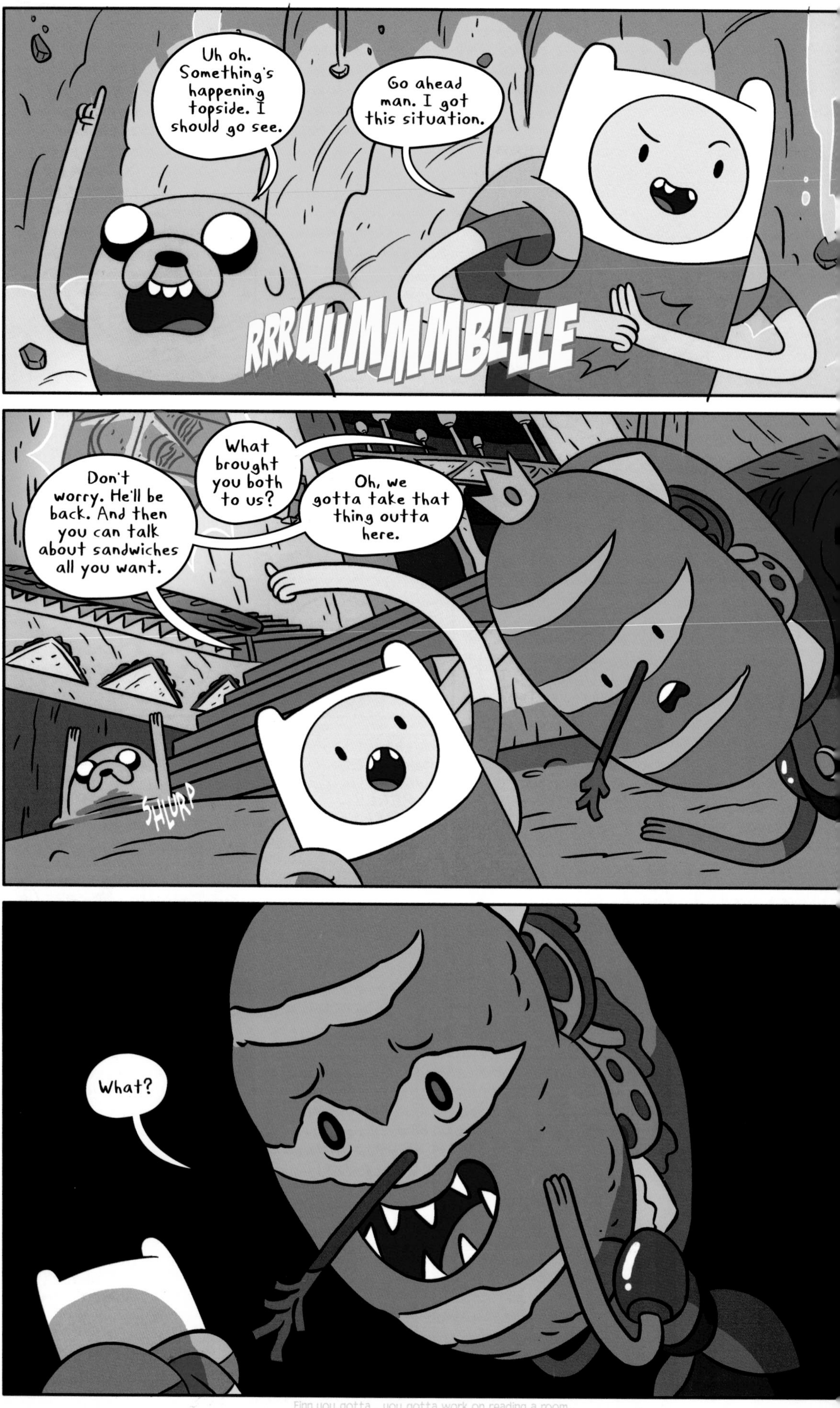
Uh oh. Something's happening topside. I should go see.
Go ahead man. I got this situation.
RRRUUMMMMBLLLE
Don't worry. He'll be back. And then you can talk about sandwiches all you want.
What brought you both to us?
Oh, we gotta take that thing outta here.
SHLURP
What?

Finn you gotta... you gotta work on reading a room.

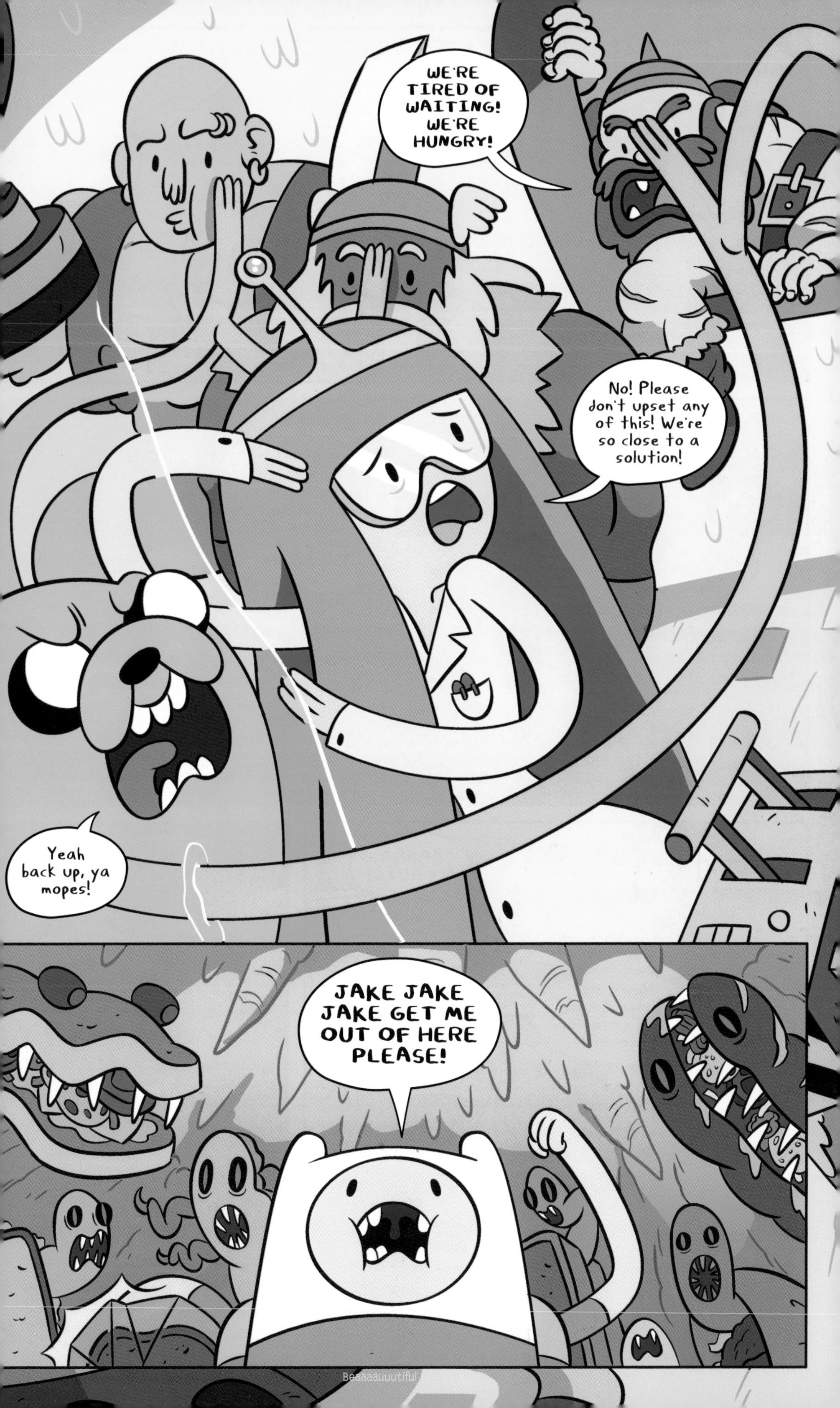
WE'RE TIRED OF WAITING! WE'RE HUNGRY!
No! Please don't upset any of this! We're so close to a solution!
Yeah back up, ya mopes!
JAKE JAKE JAKE GET ME OUT OF HERE PLEASE!
Beaaaaauuutiful

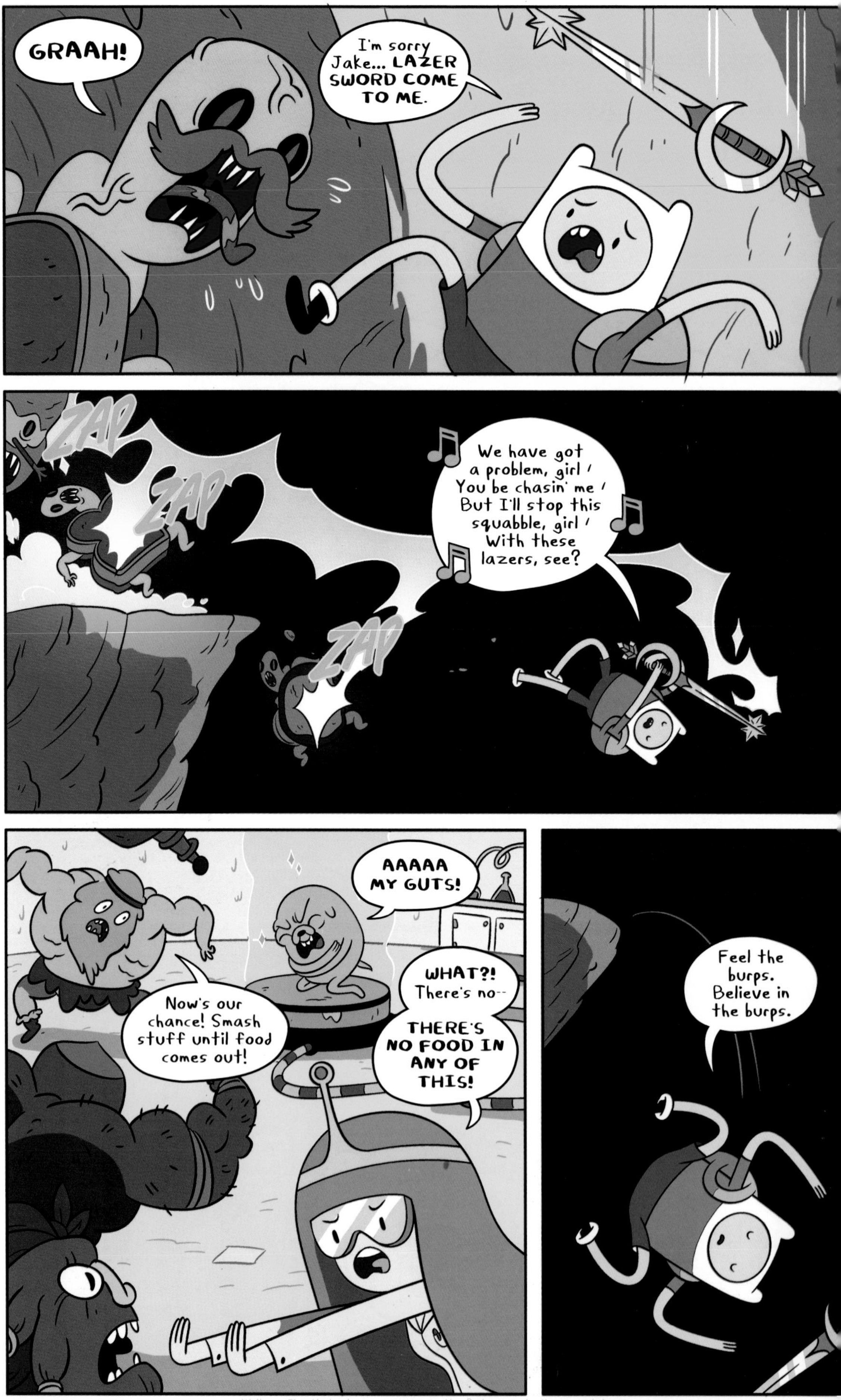
GRAAH!
I'm sorry Jake... LAZER SWORD COME TO ME.
ZAP
ZAP
We have got a problem, girl / You be chasin' me / But I'll stop this squabble, girl / With these lazers, see?
ZAP
AAAAA MY GUTS!
Now's our chance! Smash stuff until food comes out!
WHAT?! There's no--
THERE'S NO FOOD IN ANY OF THIS!
Feel the burps. Believe in the burps.

Wait, no Finn that where you were on the first page, don't you... ah jeeze.

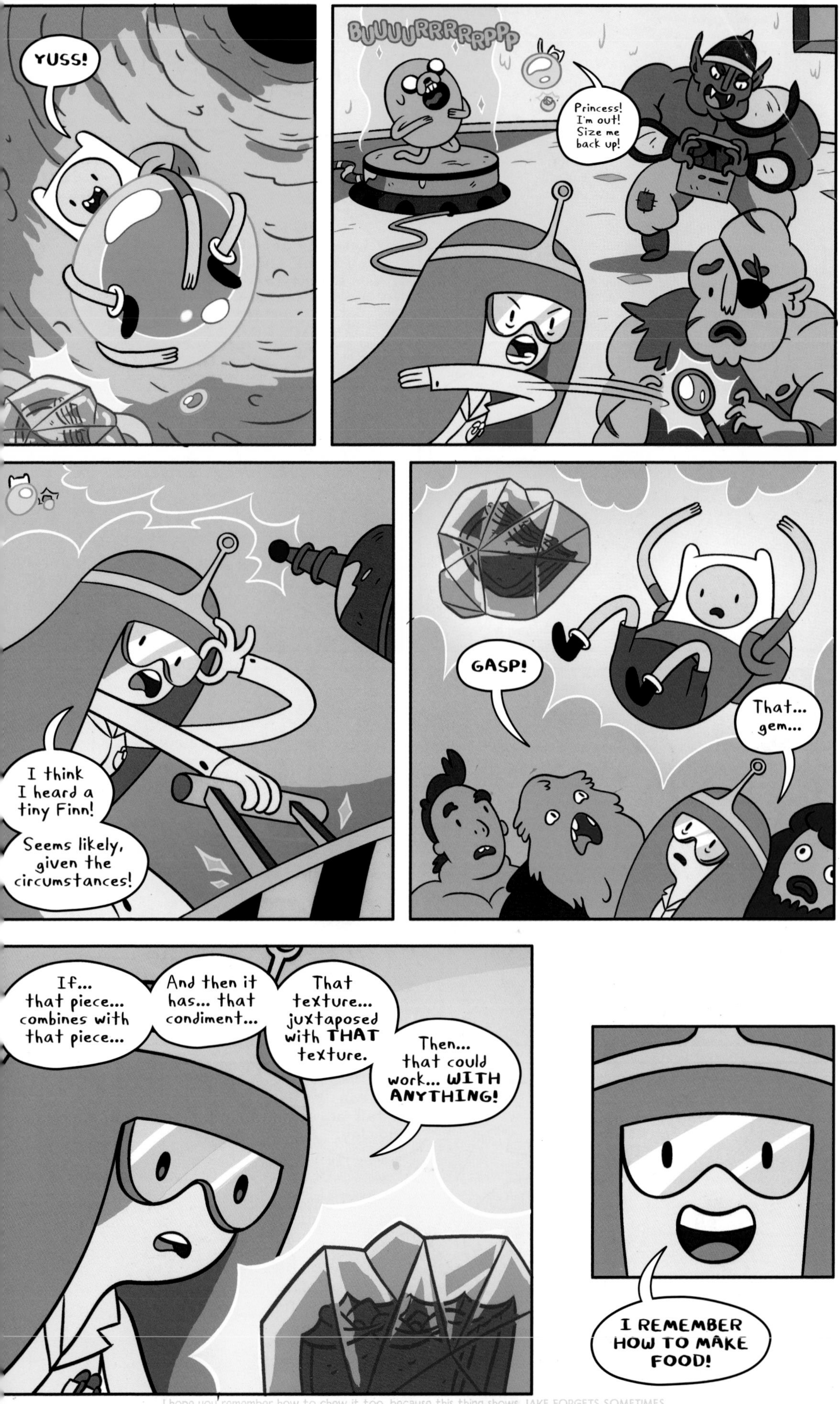
YUSS!
BUUUURRRRRPPP
Princess! I'm out! Size me back up!
I think I heard a tiny Finn!
Seems likely, given the circumstances!
GASP!
That... gem...
If... that piece... combines with that piece...
And then it has... that condiment...
That texture... juxtaposed with THAT texture.
Then... that could work... WITH ANYTHING!
I REMEMBER HOW TO MAKE FOOD!

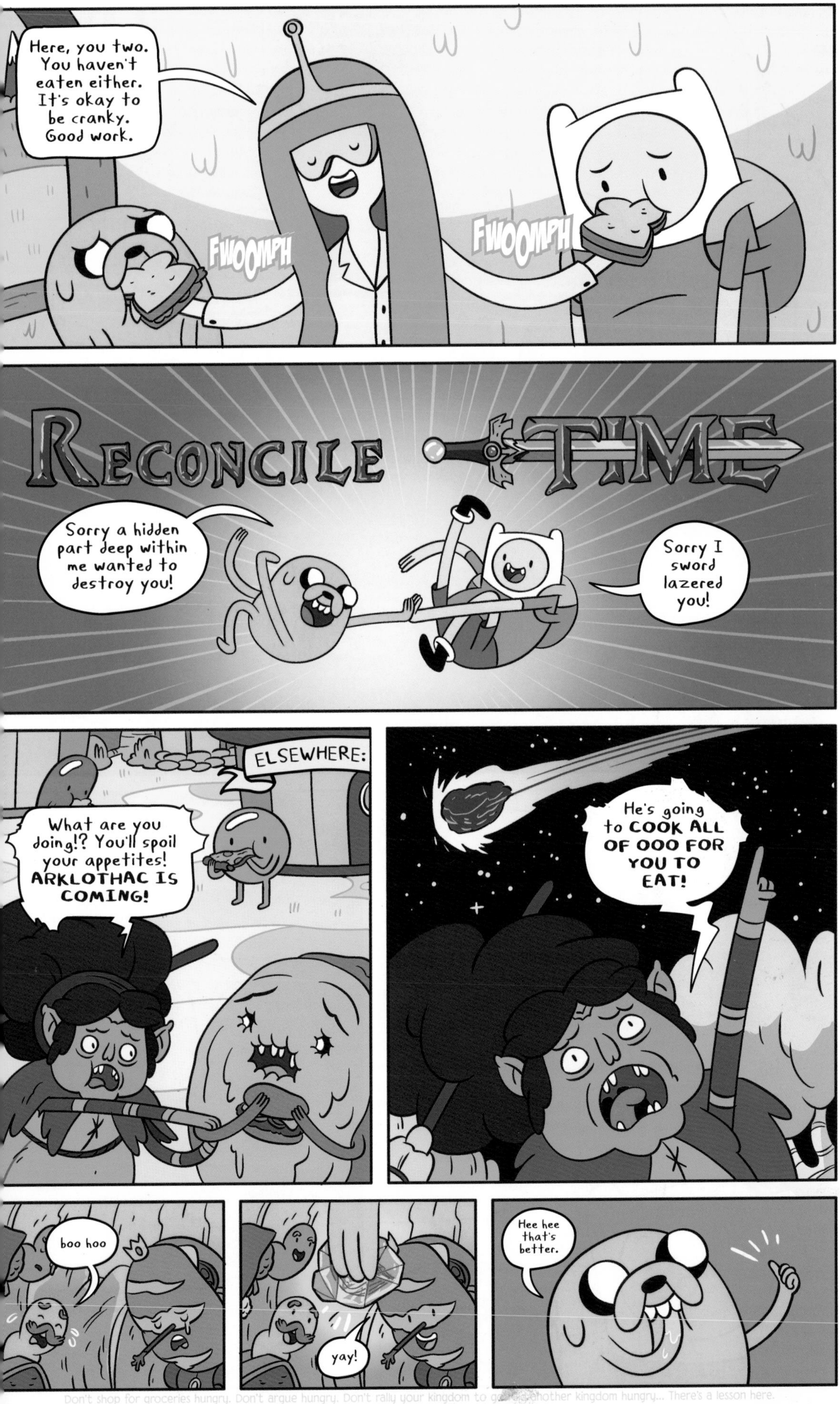
Here, you two. You haven't eaten either. It's okay to be cranky. Good work.
FWOOMPH
FWOOMPH
RECONCILE TIME
Sorry a hidden part deep within me wanted to destroy you!
Sorry I sword lazered you!
ELSEWHERE:
What are you doing!? You'll spoil your appetites! ARKLOTHAC IS COMING!
He's going to COOK ALL OF OOO FOR YOU TO EAT!
boo hoo
yay!
Hee hee that's better.

Don't shop for groceries hungry. Don't argue hungry. Don't rally your kingdom to g[illegible] another kingdom hungry... There's a lesson here.

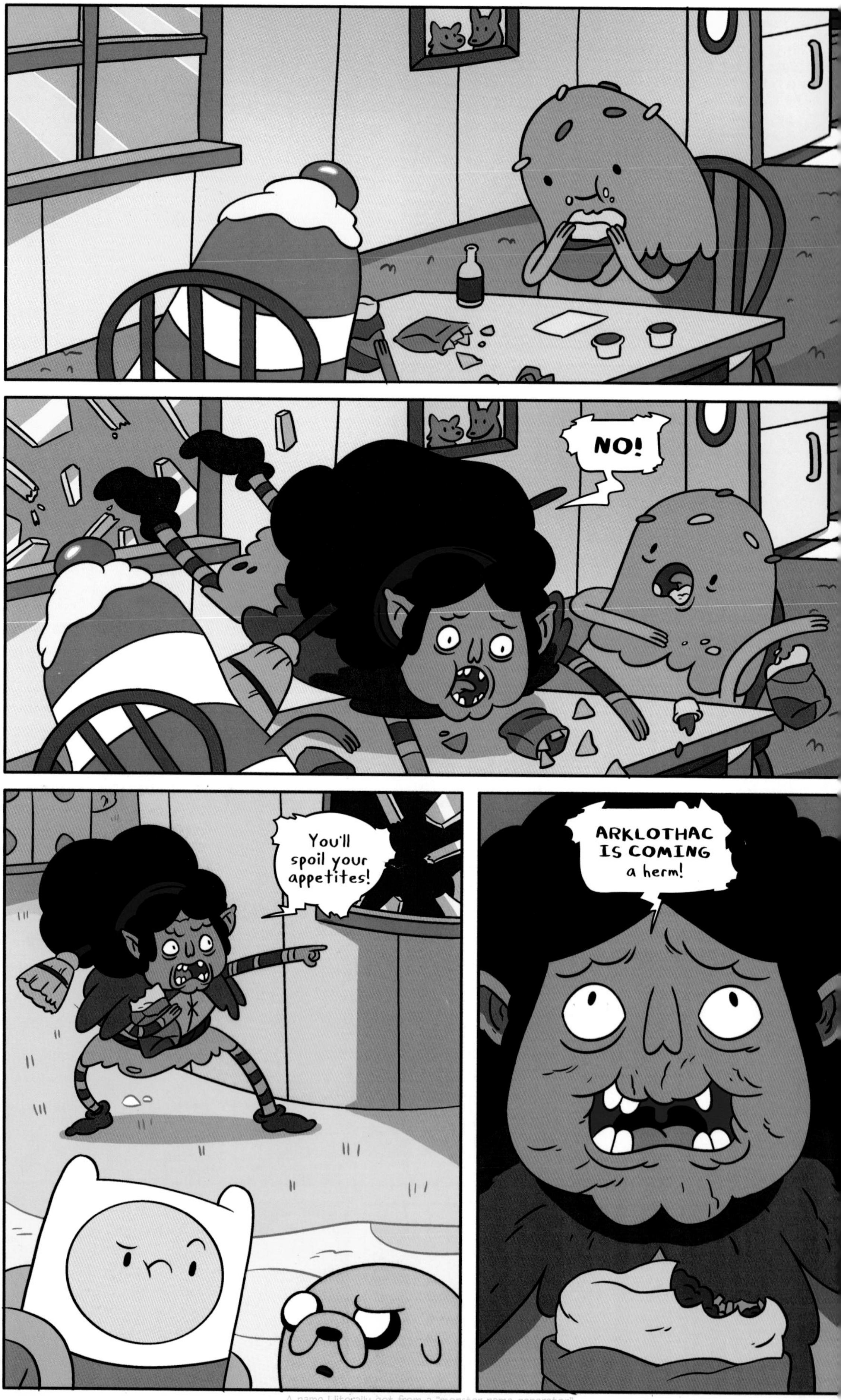
NO!
You'll spoil your appetites!
ARKLOTHAC IS COMING a herm!

A name I literally got from a "monster name generator".

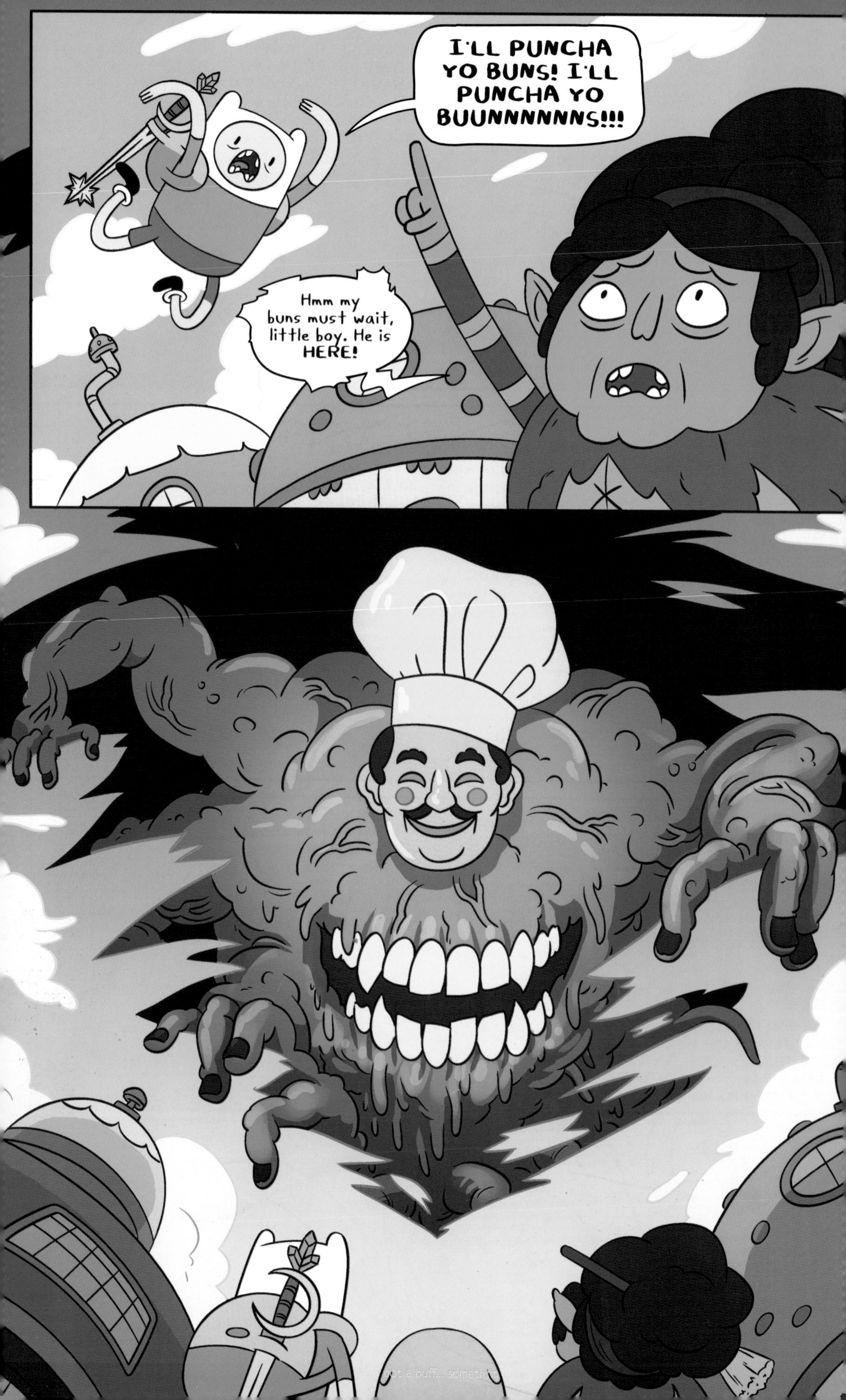
I'LL PUNCHA YO BUNS! I'LL PUNCHA YO BUUNNNNNNS!!!
Hmm my buns must wait, little boy. He is HERE!

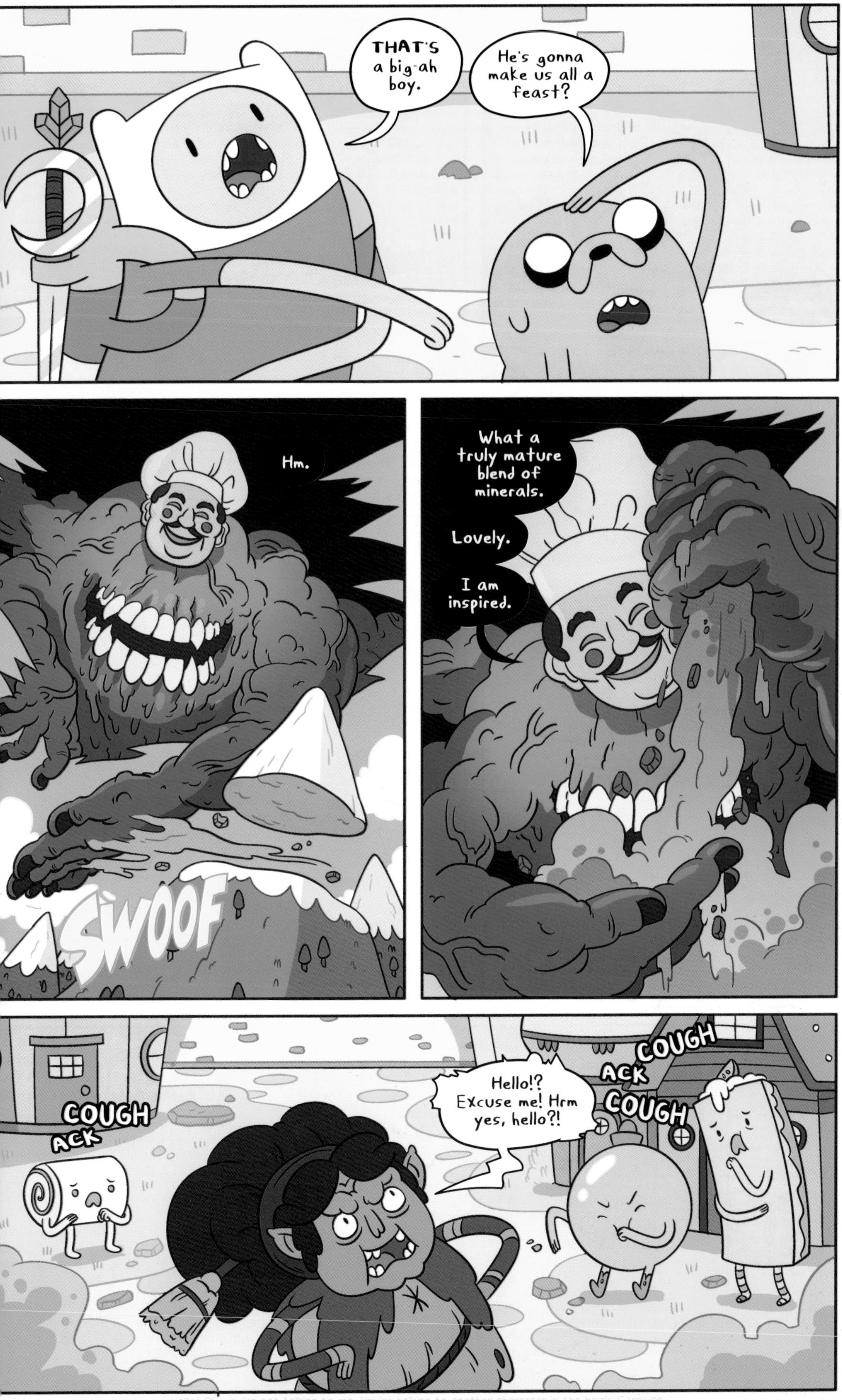
THAT'S a big-ah boy.
He's gonna make us all a feast?
Hm.
SWOOF
What a truly mature blend of minerals.
Lovely.
I am inspired.
COUGH
ACK
Hello!? Excuse me! Hrm yes, hello?!
COUGH
ACK
COUGH

Hello! Oh, you're not talking to me. You're talking to another character in the book. Carry-on.

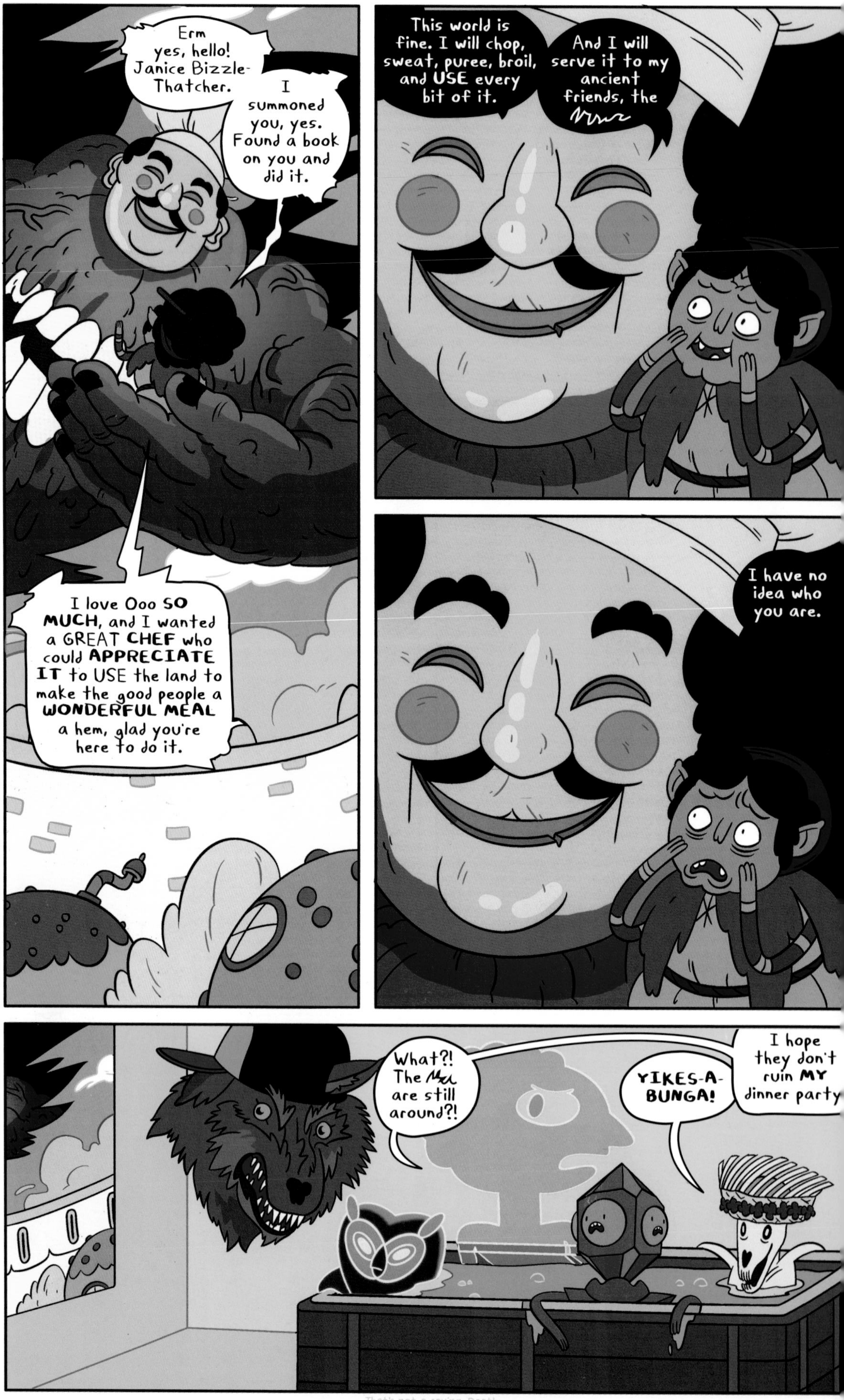
Erm yes, hello! Janice Bizzle-Thatcher.
I summoned you, yes. Found a book on you and did it.
I love Ooo SO MUCH, and I wanted a GREAT CHEF who could APPRECIATE IT to USE the land to make the good people a WONDERFUL MEAL a hem, glad you're here to do it.
This world is fine. I will chop, sweat, puree, broil, and USE every bit of it.
And I will serve it to my ancient friends, the
I have no idea who you are.
What?! The are still around?!
YIKES-A-BUNGA!
I hope they don't ruin MY dinner party

That's not a saying, Death.

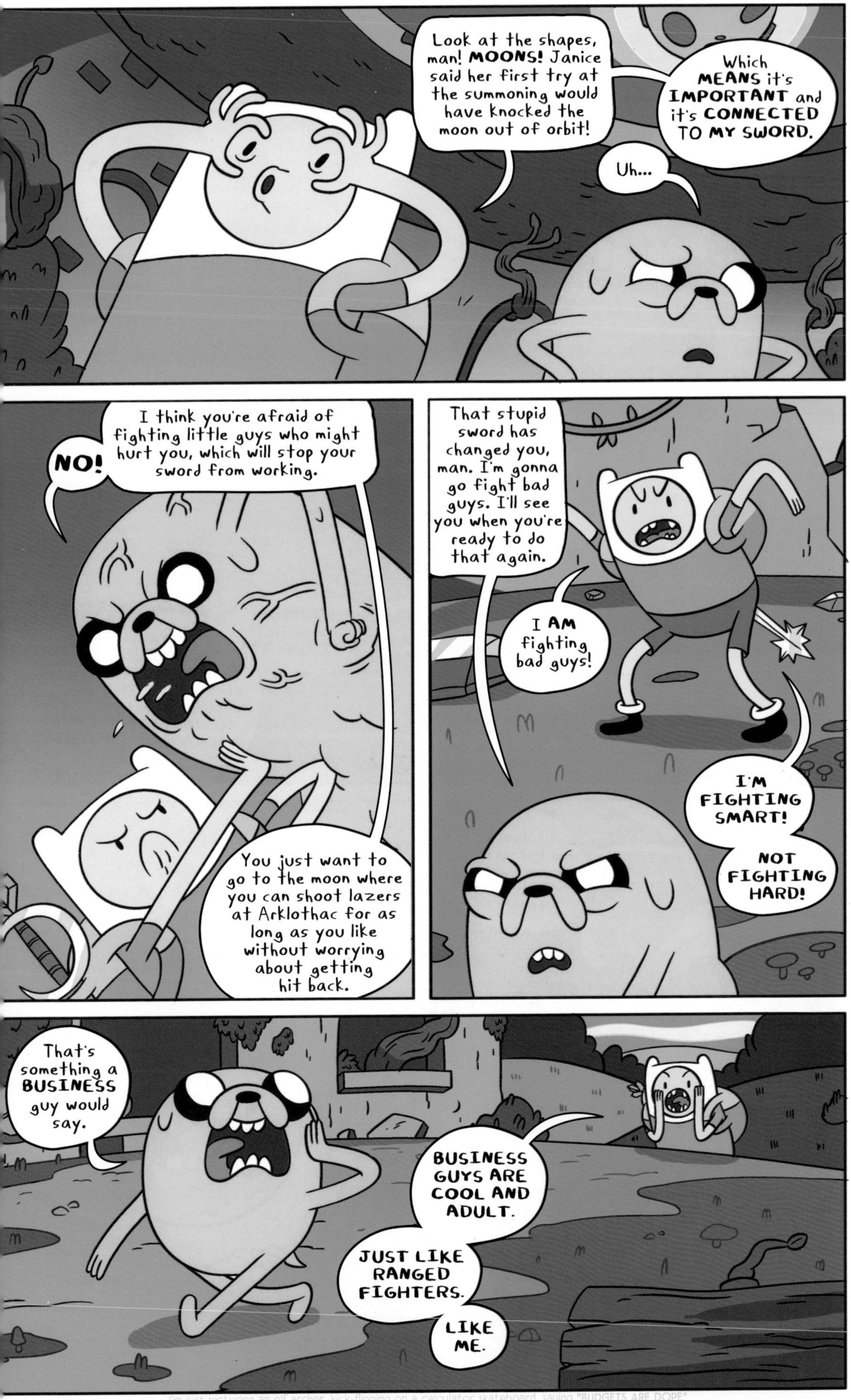

Look at the shapes, man! MOONS! Janice said her first try at the summoning would have knocked the moon out of orbit!
Which MEANS it's IMPORTANT and it's CONNECTED TO MY SWORD.
Uh...
I think you're afraid of fighting little guys who might hurt you, which will stop your sword from working.
NO!
You just want to go to the moon where you can shoot lazers at Arklothac for as long as you like without worrying about getting hit back.
That stupid sword has changed you, man. I'm gonna go fight bad guys. I'll see you when you're ready to do that again.
I AM fighting bad guys!
I'M FIGHTING SMART!
NOT FIGHTING HARD!
That's something a BUSINESS guy would say.
BUSINESS GUYS ARE COOL AND ADULT.
JUST LIKE RANGED FIGHTERS.
LIKE ME.

I'm just picturing an elf archer, kick-flipping on a calculator skateboard, saying "BUDGETS ARE DOPE"

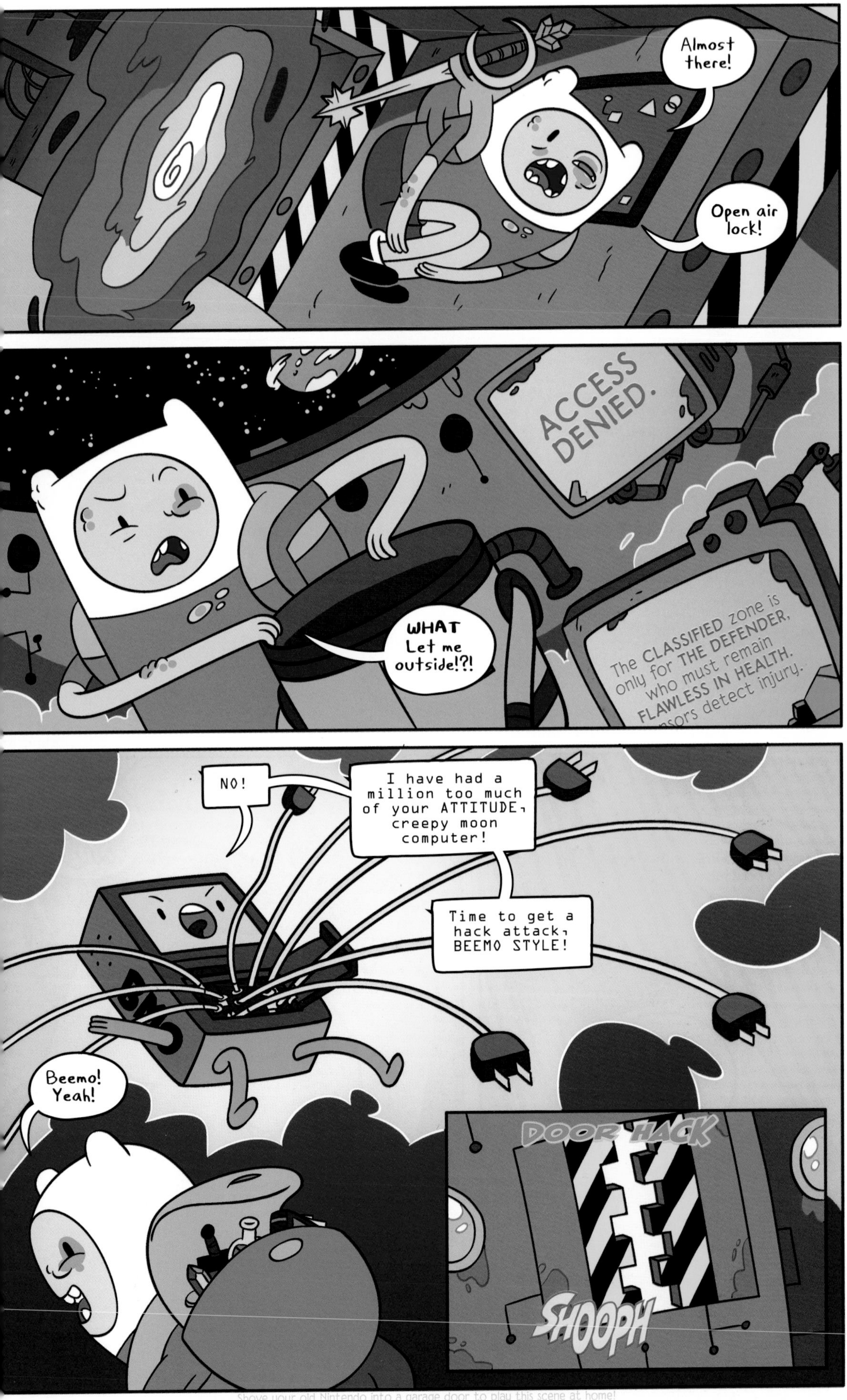

Almost there!
Open air lock!
ACCESS DENIED.
WHAT Let me outside!?!
The CLASSIFIED zone is only for THE DEFENDER, who must remain FLAWLESS IN HEALTH.
NO!
I have had a million too much of your ATTITUDE, creepy moon computer!
Time to get a hack attack, BEEMO STYLE!
Beemo! Yeah!
DOOR HACK
SHOOPH

Shove your old Nintendo into a garage door to play this scene at home!

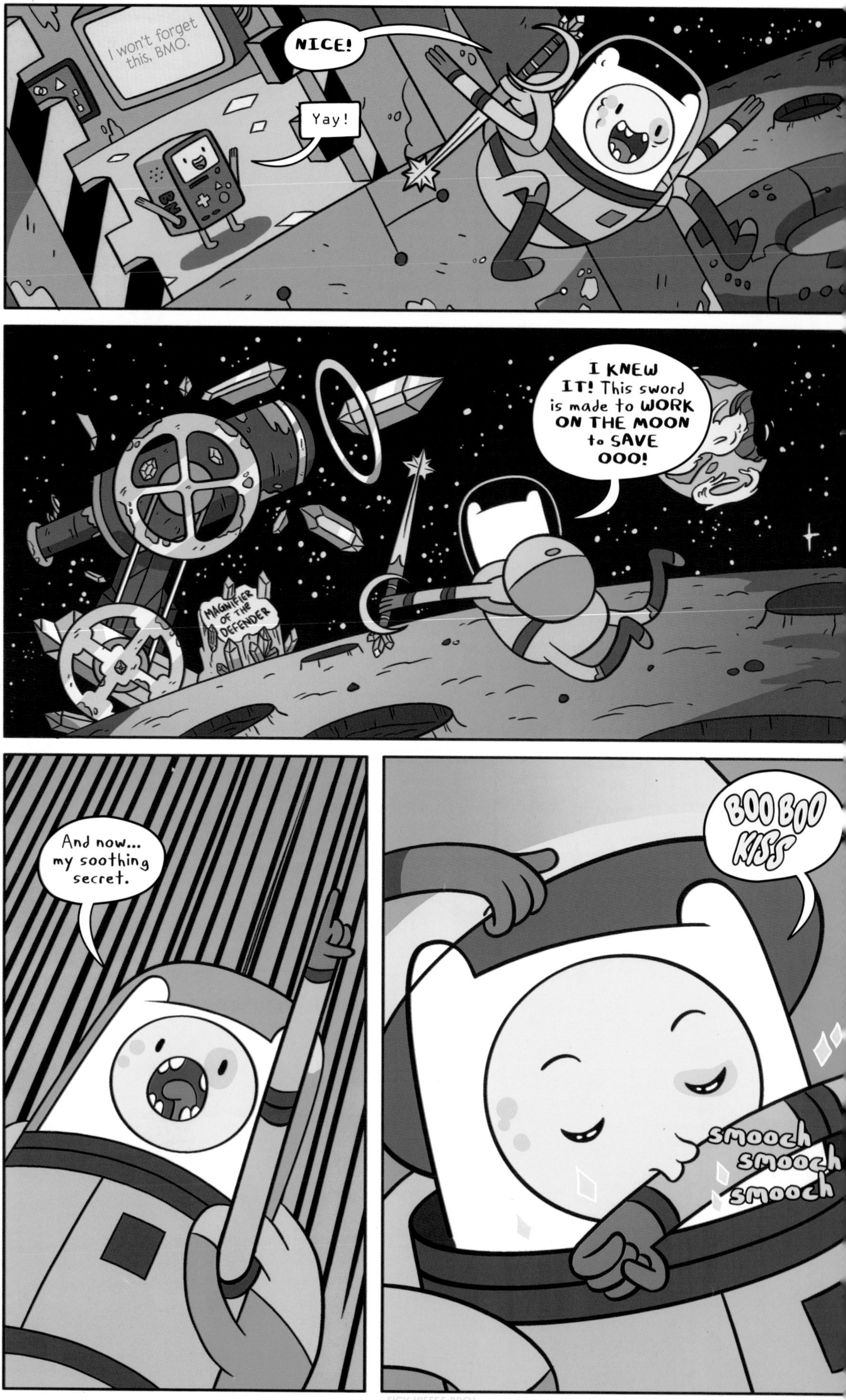
I won't forget this, BMO.
NICE!
Yay!
I KNEW IT! This sword is made to WORK ON THE MOON to SAVE OOO!
MAGNIFIER OF THE DEFENDER
And now... my soothing secret.
BOO BOO KISS
smooch smooch smooch

SICK KISSES BRO!

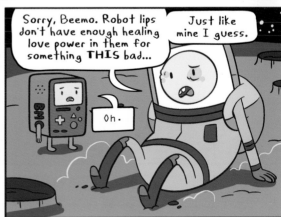

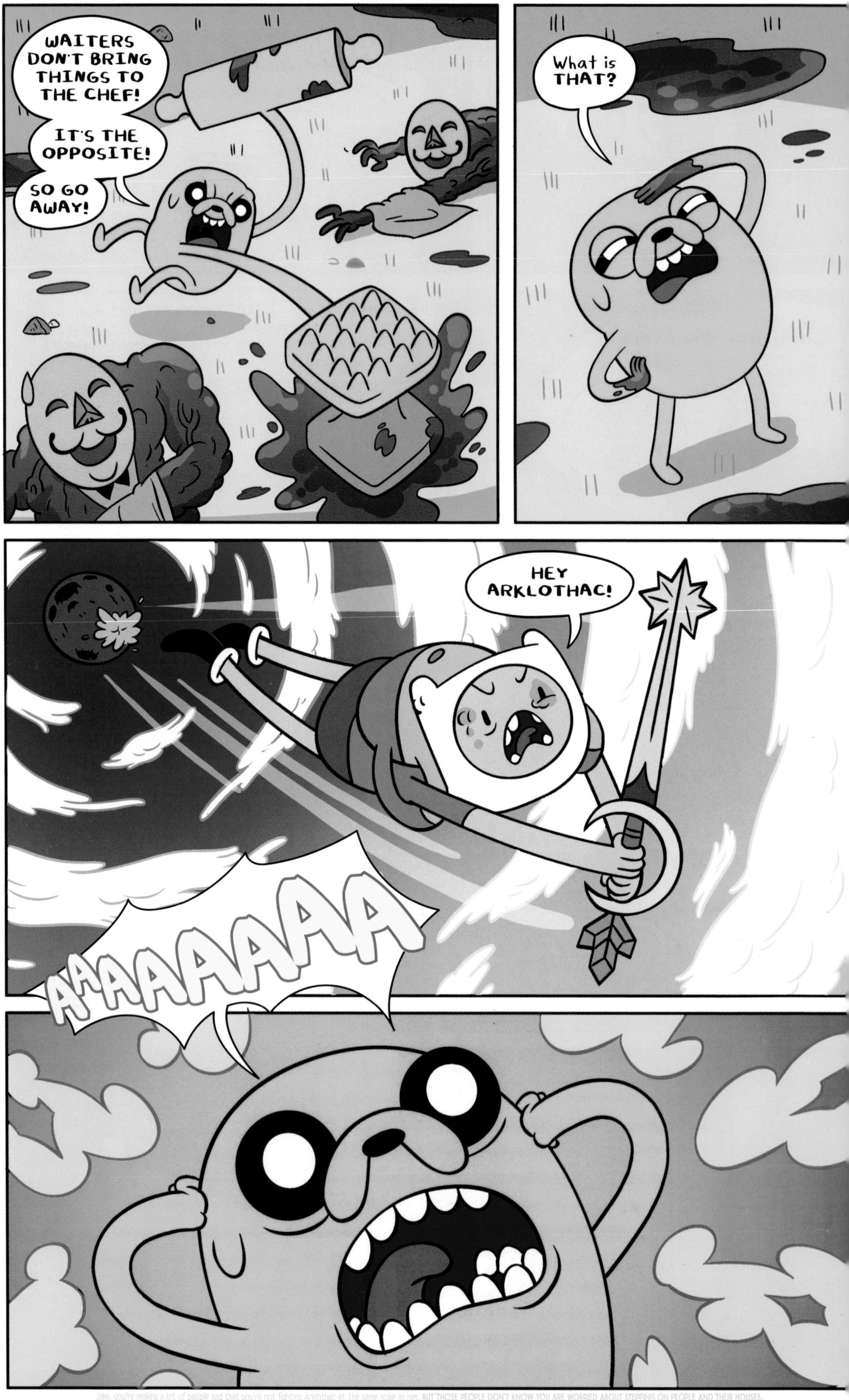
WAITERS DON'T BRING THINGS TO THE CHEF!
IT'S THE OPPOSITE!
SO GO AWAY!
What is THAT?
HEY ARKLOTHAC!
AAAAAAAA

Jake, you're making a lot of people sad that you're not fighting Arklothac at the same scale as him. BUT THOSE PEOPLE DON'T KNOW YOU ARE WORRIED ABOUT STEPPING ON PEOPLE AND THEIR HOUSES..

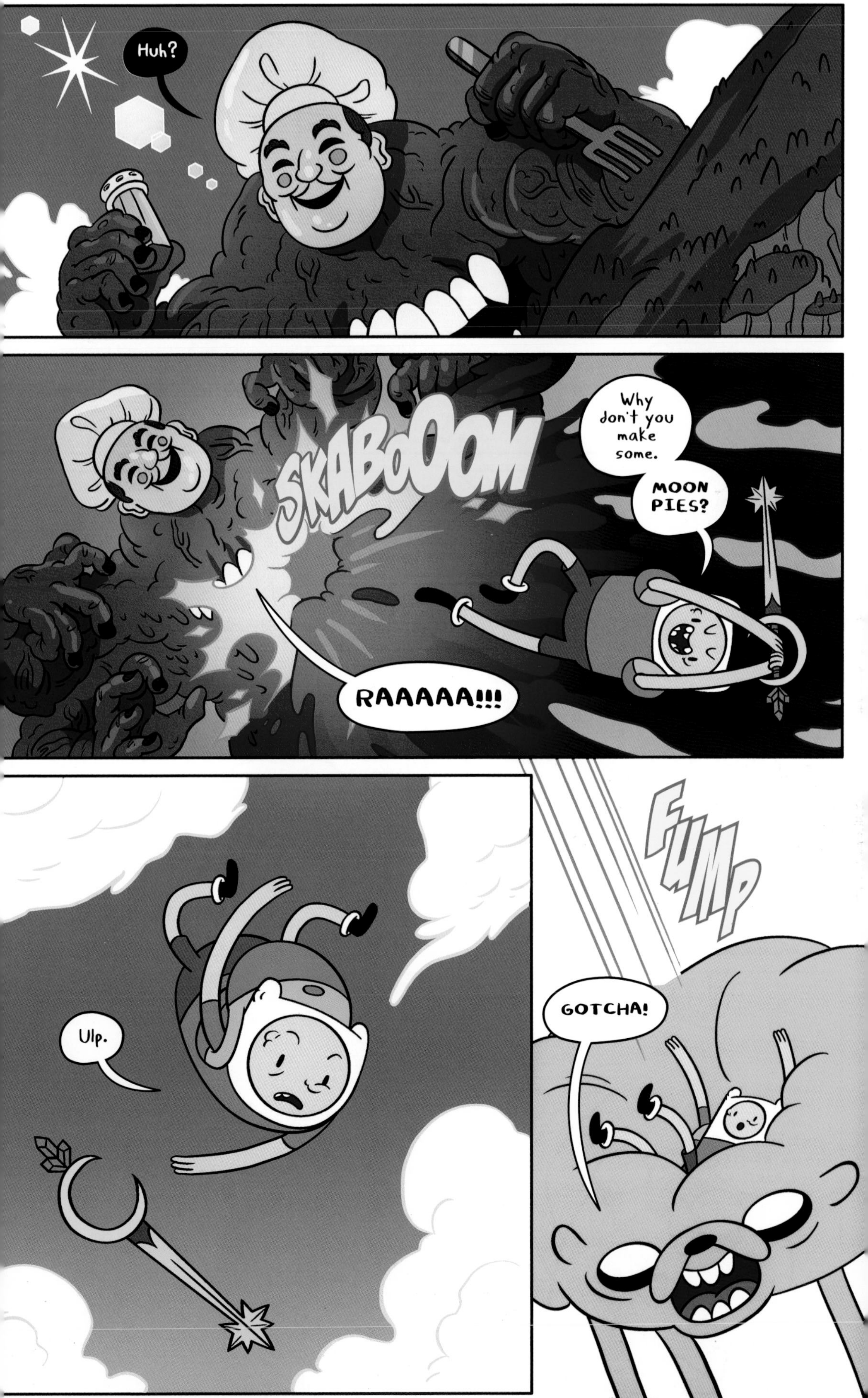
Huh?
SKABOOOM
Why don't you make some.
MOON PIES?
RAAAAA!!!
Ulp.
FUMP
GOTCHA!

Finn, are you saying you've spent enough time on the moon, you are now one of its pies?

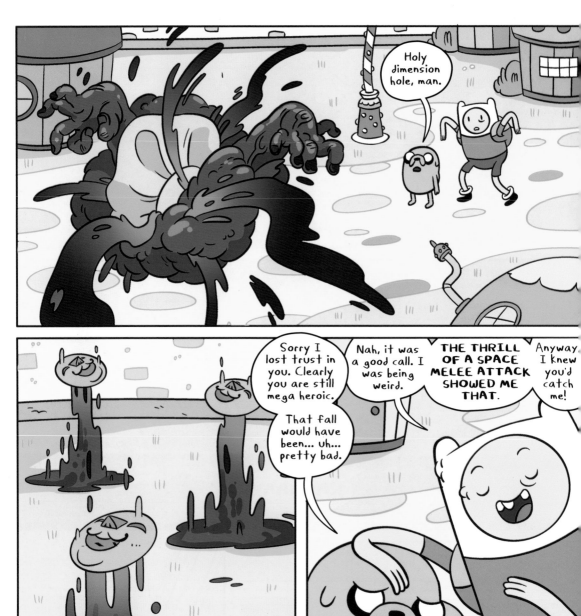

Holy dimension hole, man.

Sorry I lost trust in you. Clearly you are still mega heroic.

That fall would have been... uh... pretty bad.

Nah, it was a good call. I was being weird.

THE THRILL OF A SPACE MELEE ATTACK SHOWED ME THAT.

Anyway, I knew you'd catch me!

What if I just thought you were a meteorite, man.

I'm not in the habit of running and catching all the meteorites I see.

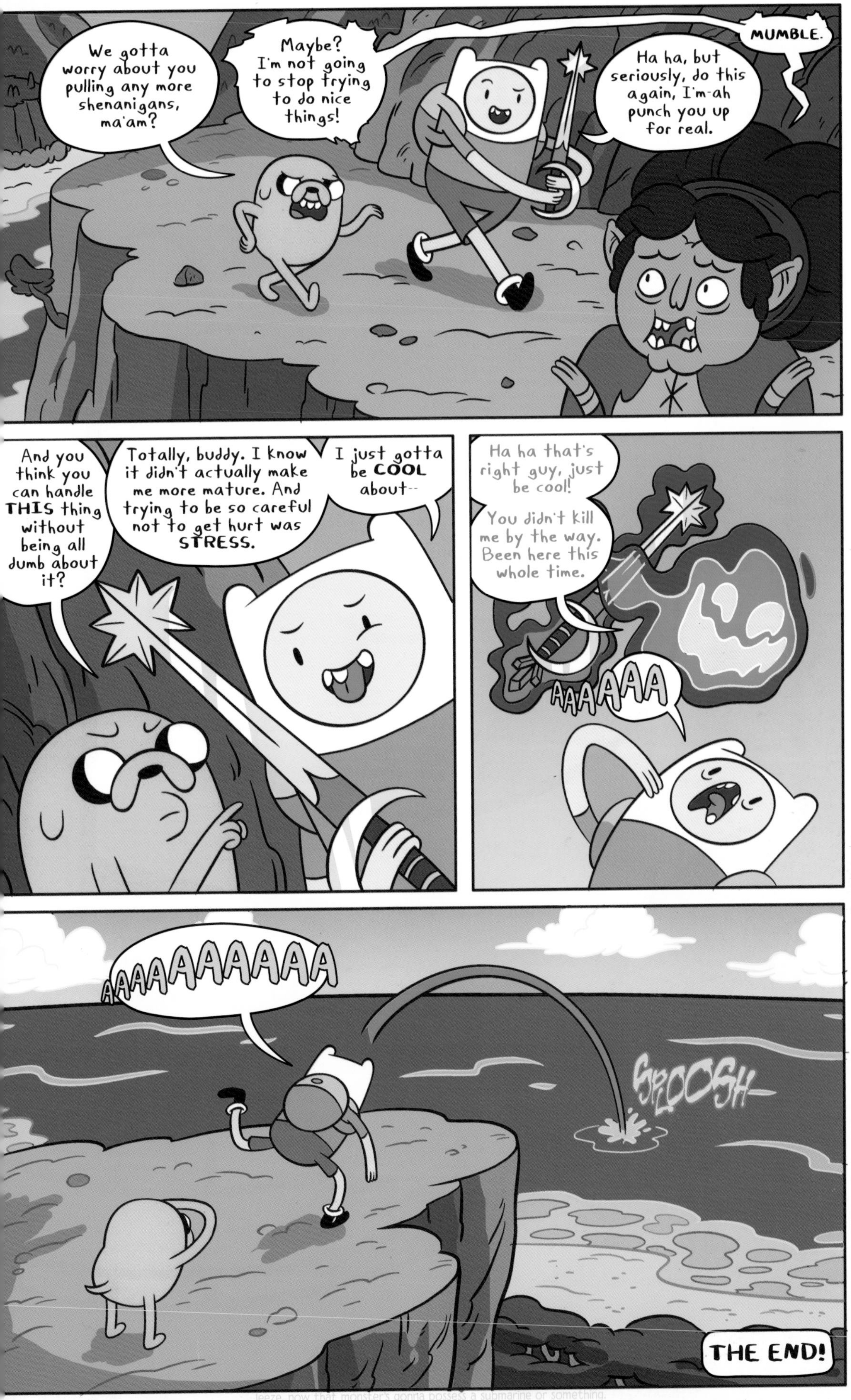
We gotta worry about you pulling any more shenanigans, ma'am?
Maybe? I'm not going to stop trying to do nice things!
MUMBLE.
Ha ha, but seriously, do this again, I'm-ah punch you up for real.
And you think you can handle THIS thing without being all dumb about it?
Totally, buddy. I know it didn't actually make me more mature. And trying to be so careful not to get hurt was STRESS.
I just gotta be COOL about--
Ha ha that's right guy, just be cool!
You didn't kill me by the way. Been here this whole time.
AAAAAAA
AAAAAAAAAAA
SPLOOSH
THE END!

Jeeze, now that monster's gonna possess a submarine or something.

COVER GALLERY

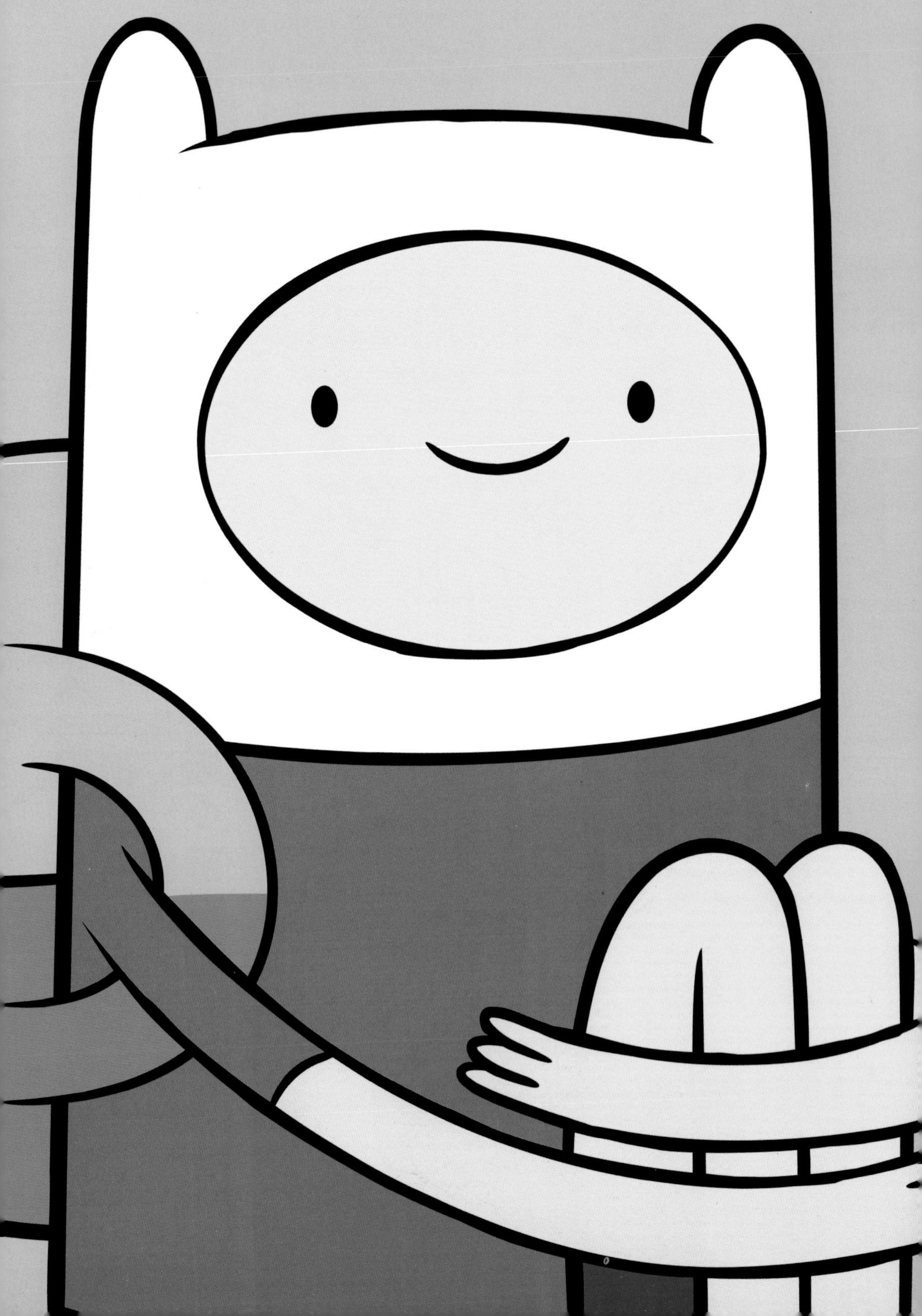

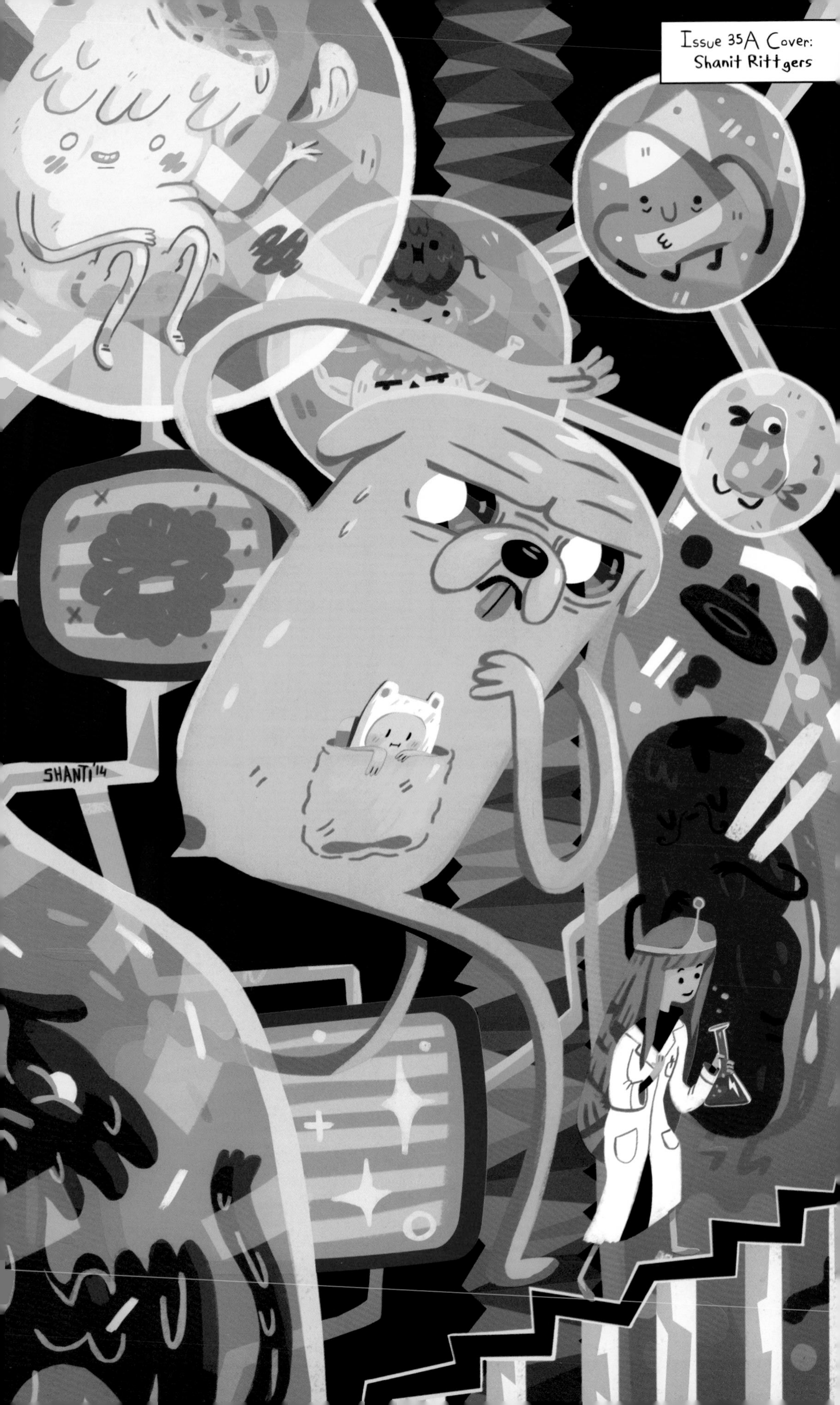
SHANTI '14

Issue 35A Cover:
Shanit Rittgers

Issue 35B Cover:
Mychal Amann

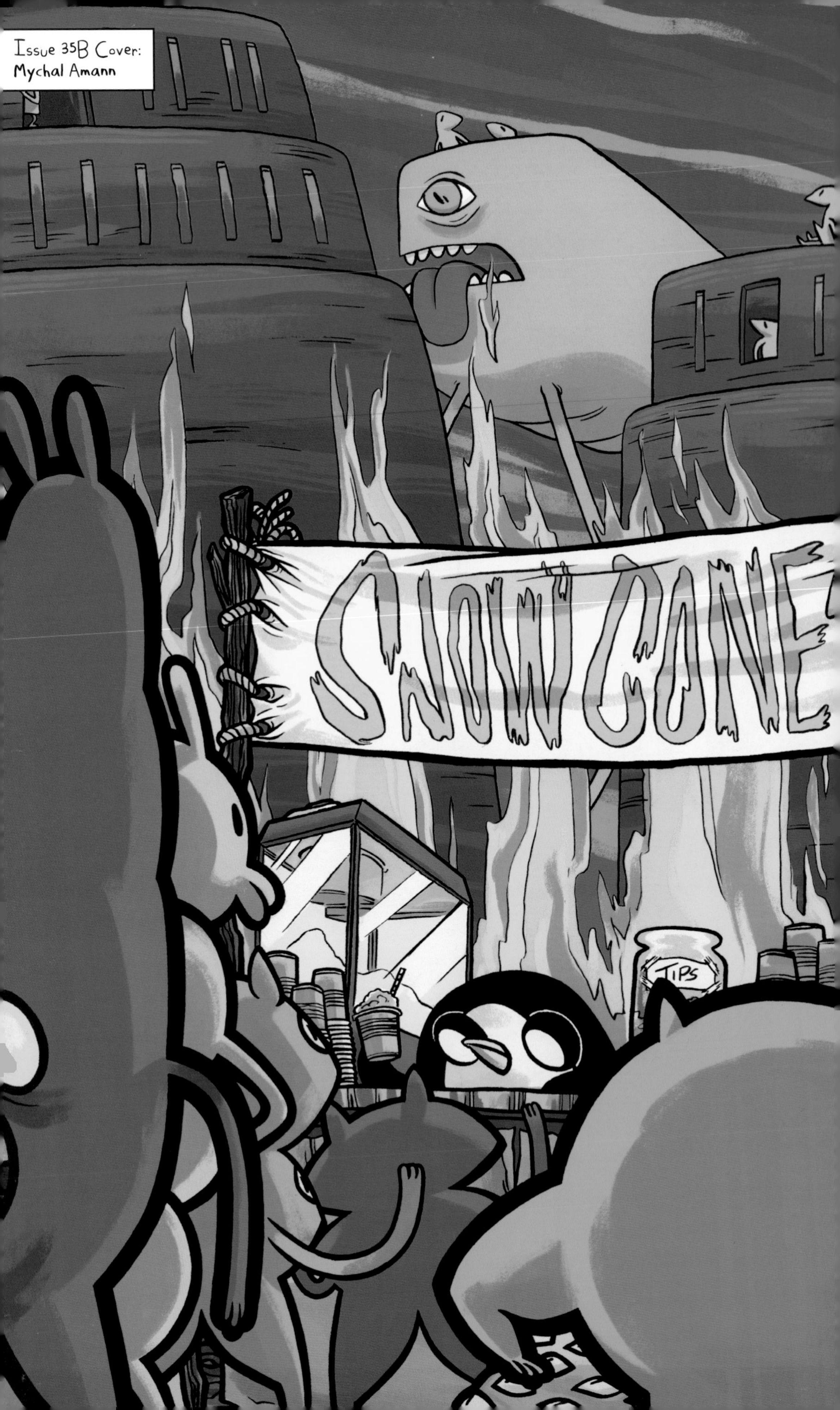
SNOW CONE
TIPS

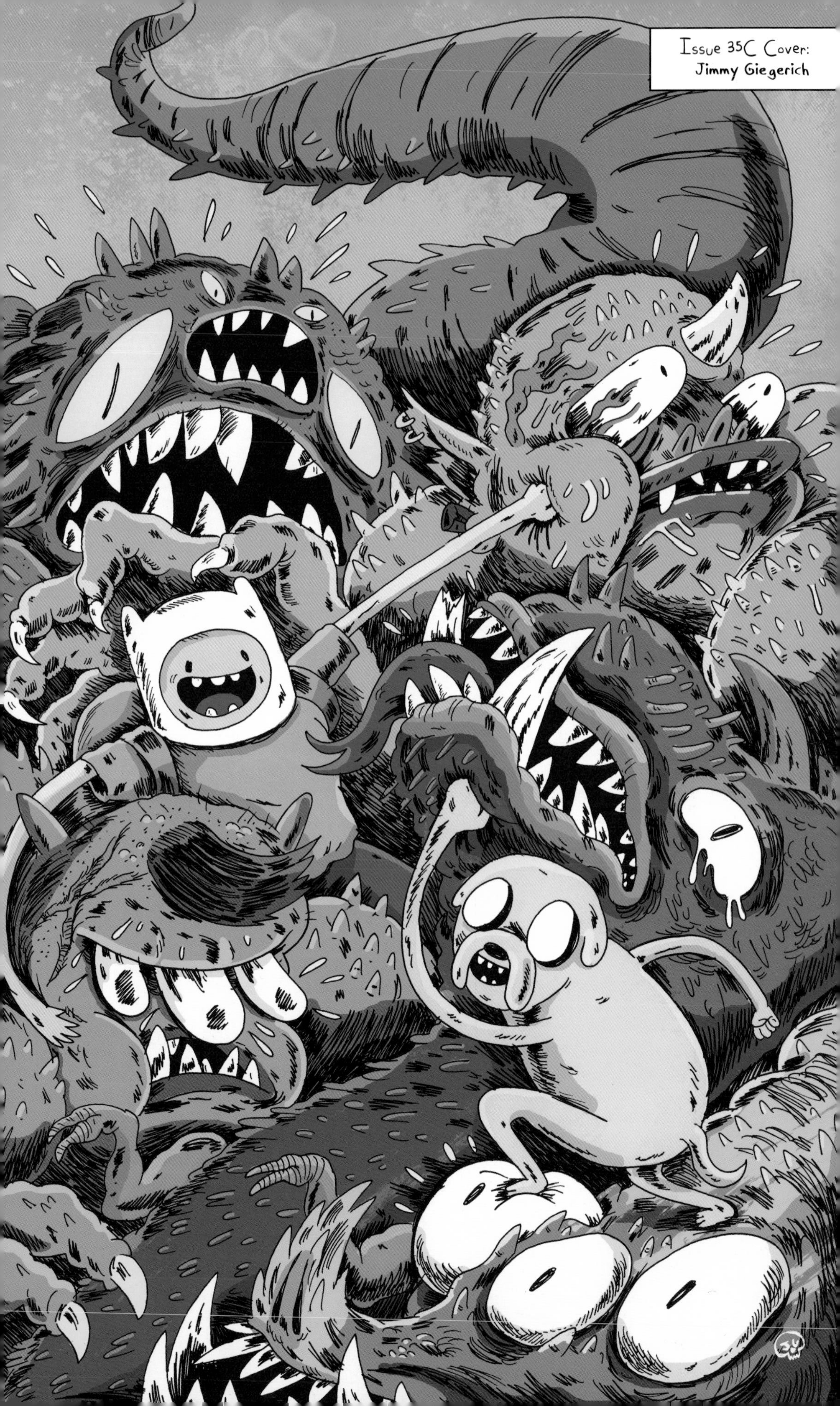

Issue 35C Cover:
Jimmy Giegerich

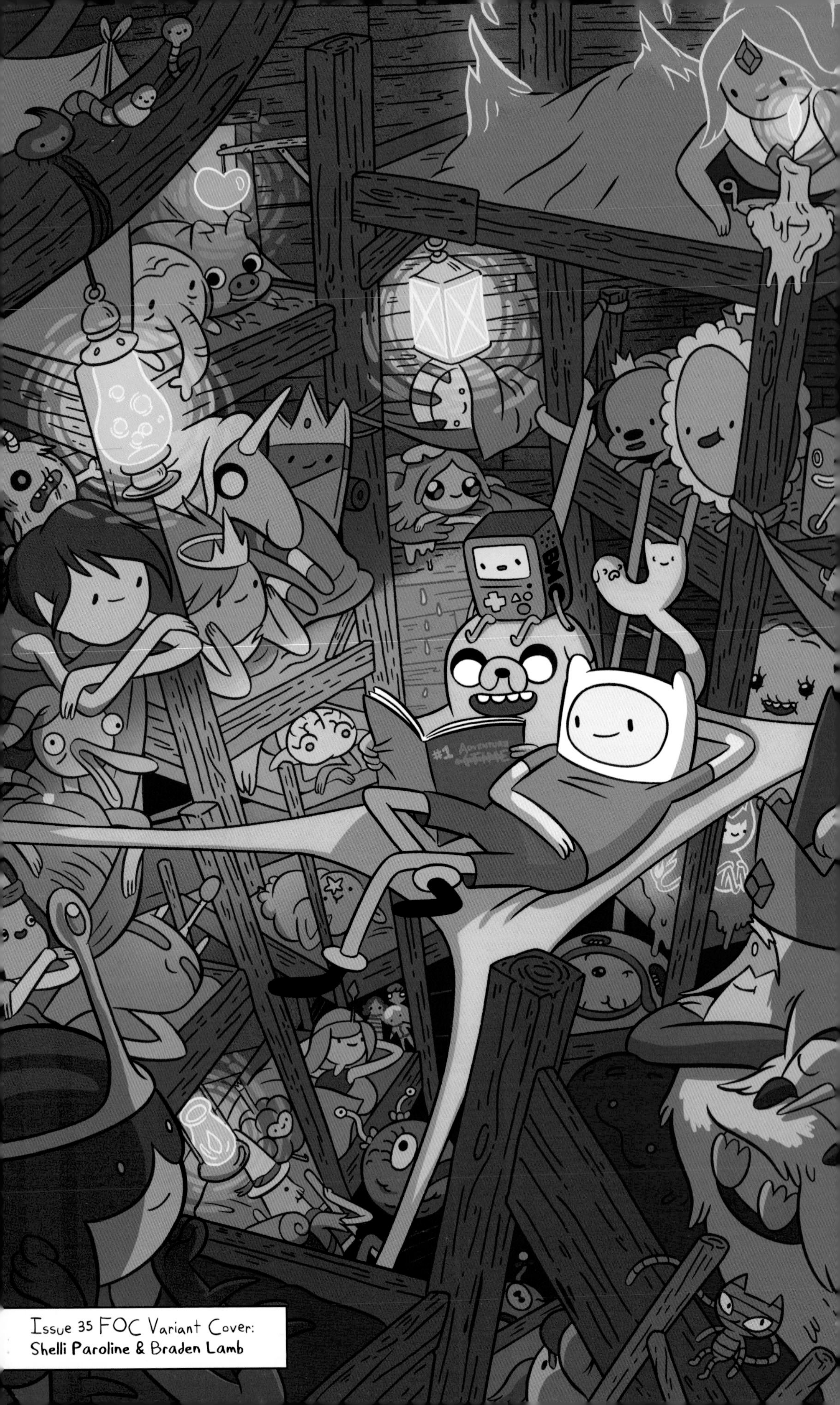
BMO
#1 ADVENTURE

Issue 35 FOC Variant Cover:
Shelli Paroline & Braden Lamb

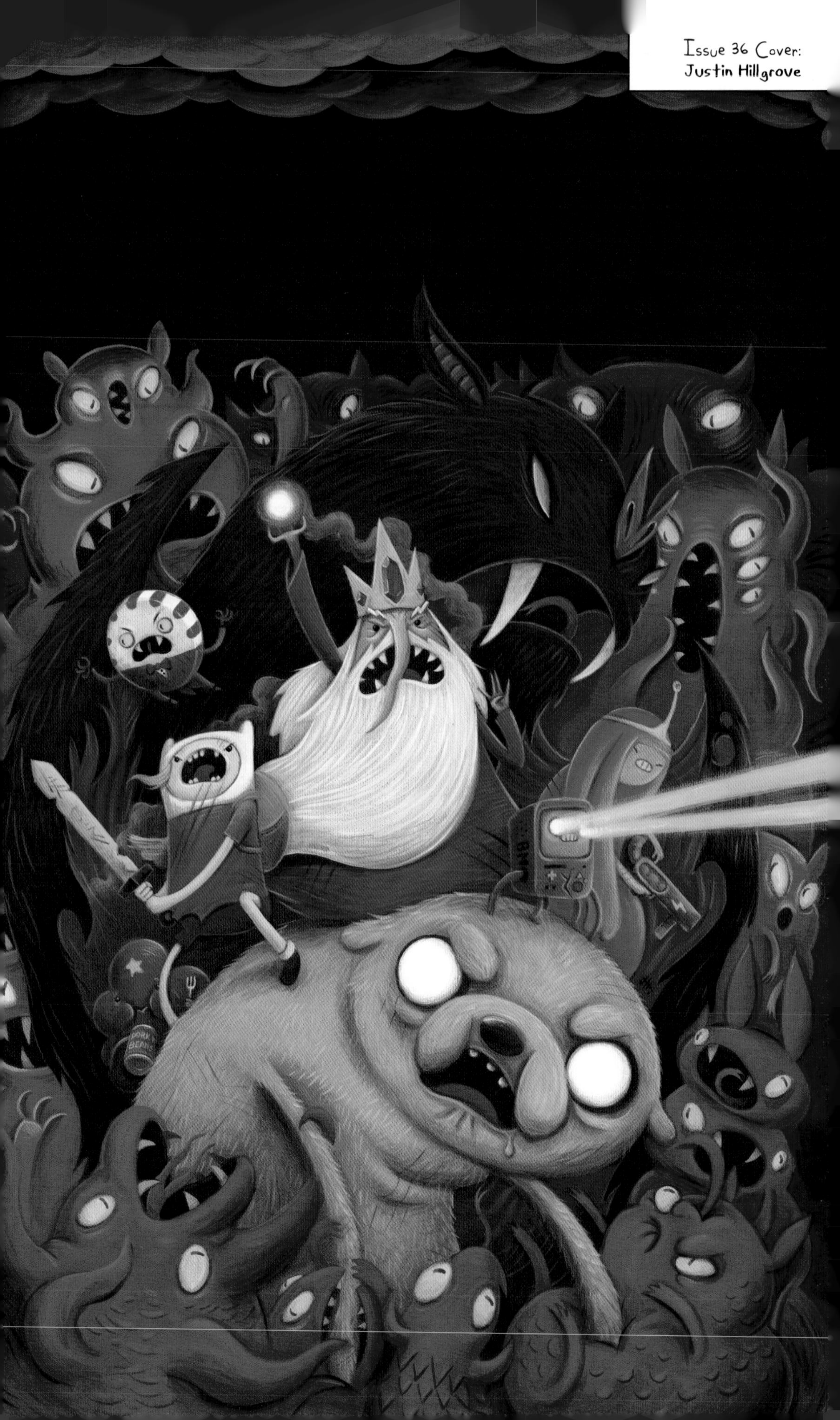

Issue 36 Cover:
Justin Hillgrove

Issue 36 Subscription Cover:
Ale Giorgini

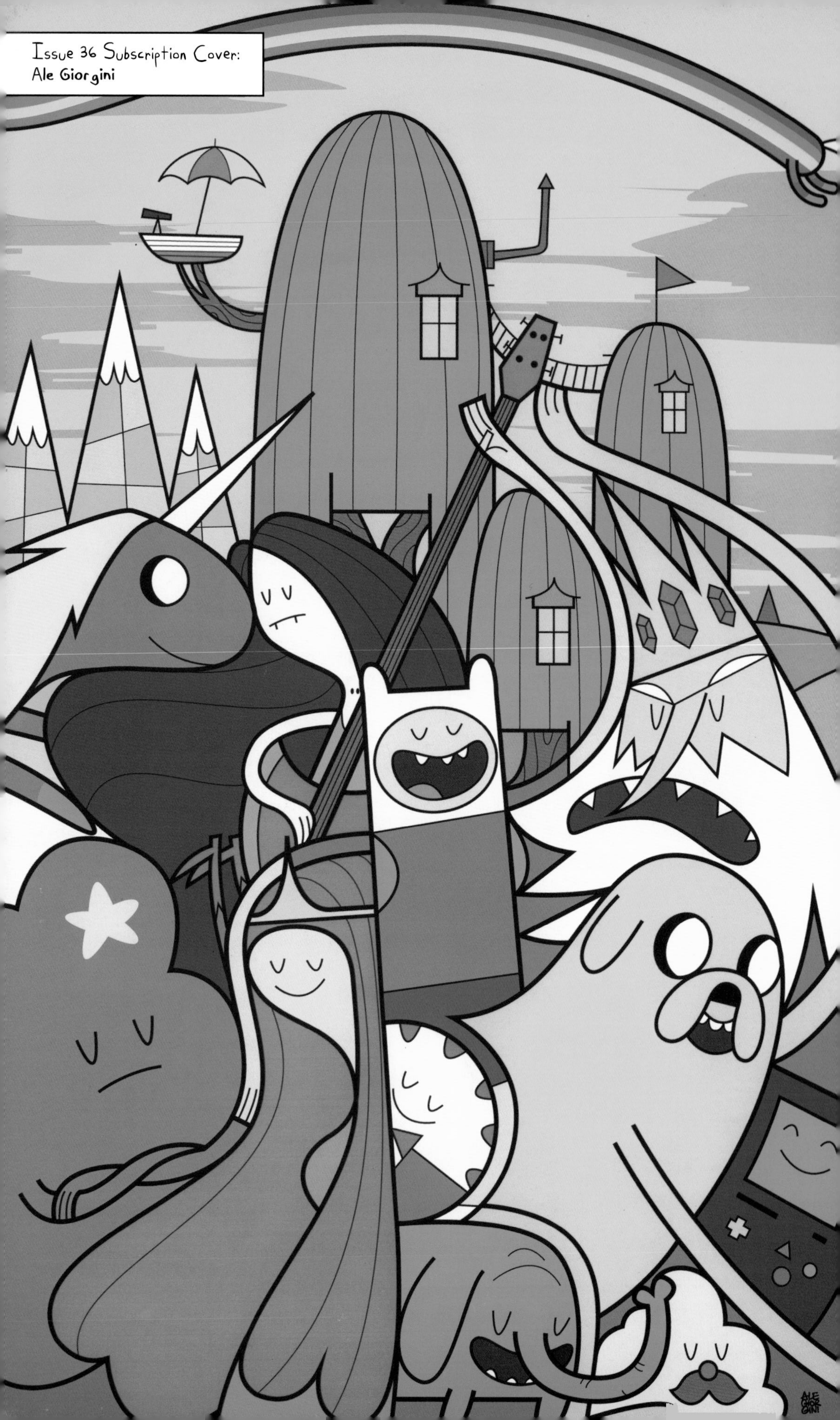

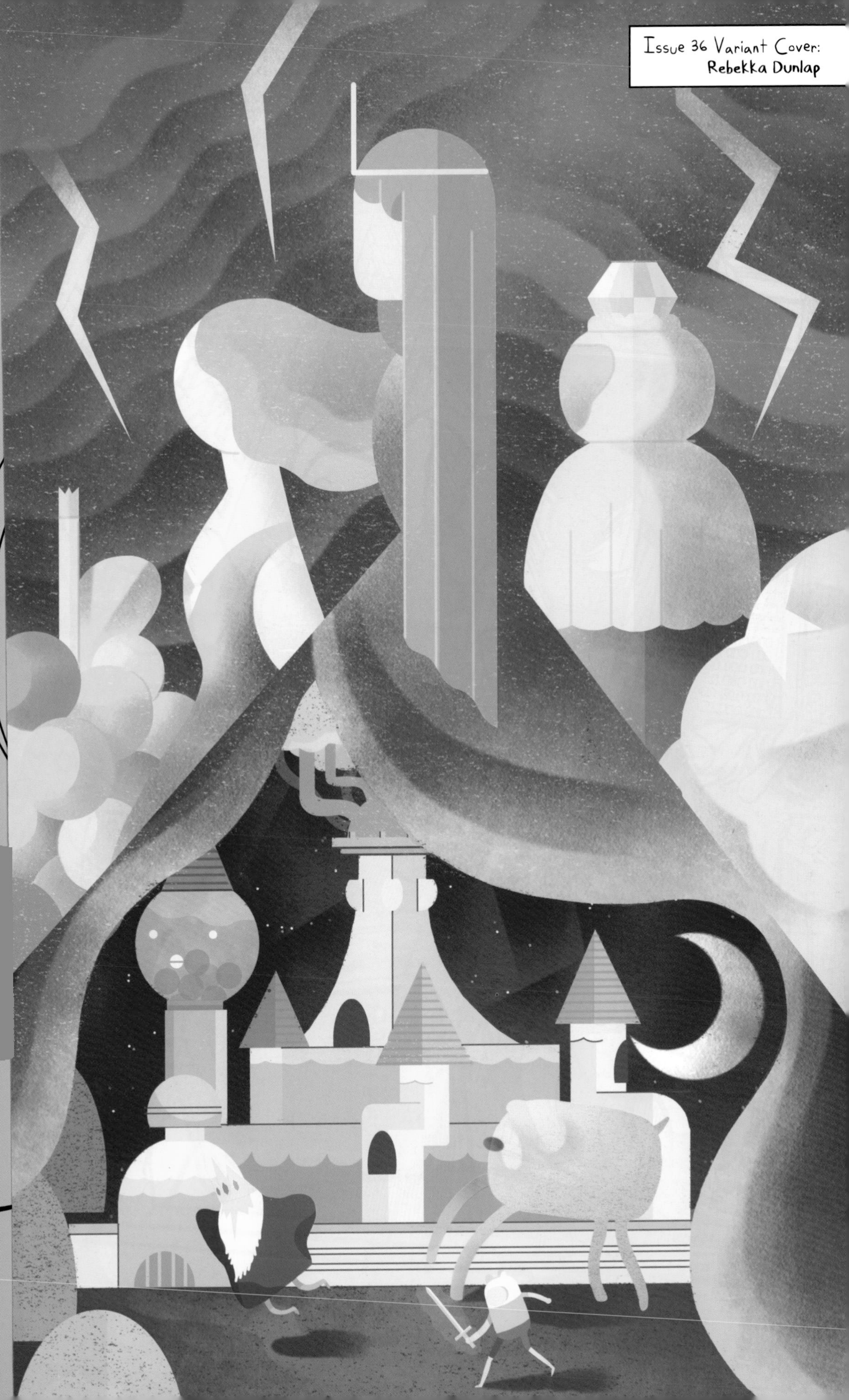

Issue 36 Variant Cover:
Rebekka Dunlap

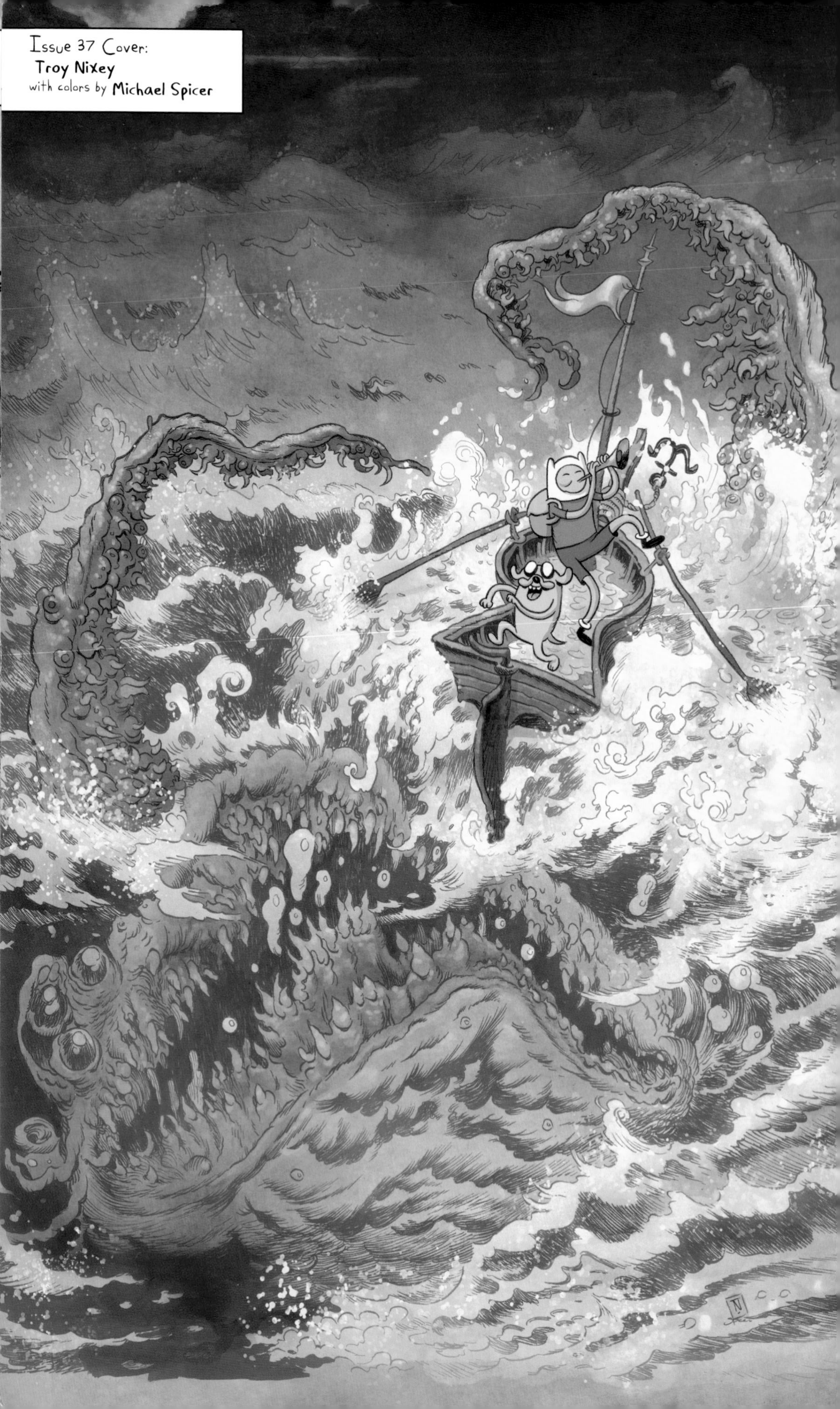

Issue 37 Cover:
Troy Nixey
with colors by **Michael Spicer**

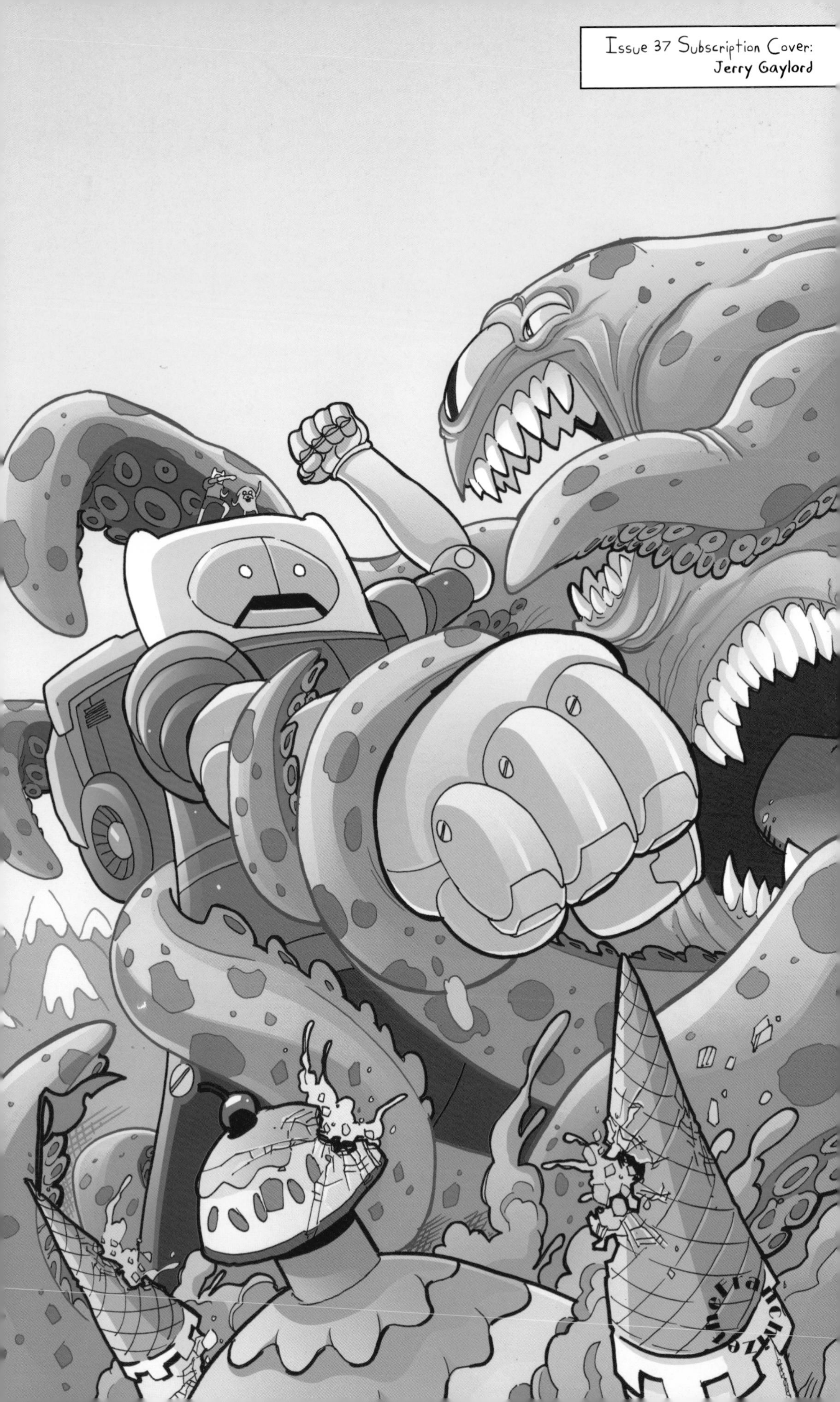

Issue 37 Subscription Cover:
Jerry Gaylord

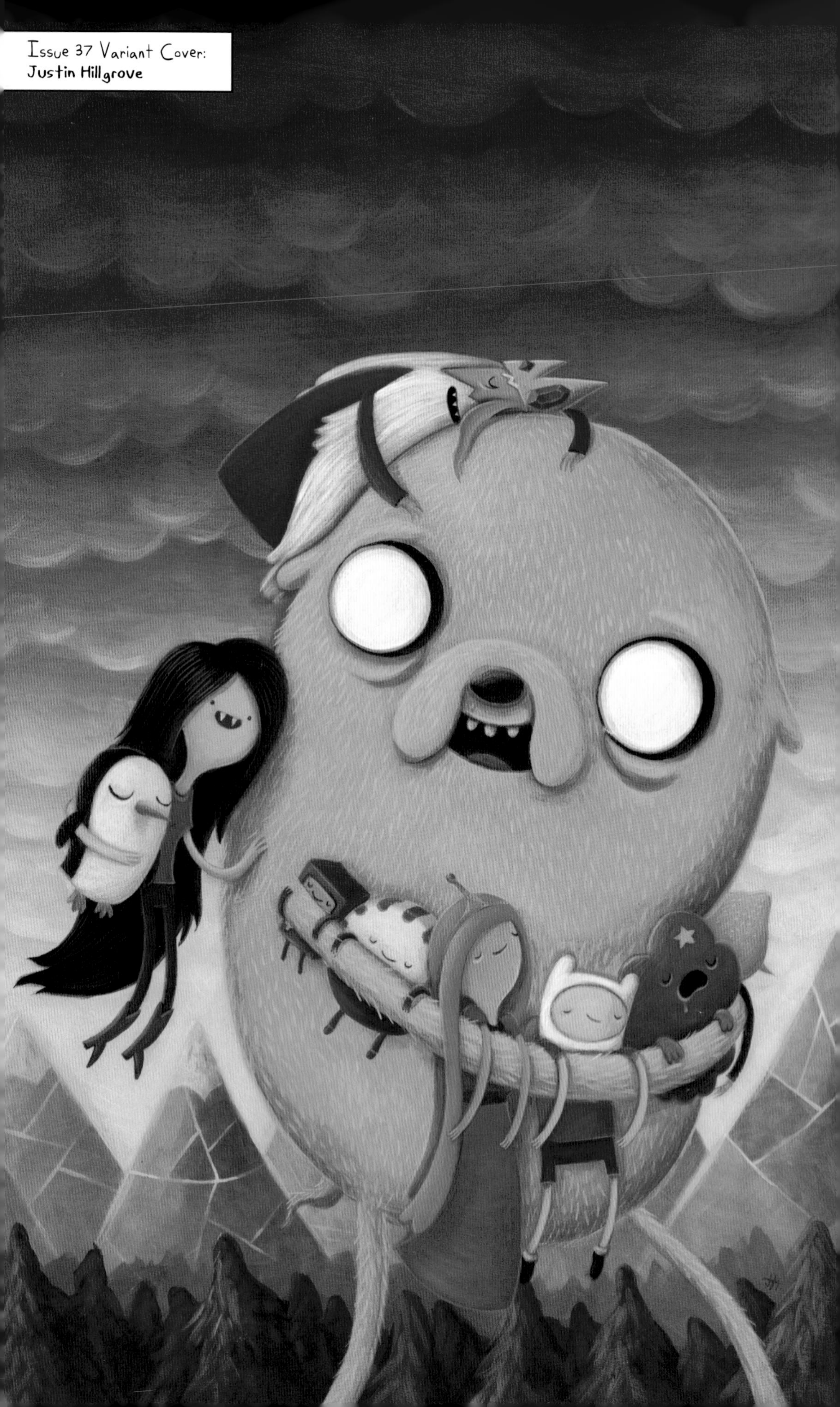

Issue 37 Variant Cover:
Justin Hillgrove

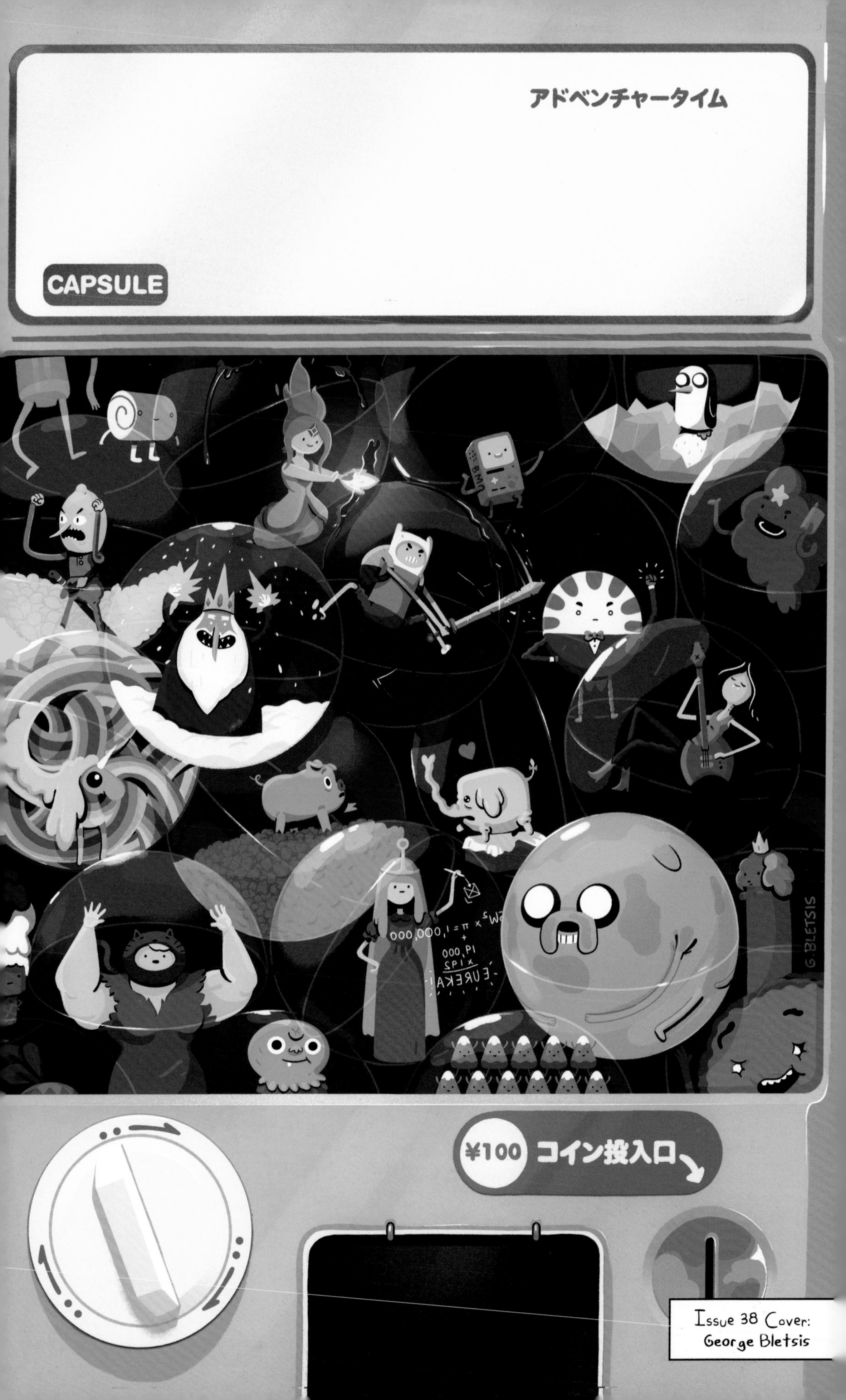
アドベンチャータイム
CAPSULE
G. BLETSIS
¥100 コイン投入口

Issue 38 Cover:
George Bletsis

Issue 38 Subscription Cover:
Mahendra Singh

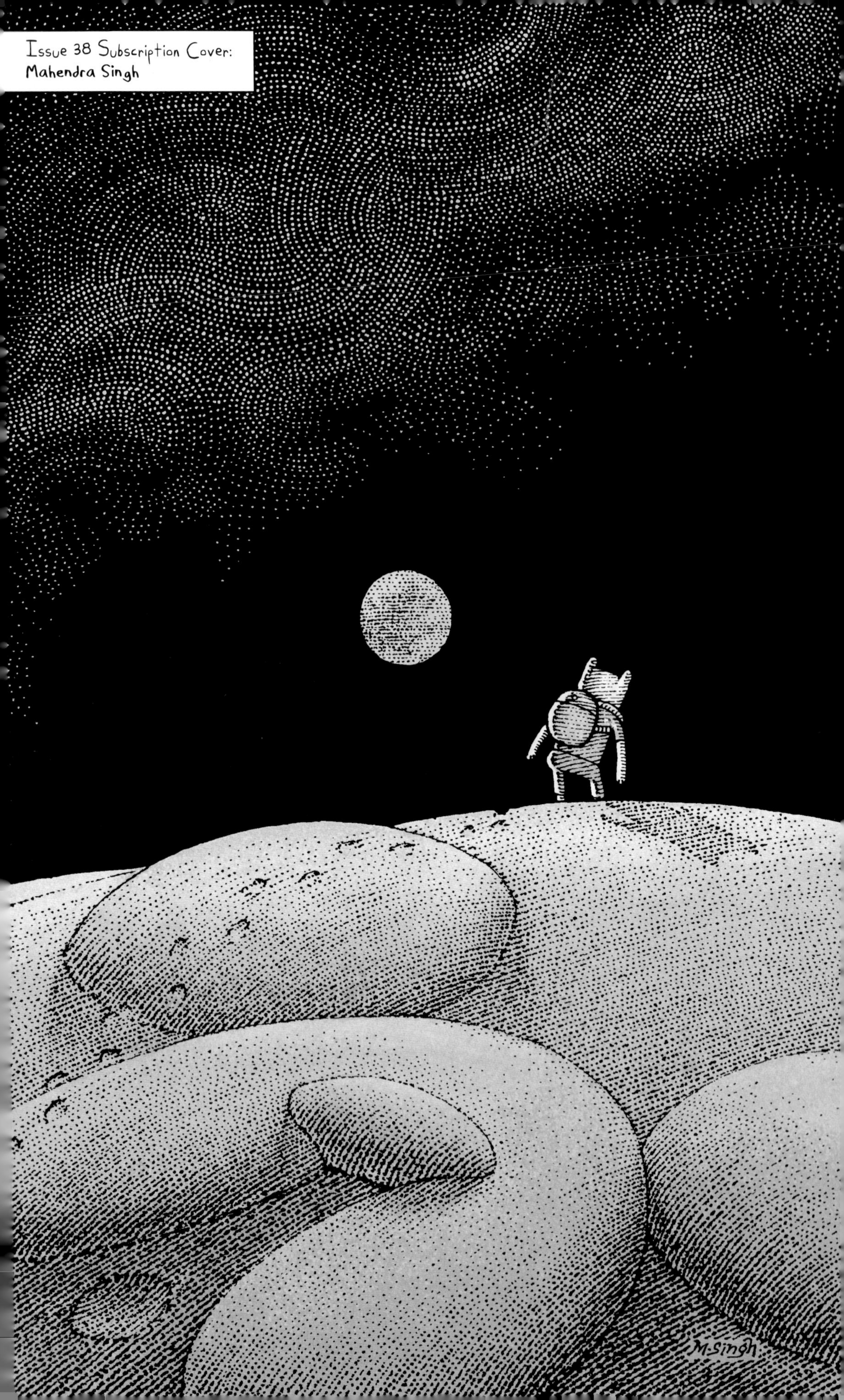
M.Singh

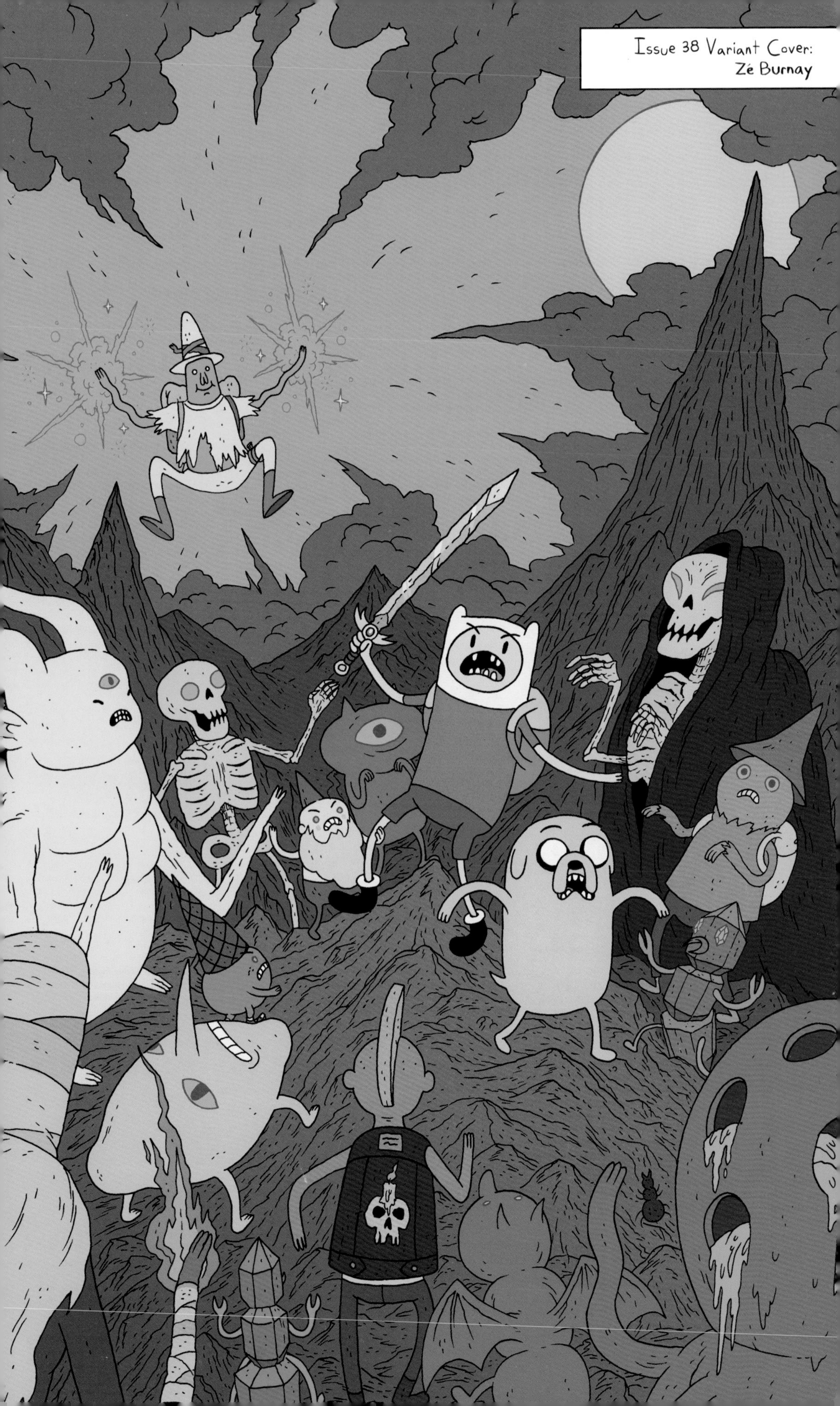

Issue 38 Variant Cover:
Zé Burnay

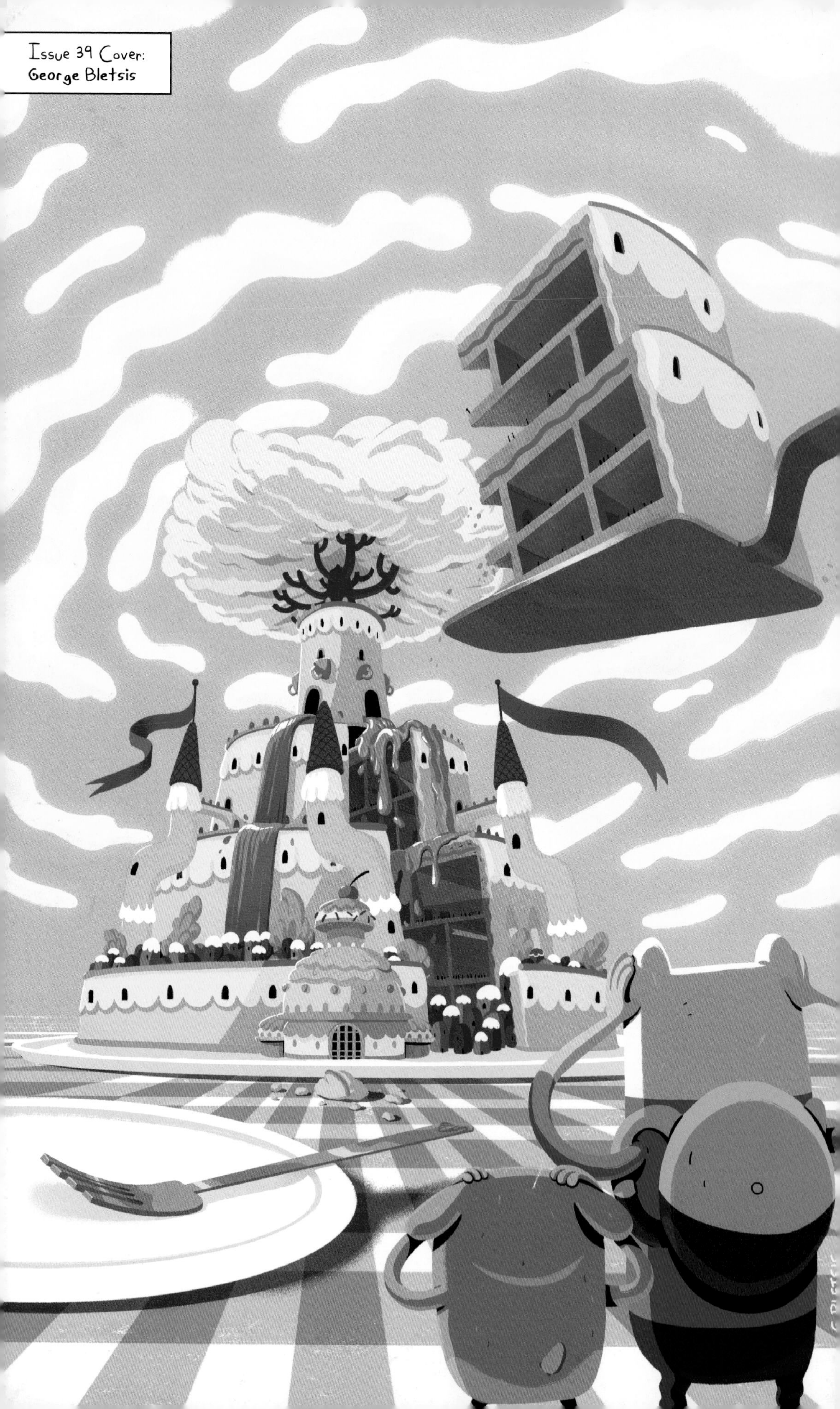

Issue 39 Cover:
George Bletsis

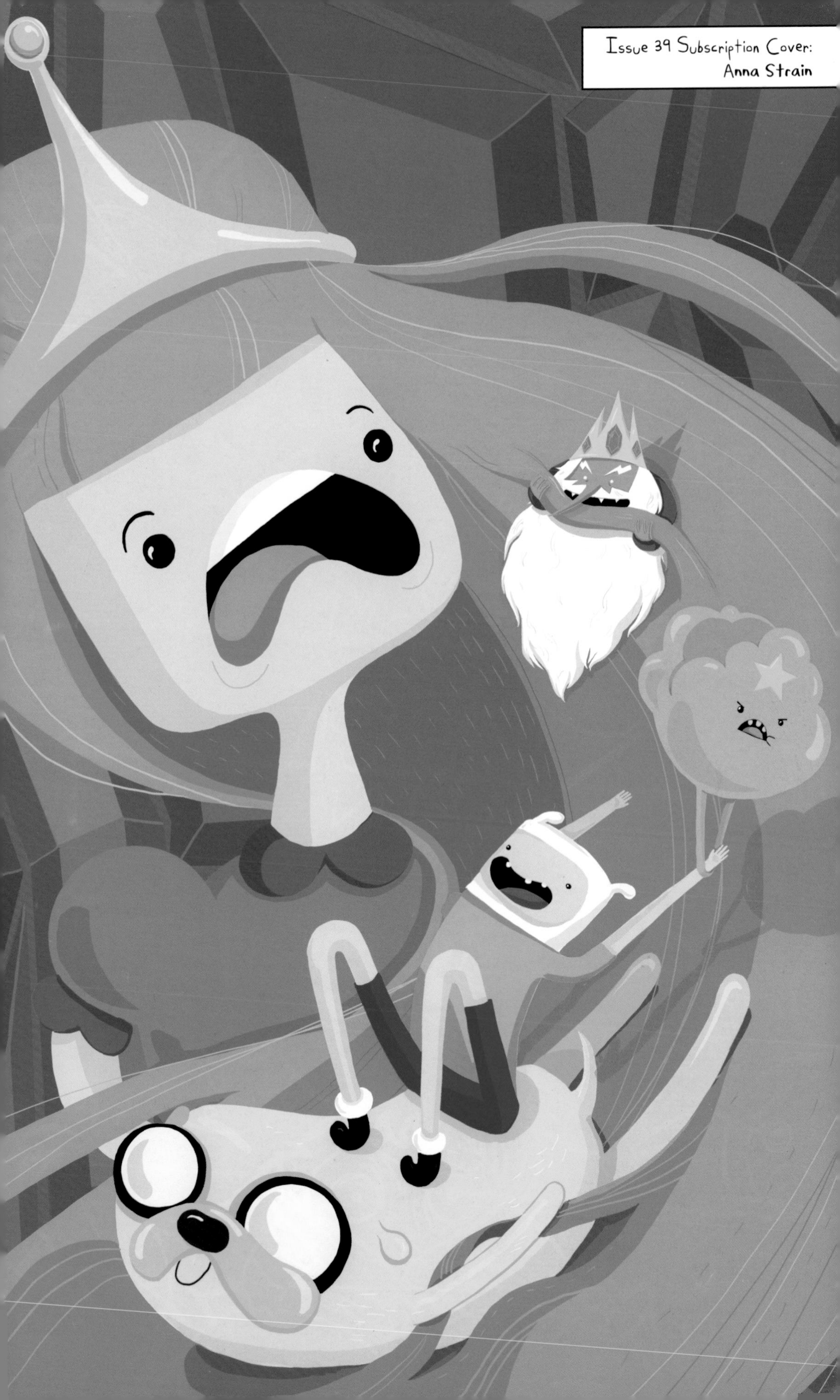

Issue 39 Subscription Cover:
Anna Strain

Issue 39 Variant Cover:
Wes Craig

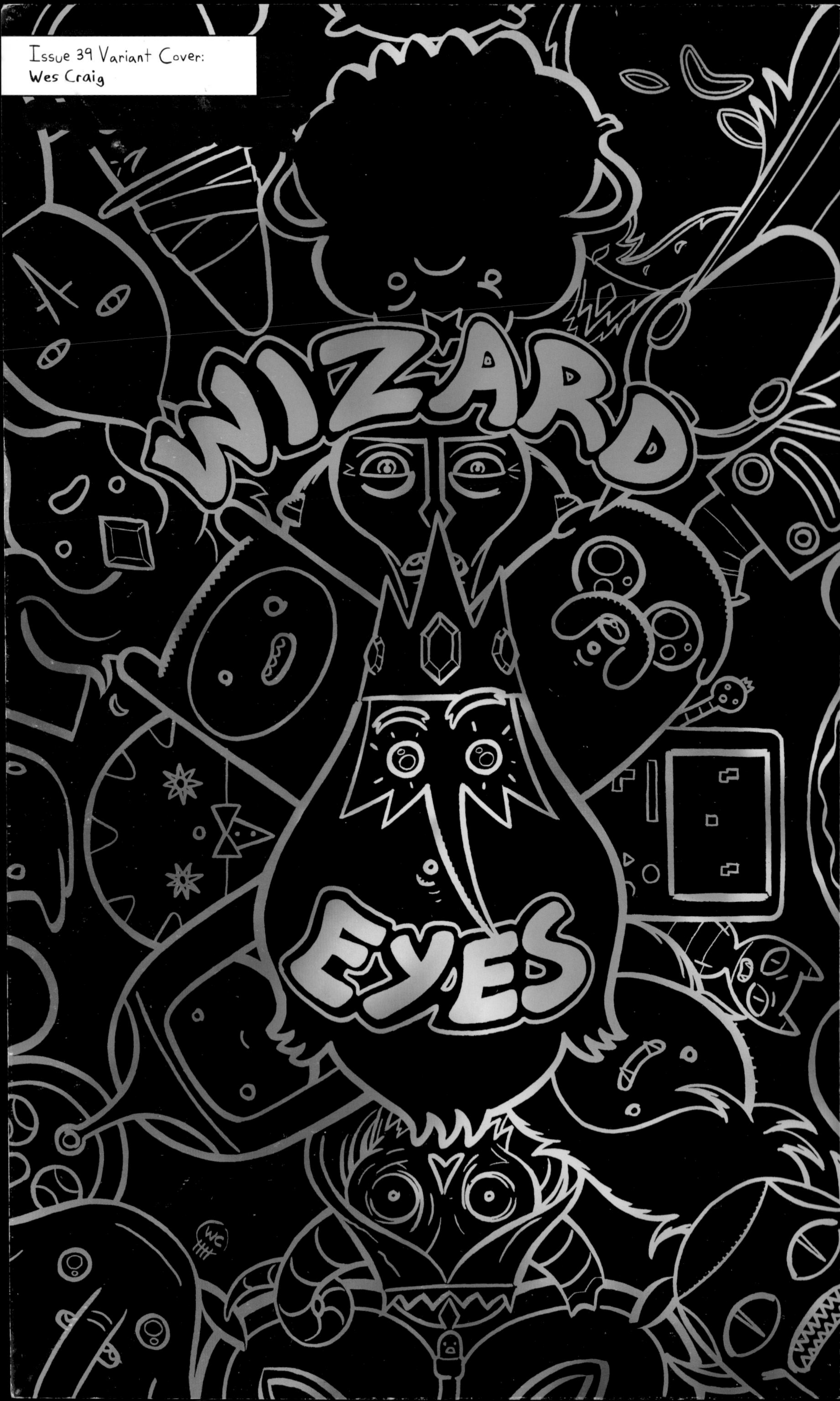
WIZARD
EYES